THE SYMMETRY OF SNOWFLAKES

Paul Michael Peters

ISBN: 1505693691
ISBN 13: 9781505693690

For Phyllis

THANKSGIVING VIGIL

1

The gray, overcast Ann Arbor sky sheds its first snowfall of the year. I watch the flakes from outside my second-floor office window at RedMitten Greetings.

It is the end of my day.

It is the Wednesday before Thanksgiving.

The cobweb on an exterior windowsill holds steady despite the cold updraft. The bank sign across Main Street alternates between "6:11 p.m." and "29°." More than time and temperature, these two points of data tell me "put on jacket" and "meet friends for dinner." Still, I sit and wait, lingering in the moments that are mine, free from the entanglements of others, alone in the last of my own thoughts.

I am on the precipice of what has become an annual trial—several long weeks that will test my character and prove my endurance. It would make me feel noble and masculine to tell you the challenges ahead involve physical speed or strength, but no, the days ahead will be a test of memory, fortitude, and tolerance.

Each Thanksgiving marks the start of a holiday season, which for me does not end until January 10, my birthday. I have long accommodated the separate parent visits, the making of compromises, the assimilation with new marriages, the new family traditions. When I live "my own life" and have a family, friends, and rituals of my own, I hope to leave this tough season behind me.

The Internet tells me that there are thirty-five types of snowflakes. Some are complex, others are simple, and yet no two are ever alike. We can grow them in a lab. They occur in nature. Alone, a snowflake can be amazing and wonderful.

I've found that there are at least that many types of people. Some are complex, others are simple, and yet no two are ever alike. We can grow them in test tubes. A person can be amazing and wonderful. However, I find that most will be big flakes during this, the coldest of seasons.

"6:15 p.m." and "28°" tell me again "put on jacket" and "hurry to friends." I am delayed, but not because of them. They are the lee of my emotional turbulence, my shelter from the icy wind. Still, I do not want to keep them waiting too long.

The bank sign is correct. It is cold outside, and I have six blocks to go before reaching our favorite Irish pub. I am the last one out of the office by over three hours.

As I walk, the backlog of work churns in my mind...staff schedules, making payroll, marketing expenses, press releases, sales, system maintenance. I decompress and try to breathe deeply with each step. After years of reinvesting every penny earned into my business, it finally may pay off. Just this week I received an offer from a large greeting card company in Missouri. They want to purchase RedMitten Greetings, pitching with phrases like *young, leading edge, investment support for such a stable, maturing goliath* peppered throughout.

Five blocks still to go, so I try to focus on the snow. Each flake melts as it hits warmer ground. This is "show snow," an opening act. The "show flakes" are large, white, full, pretty. It is the snow of movies and songs tied to the holidays, but it will not last. "Show flakes" want to be something more substantial, like a December blanket or February blizzard, but their dendrites are no match for the warm earth still cooling as the hours of daylight become shorter and shorter.

Snowflakes are symmetrical. "Symmetry" can be precise, mathematical, scientific, or, simply beautiful—balanced by both form and proportion. Closing my eyes to think of the perfect snowflake,

I visualize the fernlike Stellar Dendrite. With six arms, spikes and spindles of crystal, and ideal ice shafts, it is a thing of beauty. Like a glass etching, done by a skilled and steady hand, the lines that form each crystalline structure are striking. Still, with at least thirty-two additional types of snowflakes, few look anything like this under a microscope.

Mathematical symmetry is different. Frozen water molecules want to align with hydrogen, but this does not form strong bonds, so they are compelled to be together in groups that fit just right, even if there is a weakness. Locked in the hexagonal shape of hydrogen, each crystal becomes a geometrical wonder of interlocked strength and delicate design, each staying with us only the shortest of time. How is it that we still do not know everything about something as simple as a snowflake?

Much debate surrounds the mechanism that holds snowflakes together. Is it electrostatic, mechanical, or some supersticky liquid state at certain temperatures? For all I know, it could be love that brings a stray partial and water droplet together in some Shakespearean drama.

He, the particle, came from the wrong side of the Great Divide high in the atmosphere; she, the droplet from a noble nimbus cloud family, who would never bond with such a piece of dirt. They unite as lovers, the "Mono-particles" and "Dropulets." We understand that something between them connects, but not why, and they form something greater than the individual parts, a beautiful snowflake.

I can see the gang at a table near the front of the bar, which is clean, dimly lit, and warm inside. They saved me a seat by the crackling hearth, and a drink waits.

My friends are lifelong. I have known them since college. We were all in a social fraternity together, which explains their funny nicknames: Pike, Knobby, and Dord. Pike, Knobby, and Dord are married to wonderful women—Michelle, Kate, and Jean. I only wish I could find a woman to love me who is equally amazing.

Our early years together were much like you would imagine for college age. Our fraternity members were known for things other than the ability to party, get girls, or play sports. We had the highest GPAs on campus and were all very involved in extracurricular organizations.

The bonds with my six-sided friend-flake include shared values. We are not in unison on issues such as politics, religion, culture, or even music. It would be a rare day when two of us say the same thing on any of those subjects. Pike, Knobby, and Dord all grew up in small farm towns near Lake Michigan. These three boys can talk farm equipment, corn crops, ethanol, and *Farmer's Almanac* like no one else I know. Four-H, Boy Scouts, and working late-summer hours with their dads are all activities that build a certain character.

Michelle, Kate, and Jean are from small towns in Michigan. They expect men to know how to fix and build things, which fortunately these men do. Honesty and integrity are important. In exchange for this, Michelle, Kate, and Jean have a loyalty to their husbands that is deep and vital.

Not having grown up on a farm, I do not have the strong farm-boy character, and I am not married to one of the greatest women of our time. Most people use my full name, Hank Hanson, as I don't have a nickname. This group just calls me Hanson. I am twenty-nine and single…have been for nearly a year now.

I am greeted by a cheer of "Hanson!" Seated with the people I trust more than any others, daresay, love, in the most comfortable of settings, I should feel better as the gin and tonic warms my blood.

"You're just in time, I was about to tell everyone about the farm report from my dad this morning," Dord says.

"Oh good, I didn't miss it," I reply.

The boys are interested in his father's take on the rise in commodities and the effect it will have on winter crops.

As my eyes begin to glaze over, Kate grabs my knee under the table to get my attention. "Hey, Knobby and I are going to be at my parents' house tomorrow morning. You know they would love to have you over if you wanted to stop in."

"Oh, that's really nice; I would do it in a heartbeat if I didn't already have to eat crepes with P3 in the morning and Entenmann's at P4's," I said.

She smiles that classic leading lady beam. "I understand. There are only so many places you can be in a day."

"Hanson," Knobby calls from across the table. "What are you saying to my wife?'

"I was saying that I can't make it over to her parents tomorrow," I reply.

"Oh, yeah, you've got that one-day expedition you hold every holiday." He chuckles. "It's your mother's third husband's cousin's brother's brunch or something?"

"No, no, his father's second wife's son," he adds with a laugh.

"I thought that you just drove laps around the city playing some geocaching game putting miles on that hoopdee you drive," Jean says.

"Ha, ha," I feign humor. "You are all right. Crêpes in Royal Oak with mother's second husband P3 as a fifteen-year tradition, followed by opening a box of Entenmann's in Wyandotte with father's second wife P4, lunch served by mother's third husband's kitchen staff in Bloomfield Hills, in the home stretch I have first Thanksgiving dinner with dad's parents at the retirement home, then finally last Thanksgiving with dad and his current wife, Midge."

They look at me with what seems pity. It might be confusion, like the first time they found out.

My epiphany that my family is different occurred in October of my first year of college. Pike and I were roommates, while Knobby and some other guy lived down the hall. I got a phone call before dinner with sad news about a death in the family. Fifteen minutes later in the cafeteria, I asked Pike and Knobby, "What's the proper etiquette for the death of your mom's second husband's third wife's father?'

An odd, and similar, look settled on their faces halfway through my question, a look that seemed painful, as if their minds could not process my question. They stared at the ceiling; their expressions suggested the quiet solving of complicated math equations. After a moment Pike asked, "You're kidding, right?"

Sadly, I was not kidding. It makes me wonder if the family isn't just blended, but pulverized.

The answer to the original question is that one can always send flowers. It came to us after dinner and video games, and three bottles of Miller High Life apiece. In fact, flowers are what you should send to any female in my family, along with a personal note if a significant event occurs. For men, a card is enough.

That epiphany inspired RedMitten Greetings; the remnants are in our marketing materials: "Helping you find the right words for any situation."

In rudimentary terms, my family starts with my dearly departed mother—parental unit number 1, or P1 for short. She remarried twice, first to a man I refer to as P3, and then to her third husband, P5. Dad is parental unit number 2, or P2. His third and current wife, Midge, is P6. Between his first wife and Midge is P4, Tess.

There are children from these unions. I have two full-blooded siblings, my brother, Mark, and sister, Lisa.

I have two half-siblings, partially connected to me, and four steps-siblings—people the courts say I am, or was at one time, related to. In addition, there are people one might think should be relatives, but who are not. These are the children of spouses born prior to when either of my parents was involved in the various families.

Looking back, I like to say that they peaked with me and it was all downhill from there, though I recognize it is a nearly cruel and pointed jab at the life choices of others.

Consider my relationships with each of them. For instance, my father's second wife played more of a role as a stepmother than his current wife, who is closer in age, like a babysitter. Neither could be as wonderful as my biological mother, yet these two women, forced into my life, require attention.

"Hanson, are you actually ready for Thanksgiving? I mean, with all those people, don't they press your buttons?" Dord asks.

My answer is instinctive. I sip my drink, and say, "They don't just press my buttons, they installed my buttons. They wrote the operation manual. I'm never really ready."

"It can't be that bad, Hank Hanson," Kate says.

"Families are funny things, Kate. You have heard that phrase, you can choose your friends, but you can't choose your family? I'm blessed and fortunate to have found you all, and well, we've all chosen one another."

"Yeah, you are blessed," Knobby says with a laugh.

"Still, my father gets to choose my family," I say.

"Is that the one your brother used to date?" Michelle asks.

"Or the one who's slightly off kilter?" Pike follows up. "There are so many."

"They are one and the same," I say.

"How is your brother, Mark?" Dord asks.

"Mark is fine. We talk on the phone. He's not coming out this year. The way he sees the family is different from how I see it, different from my sister, Lisa. I look back and remember things they don't. Maybe it's age, maybe interests, maybe just awareness."

"Anyone know what the lottery is up to this week?" Michelle asks, finding a break in the conversation.

"It's only at nine million," Knobby says.

"Only?" Dord asks.

"Listen," Knobby says from behind his dark, thick-rimmed glasses. "If I win one million dollars, that's nice, that's great. Kate and I are going to put it in the bank, square off with everyone, and take a nice trip. It is not enough after taxes, which takes half. I don't want to suffer the Oprah Effect."

"You've given some thought to our future," Kate says with a smile. "What's the Oprah Effect?"

Knobby wrinkles his nose in feigned disapproval at his own wife not knowing. "Please, the Oprah Effect, when she has this big giveaway a few years ago, and everyone gets a free car. What the winners do not understand is that they have to pay taxes on the car—and most people do not have the cash to pay the government at the door of the studio to take over the title. What are guests left to do, not take a car? Make Oprah look like a liar? Sell the car and take cash? There's no easy way out. Honey, we need to go big, or not go at all."

"You've given this considerable thought," Kate says.

"I have, honey, and you, my love, deserve more than five hundred thousand after taxes to build interest. You, my dear, need at least twenty million dollars to leave your job," Knobby says with a slap of his open hand to the table, making dishes jump up and rattle.

"Twenty is a lot," I say in response to his excited energy on the topic. "What's the thinking behind twenty?"

"Well, Hank Hanson, it's simple. I win twenty. Right away, I say, I'll take that all in cash, thank you. I do not trust them to pay it out over a lifetime; the lottery commission could change the rules. Now down to say, eighteen cash, after the full payout penalty, and then the government takes its half. Now down to nine, and I put that nine million in a credit union savings account making minimal interest. I'm good with that. If I put part of it into a higher-risk investment, I can do that. I am still covered. That's a good life."

"Won't there be a lot of people asking you for donations to their cause? Family lining up with open hands?"

"No," he replies emphatically. "In fact, Hanson, you may never know that I've ever won money. I'm going to take every precaution to not let anyone but my beautiful wife, Kate, know."

During this, the busiest night of the year for every bar, pub, and pool hall in Michigan, we feel the crowd start to press against our table and the volume of the music rise. It is time to go.

With reassurances to everyone that I will be fine walking the six blocks to my loft apartment over RedMitten Greetings, the ladies kiss me good night. Kate gives an added embrace, saying, "Call if you need anything." The guys give hearty handshakes and the masculine half hug.

Minutes later I am in my apartment and listening to my old-fashioned two-tape answering machine, which sounds off several reminders of the Thanksgiving Day itinerary.

THANKSGIVING

2

I still have a half hour before my alarm will sound, but I am wide-awake. My cat, Perry Winkelberry, sits on my chest and looks into my eyes. He purrs and gives me a gentle head butt. After showering, shaving, and pretending that my hair pushed and parted a certain way makes a difference, I grab my overnight bag, pull my blazer from its hanger, and head to my car.

It is still dark outside. The fresh cold air of morning feels good and wakes my senses. Last night's snow remains in a thin layer over the green grass. Only the watery remains of snowflakes cover the concrete sidewalk to remind me they tried to establish a cold front overnight.

My 1986 maroon-colored Pontiac Parisian Safari Station Wagon with wood trim and a "back-back" backseat, which I've named Paris, waits patiently in my assigned parking space. Paris is the only car I've ever owned. I purchased it from my mother. Paris is roughly eighteen feet long and just shy of ten feet wide. After three preliminary pumps on the gas pedal and a turn of the key, she roars to life.

My itinerary today is the same as it has been for five years. As was described to my friends last night, my total time with Paris today should take four hours and fifty-four minutes, and put approximately 268 miles on her chassis.

Breakfast is uneventful. Sweet and delicious toppings are available to cover the crepes as three generations of P3's friends pack into a small house for a Thanksgiving tradition. The people there knew my mother and say they still see her when they look at me, which pauses any conversation with an awkward stir of the emotional sediment that has gone untouched since our last meeting.

After repeating my holiday mantra to nearly each of them—"I am fine. The business is fine; and of course, I will tell everyone you said hello"—my family duties are fulfilled, and I return to the warmth of Paris and her V8 engine for the forty-five-minute drive to what is commonly called Downriver, just south of Detroit.

Near the steel mill, Downriver has several middle-class suburbs along the Detroit River. They have names like River Rouge, Taylor, Southgate, Allen Park, and my favorite, named after a Native American tribe, Wyandotte.

I find a note on the door of P4's red-brick split-level. Last night Tess decided to drive to her son's home to see her grandchildren. I find this to be typical of her behavior, but now I am ahead of schedule, giving me enough time to do something I have not had the chance to do since childhood: to attend the Thanksgiving Day Parade in Detroit.

I find a parking space close to the parade route and step quickly toward Woodward Avenue. As a single adult, I can move past herds of families with small children to the strips of newly refurbished streets between Cass Corridor and the casinos built in Greektown.

I find a good viewing location by an electrical box. I check; I am not blocking the view of kids. I am tall enough to see over others in front of me. A light flurry of flakes falls.

My favorite part of the parade is watching the high school marching bands. Marching bands from across our mitten-shaped state get a chance to drive in and be part of the annual festivities. The Detroit

All City Marching Band attends, as well as bands from local high schools, including Troy, Chippewa Valley, Macomb, Walled Lake, Cadillac, and Henry Ford II. They provide some of the highest-energy, best-marching music for this event. Other groups also march in the parade, with banners such as "Vikings," "Matadors," or "Woodsmen" from other parts of the state. What really gets Motown thumping is a local group playing "Smooth Criminal" by Michael Jackson, with a dance team working it out in front of the cameras.

"Now that was a great band," I hear from my left.

"Amazing," I reply with a smile.

I look to my left; she seems close to my age. She is slightly shorter, wearing a plum-colored jacket and a white knit hat, and her large blue eyes are beautiful. A small, perfectly constructed snowflake catches in the tip of an eyelash.

"I love that song," she says, taking a sip from her white cup. "And they had such a fun twist to it."

I try not to look at her directly, but cannot help myself. "Yeah, that was maybe the best I've seen today."

"You bring your kids here?" she asks.

"Ah, no, I don't have kids," I say, putting my hands in my jacket pocket.

She smiles. "Friends?"

I chuckle a bit and shuffle my feet.

"I have those, but not with me today. I was on my way to my next stop to visit some family when I decided to steal away for some time. I enjoy the parade. It's a rare treat for me."

She is confident, direct, and has a presence that lacks reservation. "I'm here with my sister and her three kids. They love to come down each year, and the guys stay for the game."

I pause, trying to think of what game might be on. For me Thanksgiving is about driving, eating, and telling the same stories repeatedly to people I see annually.

"Oh yeah, that's right, the football game is down here now."

"Duh. Are you new to the area?" She is teasing me.

"No. It is just that I haven't been to the parade since I cannot remember the year, and I only catch the game on TV here and there. Games were always at the Silverdome, in Pontiac, the last time I came down for the parade." There is a beat of silence, and I worry I have lost her interest. "It really is a full day in Detroit."

She smiles intently, listening to each word. "If you like to run, they start the day early with the Turkey Trot. They run the parade route."

"Most of my running is while being chased, but that makes sense now, all those people with numbers on."

She looks as if she is trying to make sense of me, and then smiles as if she has decided what her judgment of me will be. "Would you like some hot chocolate? We have an extra cup."

"Yes, please, that would be great, thank you."

She reaches over to a backpack to remove a thermos and another white paper cup. Carefully pours and hands it to me. It is hot and tasty.

"Mmm. I think there's a little something more than hot chocolate going on here," I say with a warming grin.

"Yeah, that would be the peppermint schnapps. I gave you some from the adult thermos. It helps one make it through the day. You are an adult, right? Not some giant minor hustling the streets for a drink." She pretends as if that were even a possible choice.

"Thank you, thank you very much." I pause for another sip. "I'm sorry, where are my manners? My name is Hank Hanson."

She removes her glove, extends her bare hand, and we shake. "I'm Erin Contee."

Our hands touch, and in an instant, I can feel the full wonderfulness of her skin press my palm, soft, tender, delightful. "It's a pleasure to meet you, Erin."

"You've got warm hands." Erin Contee smiles.

The next band starts to thunder, eliminating any chance for conversation. We pause. The music is a fun version of "Take on Me" by A-ha, a song that Erin and I seem to know every word to as we move in time to the music. As the band moves on and we can talk again, I fumble for another question to learn more about Erin.

"What do you like about the parade? What brings you down here every year?" I ask.

She leans in closer, as if it were a secret between us, and says, "I like people watching. There are so many interesting people here. Last year we stood next to Jack White from the White Stripes for a while. We talked a little bit. He was supernice. Are you someone famous?"

"No, no, I'm just a small business owner from Ann Arbor," I say.

"I like Ann Arbor. What type of business do you own?"

Humble is the way I always talk about my achievements to new friends. "A small greeting card company. We make a line of greeting cards that's slightly popular these days, and we have this online service where you can make and send your own designs."

"RedMitten Greetings?" she asks.

"Oh, you know about us. That's cool."

"Oh my God, yeah, I know about you guys. You are world famous in Michigan. You have the coolest cards. I share those online all the time."

"Yep, that's what I do. What about you?"

"Graphic designer. I live in Plymouth," she says as if it were a small or disappointing fact.

"I like that area, very friendly," I say with encouragement.

"Yeah, but it's not cool like Ann Arbor."

"I don't know; Plymouth is pretty fun."

"It's OK, very family friendly, but if you don't have kids or a husband like me, it's just OK."

I pause for a moment, not knowing what to say. She is telling me she's single, and she did offer me a drink; she must be interested, not just friendly.

"Are you going to the game later with the boys?" I ask.

"No, they drove separately. After this we'll go over to the tailgate and eat some lunch, then head home. After the guys get back from the game, we will eat a big turkey dinner at my sister's. How about you?"

I smile, hoping she won't freak out from my answer. "My next stop is my mother's third husband and his family in Bloomfield Hills; then I'll drive up to St. Clair, not St. Clair Shores, to see my grandparents, and after that, over to Brighton to see my father and his family."

"That's like, five hours in the car, not including time with people," she says, processing the time and distance as she speaks.

"Yeah. And I've already had two stops and three hours in the car this morning."

She leans in again. "I bet you don't really like the way you spend Thanksgiving, do you?"

I look her into the eyes, "You know me so well already, Erin, and we've just met."

"Why don't I put my number in your phone," she says, exposing her hand again, "and if you need a friendly voice while you drive the day away, you call me. I want you to call and tell me about your adventures."

I pull my phone from my jacket and surrender it under the power of her will. She begins to type.

Trying to be interesting I ask, "Did you do this for Jack White last year too?"

"No, we just had dirty sex in an alley," her quick wit fires back.

"Really?"

"No, Hank Hanson, I'm just messing with you." Her delivery is dry and her smile is nearly sinister. "Hank Hanson, are you really a superhero?"

With a wink, I reply, "Super, maybe. Hero, can't say yet."

"Hank Hanson, if that is your real name, call this number. Tell me about your adventures." She returns the phone.

"Erin Contee, it's been a pleasure watching the parade with you."

She says eagerly, "Are you leaving?"

"I have to get to my next stop of the day."

"You're not going to stay for Santa?"

I smile and before I can stop myself from being too cheesy, I say, "I already have the best present I could ask for—your number."

Her white cheeks flush on pale skin, nearly matching her plum jacket.

"Don't be afraid to use that gift. Don't let it expire."

We are both full of smiles as I step away from the electrical box. I turn back twice, watching as she glances back at me. Finally I force myself to walk down Grand River to where I parked Paris.

3

It is too soon to call Erin Contee. I am driving to Bloomfield Hills. After my detour to the parade, I recalculate the map in my mind to get to my next destination.

In previous years I would have had to consider football traffic on this end of Woodward Avenue, where the Detroit Lions once played.

Bloomfield Hills is nice. I am not sure if Mom married P5 because he is the world's most interesting man, or it was just good timing. Maybe she married him for money. Mom had her practical side, after all. I recall P5 appearing embarrassed about Paris a few years back, when first invited to the house for dinner. She is older, well run, carrying lots of miles, and showing slight signs of patina. In this area people have nice homes, nice cars parked in heated garages, next to in-ground heated pools.

I certainly find P5 the most accomplished of my mother's husbands. He has circled the globe, been to every continent. He has a gun collection in what I would call a furnished basement, but it serves as his showroom, which is well lit. Running the full length of one wall, guns from nearly every century since the invention of firearms hang on display. Pizza moguls live to the right of him; the owners of the largest family-owned publishing company live to the left.

Despite all this, P5 is one of the kindest people I know. I am always grateful that my mother's final years were happy with him.

I am here for lunch. There are several cars in the circle drive ahead of me. I attempt to put Paris in a part of the drive that people can get around, but I make sure that it's a spot where I can also get out quickly in the next hour. On a hanger behind the driver seat is my navy utility jacket for lunch. I look at it with hope. I hope it is the right thing for this occasion. I hope that the hair from Perry Winkelberry has disappeared, following cleaning. I pull out my blazer, which I can pair with nearly everything I own, including today's khaki pants and blue button-down shirt.

A flutter of snow remains lightly adrift on the currents of the wind. It is refreshing to feel the cold air against me as I walk back up the drive to the house where P5 stands under the portico with a glass of wine in each hand.

"I heard you pull up and thought I'd pour you a glass. It is from this little place called Frog's Leap. Your mother and I fell in love with it the last time we were in Napa Valley. It's a 2010 Sauvignon Blanc that is like butter."

"Thank you."

"You're welcome." He hands me the glass and then gives me a strong embrace without spilling. "It's so good to see you again." I can hear him smell my hair and start to well up with emotion. "I'm so glad you're here."

"Thank you for inviting me. It was such a good time last year having lunch with you, I couldn't pass up the offer."

He leads me in the front door, down the hall with hand-laid Spanish tile, around to the back of the house to the entertainment room and entertaining kitchen. Leather reclining couches line the walls of the room, facing what may be the largest and thinnest television ever made. Many of the faces are semifamiliar from the wedding. I know his three children, one older than me, one in college, and the third in high school. They are nearly as nice as their father and understand the logistical challenges involved in the holiday.

"We were watching the parade earlier," he says. "The game is going to be on soon."

"Yeah, I was able to get to the parade for about an hour this morning. I enjoyed myself downtown."

"We were just talking about next year and having lunch in the company's luxury suites in Ford Field instead of here. You interested?"

"I would love to be there, but don't make a decision based on me. If I can be there, you know I will."

"We'll put you down as a maybe," he says with a smile.

In the kitchen are two women with white, pressed shirts and black skirts. They are preparing food and placing things on a counter that is normally reserved for barstools and drinks. This is something I am still not accustomed to, having staff, especially on a holiday, though I do suspect many people are looking for additional money this time of year.

I provide an accurate, optimistic picture in response to the obligatory, exploratory, question: we just increased staff to twenty-one and are working hard; our online business is primary, the on-demand publishing is a close second, and yes, offers may have come in to buy the business, but no, I am not allowed to talk about them. If anyone was truly interested in my business, it would be P5. He cosigned the loan for the building housing RedMitten Greetings when no one else could. He never has to worry about his act of generosity. I have paid ahead on the mortgage, invested in upkeep, and moved in myself, to the upper floor, to keep all overhead down.

Most of my business phone calls and meetings cover an introduction, identification of every party, and a clear articulation of my point of view, including lots of listening before wrap-up. I find that working this holiday crowd is similar, with an opening question, followed by an update from every participant, an articulation of my point of view, and lots of listening, before wrap-up—although here it is questions about whether I have heard this or that, what's the latest update on a family member, and what do I think? I respond, listen, and listen, and there is a wrap-up of what will happen before we meet again.

P5 would like a moment of my time. This breaks the cadence. He offers me a seat in his home office. One wall is lined with books, a leather couch positioned across from his large well-organized desk. His vantage is a seat of power.

He starts directly. "You know I loved your mother. She was a great friend and greatest love to me. Our short time together was the happiest time I have ever had. You remind me of her in many ways. It's always good to have you here, and I want to make certain you know that."

I can see where this conversation is going and prepare for the comparison. I'm not against emotions, but have become less compassionate over the years to Mother's friends and loved ones treating me this way, although you wouldn't know it from my expression.

"I really like being here, and truly, I understand why Mom was so in love with you. I know she felt the same about you as you did about her."

I look in his general direction, but do not make eye contact so as not to upset him further, but it is too late. His eyes fill with tears, and he swivels his chair to look out the window.

"I'm glad to hear that, Hank. I am very glad to hear that," he says, fighting back tears. "I wonder if you might be able to talk to your brother and sister for me, because they are just as welcome here. I want them to know I feel they are just as much a part of my life and family as you are."

"I understand," I say, but I don't, really.

"You understand that you and my kids, and your brother and your sister, they are the only family I have. It is important to me—these relationships. Your mother's passing…It just made me so aware of how short life can be."

"I understand. I do."

He reaches for some tissue on the edge of his desk. "And after all my years of travel, of seeing the world, it's still difficult to find someone to really connect with, and when you find something that rare, something that important, you want to hold on to it."

"I understand what you're saying, and I can appreciate that you're still getting over the loss. It might be even more than that. And I'm sorry I can only make it over here once a month."

"No, no, don't apologize," he interrupts.

"It would be nice to see each other more, I understand that. I'll mention it to my brother and sister, but they have their own lives, and they live farther away, so it's difficult to make it back here with any frequency."

"I know, I know that, and I understand. I was only a stepfather for a few short years, and that is not much to go on."

"Think of it this way: at least they're not asking you for money or favors. They're pretty honest people in that respect."

"You're right. I do appreciate the connections we have; I just wish it could be better."

"It's tough. I get it. It can be lonely, I understand. I think it is great that you open your heart and home like this when you don't have to. It shows what a generous person you are. Would you like to meet someone new?"

"I don't think anyone could replace your mother, Hank," he says with a deep sigh.

"No, I don't think so either. But maybe someone who is interested in similar things, someone to spend time with, not true love, but companionship."

He tries to say something through the emotions. "Maybe, Hank, maybe."

"Well, if I meet the right lady for you, I'm going to bring her to dinner next time. Fair?"

"Fair."

He swivels back in my direction and quickly grabs some tissues, before we exit his office. Another bear hug lingers longer than I would like, but I let him squeeze away, feeling like a surrogate for the loss of his best friend and my mother.

The very core of his expression is the reason my brother and sister avoid contact with P5. Apparently, there is something about each of us that reminds other people of our mom, but I will never completely understand it. It triggers a longing and emptiness in those who have lost her, but we cannot replace her. Since her death they have slowly drifted away, and I am not sure if they remove themselves out of protection, or if they were never really engaged in the relationship from the start.

I am not my mom. I am not the one P5 is missing, but even I understand that three genetic half versions of her showing up might feel as though it could fill that emptiness. Like any crutch, you need to wean, and slowly, or you will be dependent on it forever.

I am stuffed after a pass at the fancy snacks and appetizers with P5 and that engorging breakfast with P3. It is only one thirty in the afternoon, and I cannot bear to eat another thing, yet I have two full Thanksgiving dinners in front of me.

With hugs and good-byes to P5, his friends, and my nonsiblings, I am finally back in Paris and making my way east to St. Clair Shores, an hour away.

Can I safely drive and call Erin Contee?

4

This morning's drive down the Southfield Freeway to see Dad's second wife, Tess, P4, has stirred up memories of my brother, sister, and me spending weekends downriver. Dad's brown Buick Regal with T-top had an eight-track player and a brown leather case in the backseat full of tapes. My older brother paid close attention to the system that allowed each of us in turn to choose a tape each time we got in the car. While my sister would always choose Donna Summer, or the soundtrack to *Saturday Night Fever*, my brother would always pick KISS (something Mother forbade us to listen to, believing we too might become knights in Satan's service). Without fail I would always choose Electric Light Orchestra's *Out of the Blue*.

When an argument ensued about whose turn it was, Dad would settle things by throwing on Bob Seger and the Silver Bullet Band's *Live Bullet*. Recorded in Detroit at Cobo Hall, this album was Dad's favorite; he knew every word and would claim that you could hear his new wife, P4, screaming in the audience during part of track two, "Travelin' Man."

Music impresses a mark upon every childhood that remains throughout one's life. My sister was far too young to know what the lyrics to "Hot Stuff" implied, or why Summer wanted to "Dim All the Lights." She may have been too young for Donna Summer, but later she was well aware of what Madonna's "Like a Virgin" suggested. The mark grew and darkened and matured into what we all called adulthood. Music matters.

When P4 took her turn, she would always pick one song: "Don't Stop Believing," by Journey. The opening lyrics scream, "Just a small-town girl, living in a lonely world, she took the midnight train going anywhere," followed by, "Just a city boy, born and raised in South Detroit." P4 never failed to take my father's hands and look at him lovingly. There was more in that look than I remember my mom ever giving Dad, and this always brought me peace of mind that my parents' divorce was the right choice.

Now safely up to freeway speeds, I hit the speakerphone on the cell phone and say, "Dial brother, home."

The female automated voice responds, "Did you say, dial brother, home?"

"Yes," I confirm.

"OK, dialing brother, home."

After a few rings, I hear a grumble. "Hank?"

"Hey, Mark! Happy Thanksgiving!"

"Happy Thanksgiving, Hank."

"Did I wake you?"

"No, no, I fell asleep on the couch while the kids were watching the parade in New York," he mumbles, slowly coming to life.

"I made the Detroit parade this year. It is a great place to be, Mark. You should think about coming back for Christmas next year."

"Yeah, I'll think about that," Mark says wryly. His lack of excitement over returning home to Michigan is clear.

"You still loving McLean?" I ask.

"Yeah, Virginia is for lovers. It is a nice area. Easy to get into the labs, the kids love their schools, and the missus has her job supporting the think tank. It's going really well out here. What about you? Are you still stuck on that holiday roll? What is it, five Thanksgivings in one day?"

"I'm between P5 and St. Clair. It'd be better if you were here, you know; you could pick the mix tape."

"Oh, the shorter of the long legs in your wagon, sounds fun. How is old P5?"

"Emotional," I say with an understanding he knows very well.

"Still missing Mom." I can hear him get up off the couch and move to a more private area of the house.

"Yeah, those two were just right for each other. I wish they'd have had more time together."

"Yeah, life would have been a lot easier without our father. You still talking to him?"

I can hear the underlying anger in his voice, the gritty tightening of muscles in his jaw. "Dad? Yes, I'm planning to see him later."

"He hasn't left a voice mail in a few months. I'm guessing he has gotten the hint I don't want anything to do with him."

"I would like to see you again sometime too. I know the others would. You don't have to see him,"

"Maybe next year," he repeats for the fourth year in a row. "You should be careful not to get tangled up with him, Hank."

"The drugs?"

"I was thinking more of what he did to dear sister. With her social security number."

"You think forging a line of credit in Lisa's name was what split them up? I always thought it was the cheating with another woman." I set the cruise control at seventy-two.

"He's lucky he didn't go to jail for that. Mom was able to remove that from Lisa's credit score, as she was a minor. The cheating," he said with a thoughtful pause, "that was just an excuse to tell the judge."

"I may have been too young to know what was going on," I say in my defense.

"Probably," he said with a turn of the subject. "Weed was not the biggest issue for me. If it were just the weed, I think I would be cool with it all; then he's just a hippie. It's the broken piggy banks, the savings account Mom set up for college that he closed, the empty birthday cards from Grandma, who later inquired about the twenty dollars she gave me."

"It's a long list, I know."

His tone starts to sound like Mom's. "What about the driving? The long drives to nowhere, and he won't stop. You told me about that awful trip to Mackinaw City when you missed three days of school for no better reason than to get away."

Looking through the same windshield, I say, "I remember."

"And he made you hold the coffee can while he pissed rather than stop at the rest area just to make good time. Good time for what?" I can hear the anger in his voice start to rise.

"Hey, I just wanted to wish you a happy Thanksgiving, not spoil your day," I say to slow him down and allow him to take a pause.

"I don't know why you still talk to that guy. He's nothing but trouble."

"He's our dad. I can't give up on him. He's the only one we get."

"Really? You have had two spares to back up the first one that went flat. It's OK to disengage from him." He sounds exasperated from reliving the experience. "Every one in two hundred people in this world is a direct descendant of Genghis Khan, but you don't see him being touted as a great father."

"Yeah, I know. I know it's not that easy," I say. We stay on the line in silence. I suspect he is counting down from twenty in his mind to clear it.

The clinical and scientific voice of professionalism returns. "How is the business?" he asks. "I see you online everywhere these days."

"Business is good," I say with hesitation. "I've gotten an offer. I am not supposed to talk about it, so I can't say. It's a lot of money. I don't think I can turn it down. It's a lot to think about."

"Well, congratulations, I'm sure you'll make the right choice." I can hear the pride in his voice.

"Says the biological engineer," I say softly.

"Yeah, I studied, I've got a PhD, but you're the smart one," says a big brother proud of his little brother.

"Thanks, Mark. Happy Thanksgiving."

"Happy Thanksgiving to you. Call again, you know, whenever."

"Give my best to the family."

"Yeah, will do."

The line goes out with a click. I press the speakerphone off, than tap it again to reengage.

"Dial sister."

"Did you say dial sister?"

"Yes."

"OK, dialing sister."

"Hello?" Her voice is a clear question.

"Happy Thanksgiving!" I burst out.

"Hi, Hank, happy Thanksgiving!" she replies with the familiar sound of my little sister putting up with my overenthusiasm.

"Did I call too early?" I tease.

"No, no, I've been up for hours. Chickens, milking cows, feeding sheep."

"How cold is it in Madison, Wisconsin?" I taunt.

"Waterloo," she replies dryly.

"How is Napoleon in Waterloo?"

"That's old, Hank."

"You could name one of the cows Napoleon. Then it would be true when I called."

"OK, Hank, I'll name one of the cows Napoleon because I live in Waterloo, Wisconsin."

"Thanks. How are things?"

"Things are starting to cool down here. Where are you?"

"Between P5 and grandparents."

"Please tell Grandma that I'm using her stuffing recipe this year." She is sweet and kind and all the great things you want in a sister.

"I will."

"How were the crepes?" she asks.

There is blandness in my tone she knows. "Still good. Same people."

"Well," she says, lacking everything but politeness, "I'm glad he has his traditions. It means a lot to him. As a person of routine, I can appreciate the comfort in getting together regularly. If I didn't have the animals, I'd come home, but you know they need daily care."

"I know. If it weren't for the job, I'd be out there to see you more often. Nevertheless, I do miss you. I enjoy seeing you." I find it easier to talk openly with her.

"In a couple years, when things are settled, we can visit more," she says for the fourth year in a row.

"I'd like that. I'd like that a lot." I can hear her step outside with the slam of the exterior door and take a deep breath of what I imagine is cold country air. "You going to see Dad?"

"I planned to swing by."

"He still married to that woman who broke your brother?" I can hear the venom build from years of protecting her bigger brother.

"Yes, they still have kids and still have a house. You know, your brother is not broken; he is a successful married man with a family. That's hardly broken."

"He may have healed, but he's not whole. You watch yourself with her, Hank. She's not right in the head," she warns.

"How do you mean, outside of the obvious?"

She laughs. "Aside from the creepy feeling you get spending time with her, aside from her past with our brother, aside from that odd stare she has?"

"Yes, aside from all that." I start to laugh with her.

"Just be careful, Hank; don't get too involved with them."

"I know, I know."

"You're a generous person; I don't want you to get taken advantage of."

"Me?" I say sarcastically.

"Be careful," she says as if I were one of her calves.

"I will, I will. Let's talk again soon," I say to get off the phone.

"Sounds good."

"Happy Thanksgiving!"

"Happy Thanksgiving!"

5

Grandma and Grandpa have the fortitude that exemplifies the greatest generation forged in the pain of the Great Depression, World War II, and parenting boomers. Many of the things I hear from them are without regard to the exploration of gender roles of the 1970s. She is in the kitchen, he in his armchair with the paper.

She is making what she calls "navy coffee," which always tastes good. I thought the name derived from putting a pinch of salt in the grounds, but it actually comes from the precise measurements the sailor's manual gives for the ratio of coffee grounds to water, and the rule never to wash the coffeepot, only to rinse it.

"Dinner," says Grandpa, "is the laboratory of American democracy. You sit around a family dinner table, you learn how to treat one another, debate the events of the day, show respect to one another by listening. Hell, you even learn how to fight for the scraps."

The two-bedroom apartment is on the fourth floor of the home. An elevator is large enough for two EMS crash carts. Its lobby is full of staff ready to help. There are craft rooms, activity rooms, card rooms, smoking rooms, and a comfortable dining room if one does not feel up to cooking.

Grandma always feels up to cooking. She is especially good at it. Even though this is not the large house with the large kitchen where they raised my father and his nine siblings, they seem very happy here.

The phone rings on the wall. Grandma answers it while Grandpa is unmoved, still in his paper. It's one of my aunts calling, and Grandma listens while the person on the phone chats away. She looks over the pots boiling on the electric stove. She prefers gas, I have been told repeatedly, but this is what they have here, so one makes do.

"Papa, your daughter is on the phone, say happy Thanksgiving to her," Grandma says, bringing the phone with an extra-long cord to him.

"Well, hello, honey," he starts.

I join Grandma in the kitchen while he spends some quality time on the phone. She stirs some things and pokes at others, making certain things are proceeding at the right pace.

"Are you dating?" she asks.

"I'm not," I reply.

"What happened to that nice girl Sandy? You two were seeing each other for a while there."

"Sandy and I were not a good fit."

"I worry that you're alone. It's not good for a man like you to be alone. So focused on work."

"Well, it's my business, and it's my responsibility."

"Still, wouldn't it be nice to give Sandy a call and catch up with her?"

"Have you been talking to Sandy recently?" I ask, knowing the two were close.

"She will call once in a while, for birthdays, holidays," she says.

"Did she call today?"

"She did, she's such a nice girl. I don't think she's seeing anyone, if you gave her a call."

"Grandma, she is a very nice girl."

Now fussing with my life as well as the food, she says, "If you say it's not a fit, it's not a fit. I just would like to see you have someone in your life before I die."

Simply, factually, I say, "I have friends, I have work, I have family. I don't know if I have time for a relationship with Sandy."

She sighs and says, "I always thought it was a nice story how you two met. It's a nice story to tell." She continues to stir and check food.

"Grandma, if that's the story you like to tell, that's fine, but I remember it a little different."

"How was it different?"

"Sandy was nice. She was a devout Christian who—" She cuts me off midsentence.

"Oh, I always forget that part, a former missionary. That would be so good for you, Hank."

I am not sure how to take that statement—as a compliment, or as a statement that I'm such a sinner or so in need of spiritual guidance, I need one of God's helpers.

"She was a former missionary," I say, stressing the word *former*. "They asked her to leave those good works when a member of the congregation impregnated her, and she returned to the US so the baby wouldn't be raised in the back squalor of some struggling former Soviet bloc."

Grandma, surprised, replies, "She had a child? Sandy never mentions that on the phone."

"No, she wouldn't have brought it up. She lost the baby. Sandy and I met in that wonderful story you love so much three months later."

"Oh, I didn't know," she says, trying to take it all in.

"I never told you, Grandma. During that year we had some good times, but she never got over the loss of that baby. I do not know that she ever will or anyone ever could. We spent many weekends at the cemetery with flowers." I felt relieved to finally tell someone the truth about this part of the story. "Sandy is very nice, but she isn't the one for me."

Grandma looks at me with a sad forced smile I don't really understand. "No parent would ever, could ever, get over the loss of a child. You were very nice to date a girl who wasn't, you know, pure."

With an uncertain smile, I say, "Yes, well, there are not many pure people out there, Grandma."

Dinner with my grandparents is pleasant. They provide third-hand accounts of all my aunts and uncles living adult lives spread across North America. Most of my cousins are adults now, providing their parents more leisure time or ability to travel. My father, I am reminded, is only a two-hour drive from here and has not been seen or heard from in some time. The disappointment is not disguised, and I agree to convey the message to him during my next and final stop of the day.

Throughout the dinner the only real question in my mind is "What do I say to Erin Contee when I call her?"

6

Erin Contee picks up on the second ring. "Well, that took a while. How are you? Where are you?"

It is a relief she's not playing out some role or precept of society to be coy and distant. She sounds genuinely interested in her playful scolding. You would think we had been married as long as my grandparents had.

"Hi, it's Hank." I pretend as if she needed the introduction.

"Hi, Hank. I knew it was you with caller ID. Thought you would play it cool and wait a few hours?"

"No, no, I wouldn't do that; I just left my grandparents and called you."

"OK, so what was your favorite part?"

"Grandma makes great dried dressing, and you put gravy on it."

"Oh my God, my grandma does the same thing. The gravy brings it back to life, and it is amazing. Where are you?"

"I'm about ten minutes from I-94 in St. Clare, and I'll be heading north for a bit, then west to Flint. We have about two hours."

"That's a lot of driving alone."

"I have my car, and some good mix tapes, and you on the speakerphone."

"You have mix *tapes*?" She cackles across the phone with excitement.

"I do. My station wagon still plays tapes. I still make mix tapes."

"Holy shit. Get out of here. I love mix tapes."

"It's a lost art. Each year I lead a thing with friends called the Great Mix Experiment. Everyone makes a playlist and sends it to me—MP3s, gift cards, some actual tapes even. I put them together and send them back out to everyone, so everyone who is part of the exchange gets a copy." I hit the turn signal and bring the wagon up to freeway speed going down the ramp.

"That's pretty cool. How many people do this?"

"Like twenty, twenty-five. Depends on the year."

"So everyone gets music from everyone else."

I check my blind spot twice and merge left.

"Yeah, some of it's repeats, some of it's new and out there. You want to put things on your list that you have been listening to that year, not what the radio has, but what you have been listening to. It's like a yearbook of music, and you share it with others."

"So you drive around with all these tapes?"

"I do. It is like Hans Christian Andersen said: 'Where words fail, music speaks.' You can tell from the mix who has had a good year, or a bad year, the ups and downs of what they are going through."

"That's so wonderful."

"Here I am going on. What about you, Erin? What are you doing? Where are you?"

"I'm still at my sister's. The others have finished with dinner and are starting to play cards. Do you play euchre?"

"It's a state law. Everyone plays euchre in Michigan. I think the nurses were teaching it in the maternity ward when I was born."

"I know how to play, but some people in my family are really competitive. They really get into the game. Sometimes they get so—uproarious—at times."

"Yes, uproarious."

"Other times they get belligerent."

"Yes, belligerent."

"Are you just repeating my words?"

"No, that's exactly how I would describe every hand of euchre I've ever played. There must be something about this game that sets people off. I've never really understood trump, tricks, or going alone."

"I've never understood going alone either." There was a change in her tone. It was deep, sexy, and seductive. "Going alone can be fun once in a while, but you need a really good hand. Going alone is not something I'm interested in doing. It's always good to have a partner."

"Are we still talking about cards?"

She giggled to my honest question. "Oh, you are fun, Hank Hanson."

7

Dad, P2, my father, winning sperm delivery system, peeks through the curtain window of the poorly lit house to make eye contact before clicking the three locks on the door to open it. This three-story McMansion monster is a project he started five years ago with the onset of his current marriage. Outside it is very nice. Picturesque, with its clean horizontal lines that merge into the surrounding green lush landscape and stone circle drive to the front entrance in an equally nice neighborhood. Inside it is very rough. He says he is saving money by doing most of the labor himself. Still, to this day, most items are covered in drop cloths and sheets to protect them from the paint, stain, and general dust. Most floors in the house are the original particle sheets contractors put in as subflooring. Two rooms are "complete," the kitchen and the entertainment room. They would be more complete if the walls, not just studs, were finished with sheet rock, mud, and paint.

P2 tilts his head and mumbles something about coming in. There is something sad but mischievous behind his eyes. He moves like an aged boxer shuffling his open-toed sandaled feet, slightly hunched from the years on the assembly line. It has been nearly five years, around the same time he started the house and current marriage, since he has been to a barber. The long gray ponytail, emblematic of that high point of his generation, is now wiry and damaged, bound by an elastic band.

"Happy Thanksgiving, Dad!"

"Yeah." He is gruff. "Happy Thanksgiving, come on in. We're in front of the television."

P6, Dad's current wife, Midge, sits on the couch watching my twin four-year-old half brother and sister, Jason and Jenna, play with a mountain of toys. The television is on mute as Dorothy and Toto meet Ray Bolger in brilliant Technicolor.

"Hey, Hank Hanson," P6 says.

"Hey, how are you?" I lean in and give Midge a kiss on the cheek. She was a senior in high school when I was a freshman. There are reasons that my older brother and she don't talk. Reasons that he has not been able to make the visit during any holiday over the last five years. One of them being they are from the same graduating class. I don't ask for details on the other reasons. I can only imagine it has something to do with the amount of time they dated and with being each other's "first time."

"You hungry? We have some turkey leftovers from earlier," she says with that slightly off expression my sister described.

"No, thank you, I've had more than my fill of turkey today," I say.

"See, I told you we didn't need to wait for him," Dad chimes in. "Everyone else feeds him." He walks to another area of the first floor to tinker.

"Well, sorry," she says, increasing her volume as he walks away. "We invited him over. I thought it would be nice to offer."

Having arguments in this house must be difficult. You can continue to walk away from someone for a good amount of time and still be in each other's line of sight through the wall studs. You have to make an effort to go up to one of the two higher floors where bedrooms and bathrooms will one day be enjoyed, or downstairs to the unfinished walkout basement/Dad's tool collection and building materials, before someone can't see you.

"There's pop in the fridge if you're thirsty," she says.

"Thanks, I'm good. How are Jason and Jenna?"

"Stompy and Screamy? These two little miracles? Oh, they are acting like four-year-olds."

"Little miracles?" I ask.

"Oh yeah, they're like the Immaculate Conception, didn't you know? Your father's vasectomy was reversed by God himself," she answers loudly. "Because your father swears he had that procedure after his last wife, and your father never lies."

This level of uncomfortable conversation is not new to me. Building a tolerance takes time. Earlier, when they met, later when they were married, and those first six months, it was fun. The two could not get enough of each other. She was his biggest fan, and I think Dad really believed he had found love again. Since then they have been more open in front of me. I don't know about others, but I get to hear every detail.

"If you two are done jabbering, Hank, I could use a hand downstairs," he says, halfway down the steps.

"Sure, Dad," I call out to him. "I'm going to help Dad. Are you good here with Stompy and Screamy?"

"Yes, you boys go ahead and do male bonding stuff." Her voice changes with the children getting louder. "If you two don't shut up, I'm going to kill Scooby Doo." Her shout brings a hush to the room. "Just kidding," she says after noticing I am still atop the stairs, witness to the loss of control.

Everything in the house is solid. It's well constructed. It is just not finished. It is a house, like an unfinished snowflake is still a snowflake, even when it's not fully crystalized. It is not perfect yet, so we just call it rain.

After five years you would think they would be closer to something like a completed house. Something besides just the television room and the kitchen. Maybe he finished some of the bedrooms upstairs, or the bathrooms, and I haven't seen them yet.

"She is like that," Dad says. "One moment things are fine, something happens and she loses it. Emotions, what can you do? How are things, Hank?"

"Things are good, Dad. Grandma and Grandpa wish you a happy Thanksgiving. They were hoping to see you and your family this year."

"Yeah, I owe them a call," he mutters.

"They're your parents, they worry. I think your dad said that no matter how old you get, they're still your kids."

He huffs. "Yeah, that sounds like something he would say. How are your brother and sister doing?" he asks without showing actual interest.

"Good, they're both good, curing cancer, milking cows. They say happy Thanksgiving as well. They're sorry they couldn't make it."

He looks at me like I'm full of shit. "Yeah, I owe them a call too. I owe everybody," he says with a deeper, almost whispered hush.

"Things down here look"—I search for the nicest thing to say—"organized. It looks like you now have the right tool for everything you might have in the house."

"Grab a seat," he commands.

"Where? Here, on the bench? Or here on the box?"

"Wherever, just sit. Take a knee if you have to."

"OK." I comply. The tone in his voice is serious. Is it desperate? I can't tell, but something is different.

"I'm broke, Hank."

"Oh. This isn't the conversation I thought we were going to have," I say.

"Well, I lost my job four years ago when they closed the Pontiac plant."

"You did? I thought you said you were one of the lucky ones transferred to the other division."

"No. That's not what happened."

He starts to pace in a row of boxes.

"Don't they have a jobs bank or something? I thought that when they rearranged things on the line, they kept top guys like you on the job with ninety percent pay until you went back full-time."

"No. Not this time. I tried to network. I looked for reassignment. Wasn't able to get anything steady. So I ended up dipping into the retirement fund and savings much earlier than planned."

Sympathetic to his plight, I say, "Well, shit, Dad, I'm really sorry to hear that."

Anxious, he says, "I was underwater on the house when the market flipped, and I couldn't borrow more, so that if the market comes back, I could break even."

"Are you saying all your money is tied up in the house?" I say with surprise.

His pacing picks up speed. "Most all of it. I'd been getting unemployment for a long time to cover some things; I cashed in at the worst moment in the market." He stops and looks me in the eyes. "I just can't seem to get a break."

We sit for a bit in silence. I try to process the details of what he has just said. Fiddling with some tool in his hand to keep busy, he finally throws it at the concrete wall, doing little damage. It dawns on me why I am hearing this story.

Slowly it forms at my lips. "Does Midge know?"

"No." He chuckles to himself. "Wives. You would think I'd have learned to stop messing up other people's lives after your mom, but that little girl and the twins are all I really have."

I could hear a quiver in his voice. This is the most honest moment we've ever shared. Despite the warnings from both Mark and Lisa of broken piggy banks, stolen social security numbers, emptied savings accounts, and broken hearts, I want to believe him. I want to believe that he has grown up at some point and is not looking to con me.

"Dad, why are you telling me this—before you tell Midge?"

"Hank—I need your help," he says with desperation.

"What kind of help? I don't have the money to pay off your debts or finish this house; all my money is tied up in my business."

"You said you had an offer on your business."

"OK, slow down. You may have a plan in mind that is not going to happen. First, I have other people counting on me for a paycheck each week. I have a responsibility to them. Second, I told you that in confidence. I cannot talk to people about it. Third, it might not happen. Everything is still in discussions. They're doing their due diligence...background checks, homework to make certain all the things we are talking about are true."

He understands the third explanation.

After a moment he says, "I need you to watch the kids while I break the news to Midge."

"I can do that. We can put them in the car seats, and I'll come back in an hour."

Jason and Jenna are great kids; they can be fussy at times, but they are four years old. Once we are in P6's Chevy Traverse, I take it to the gas station to fill the tank. We drive it through an automated car wash. When I pull up to the house two hours later, both kids are asleep.

One at a time, I take them upstairs and tuck them in.

"Hank," Midge says with a serious tone. "Could you join us for a few minutes before you go?" Her voice comes from the television room.

The room is clean. The television is off.

"Hank, your father and I talked about our situation, and we have a big question for you," she says.

"Go ahead."

"Can we come live with you?"

My initial reaction is to sit down. Right there where I'm standing, I just sit down. Deep in my gut, I know yes is the right thing to say. That would make them happy. Still, I hear my siblings' warnings in the back of my head. Then, practical questions fill my mind. Three adults and two kids in my loft, is it large enough? Maybe, but it would be tight.

How would Perry Winkelberry react? How long would it be? Where else would they go if I do not take them in? My siblings wouldn't do it, or couldn't. Can I afford to put them up in an apartment? Not really, not at this moment. His parents and siblings are out of the question. I don't know much about her family, maybe her parents.

"I can see you're giving it serious consideration, and I appreciate that, Hank," she says.

"It's not"—I stop, still taking it all in—"It's not what I thought you were going to ask. I thought you were going to ask for money." Then I instantly add, "Which I don't have."

"We considered that question as well, but the amount of money we would have to ask for is far too much. Your father showed me the checkbook and told me the numbers he's been struggling with. We're going to have to find a lawyer and file for bankruptcy."

I mumble some encouragement. "Well, lots of people do that. It's a valid financial tool to use in life."

She sighs and with a tinge of sadness says, "It's a bit embarrassing; but you're right. It's the option it looks like we are going to have to take. It makes sense."

"What's the time frame you're thinking about? When are they going to call in on the house?"

"Your father tells me that's already happened. We're looking at fifteen days before our things are on the curb."

"That's fast."

"It is. I would have liked to have had this information earlier, six months ago, four years ago, when he found out about his job, but we're past that point."

"Look," Dad starts to say.

"Don't talk," she snaps. "We agreed I was going to do the talking from now on."

I watch my father recoil like an obedient dog before saying, "I understand."

"Hank, we're in a very tight position, and I don't think we can ask anyone else," she says.

"Yes, yes, the answer is yes. You are family, and you're in need. I want to help you, so the answer is yes. It's just a matter of logistics at this point, making sure that the three of us and the kids can fit in my loft."

"Thank you, Hank," she says.

"Yes, thank you, Hank. Thank you very much," he adds.

"Is anyone allergic to cats?" I ask.

8

The phone rings in wait for the other line to pick up. "Hey, Hank Hanson," Kate says with the joyful greeting of alliteration she's claimed as the number-one reason to take my every call. "Happy Thanksgiving! What tale of sorrow and adventure do you have this year?"

"Where are you?" I ask in response to chatter in the background.

"Michelle, Jean, and I are camping in front of Best Buy for Black Friday," she says.

"Hi, Hank Hanson," Michelle and Jean chime in, like high school girls talking to a boy they like.

"Hello, ladies," I respond.

"What's the poop? Shouldn't you be in bed by now? How did things go?"

"It wasn't what I expected," I say into the cell phone mounted on the enormous gray plastic and wood-like dashboard of the car.

"Interesting good? Or interesting bad?"

"If your parents came to you for money, would you give it to them?"

"In a heartbeat. I'd be really surprised, but yeah, I'd give it to them. I can't see them needing it," she says, trying to work through the ramifications in her head. "Did your dad ask for money?"

"No, he asked to move in with me. He, his wife, and the twins."

"Wow," she says, trying to find the right words. "That's…I don't know what to say."

"I said yes."

She takes a breath and says, "You did the right thing."

"Did I?"

I turn the car down the on-ramp as the engine roars, building up speed for the southbound interstate.

"Yes. I cannot imagine that many people in your loft, but hey, Soviet Russia was good at maximizing apartments. I'm sure you'll figure it out. It'll give you time to get to know him better."

"But you think it's the *right* thing to do?"

"I do. You are now officially part of the sandwich generation. You are stuck between two slices of different generations and have to support them. You are the bacon in bringing home the bacon." She makes me smile.

"I do like bacon."

"Everyone loves bacon." She giggles.

"I don't know that I want to *be* bacon."

"Nobody wants to *be* bacon." She laughs. "All that grease and sputtering, but you get to be hot and sizzle."

Changing the course of the conversation, I drop the news quickly. "I think I may have met someone special."

There is a pause before she says, "Oh really? Is this someone a female?"

"Yes."

I can hear her put her hand over the phone and whisper to the other two, "Hank Hanson met a girl. Where did you two meet?" she asks me.

"I stopped at the parade between visits and ended up standing next to her."

"He met her at the parade," she conveyed to the others, without any effort of hiding it.

I roll my eyes. "You can just put me on speakerphone if you want."

With a click I could hear all three of them taunt me like I was in school again. "Woo, Hank Hanson met a girl, Hank Hanson met a girl."

"How is this bigger news than my dad moving in with me?" I ask.

"Your dad's moving in with you?" Michelle asks.

"Yeah."

"With his *interesting* wife and twins?" Michelle asks.

"Yes."

"Isn't this the one who dated your older brother in high school?" Jean asks pointedly.

"Yes," I say, almost defeated.

"Well, that is awfully big of you," Jean adds.

"Yeah, I wish your loft was as big as your heart." Michelle cackles.

"We will tell the boys that you're going to need them and their trucks to help move," Kate says.

"Thank you."

"We want to hear more about this girl when we see you." Michelle giggles.

"I'll tell you every detail," I say and end the call.

"Dial brother, mobile," I say slowly and clearly into the device.

"Did you say, dial brother, mobile?"

"Yes."

There is a slight pause as I hear the connections cross the vast distances between Michigan and Virginia.

"Hank?" I hear the bleary voice of my brother as he wakes in what I imagine is the darkness of his bedroom, his beautifully toned blond wife nearly naked at his side. "Is everything all right?"

"Yes. There is no emergency, but I wanted to tell you about Dad."

"What?" he says with disbelief. "Why do I care about Dad?"

"He's lost the house, his job, and he's broke."

"Good, karma's catching up with him," he says.

"So they are moving in with me."

"Shut the fuck up," he says bluntly. I can hear him console his wife a bit before moving from the bedroom to a more private place. "Why the hell would you let that happen?"

"He's our dad, they're our siblings," I say to draw out the humanity in my beloved brother. "It's got to mean something, to be our father, doesn't it?"

"I'm not going to be involved in supporting him in any way," he says coldly. "That fucker. Now I'm going to be up all night, another night lost to that idiot and his problems."

"I'm sorry," I say with true sentiment. "I shouldn't have called."

"No, you shouldn't. I'm not mad at you, but let me make it clear, I want nothing to do with that man, or his whore bitch of a wife."

"Understood. You should call my cell going forward." I feel my jaw start to strain. "They might answer the phone at the loft."

"OK, thanks for the heads-up."

"Can you tell our sister in the morning?"

He chuckles. "Me you'll wake up, her you'll let sleep?"

"You're the oldest, you get all the crap."

"True." He pauses and says, "Be careful, Hank."

"I will," I say instinctively.

"No, Hank, be careful. You can't trust him, and she's…she can be manipulating."

"Understood," I say.

"I worry about you, little brother. This might have been the *right* thing to do for any random stranger on the street, but there's history here, bad history."

"OK. Talk soon?"

"Get home safe."

The lines disconnect, and the light from my cell phone dims and fades to black. When I turn up the volume on the tape deck, eerie sounds of the Electro-Theremin from the Beach Boys' "Good Vibrations" fill the wagon.

How appropriate, I think to myself.

All I can do is what I think is best, and right, and true, even if my brother and sister can't see that.

In the morning, my other brothers, Pike, Knobby, and Dord, and I get into a booth of the best breakfast location in town, Zingerman's Roadhouse. The food is amazing; the quality of the selected vendors is impressive and all local. Eggs and meats are farm fresh, according to my three agriculture expert companions. The care in making each dish is notable in the attention to detail. Even better is the coffee, a silky-smooth elegant blend that is the perfect balance to the atmosphere.

Halfway through my first cup of java, waiting for food, it begins. Knobby starts with his slightly vain confidence built from years of being a high school quarterback at a very small school with a poor program built around sportsmanship and play.

"So, I hear you need a favor."

Already beaten, I give no challenge to his sporting taunt. "I'm going to need a big favor."

"How big?" Knobby toys with me.

"Pretty big."

"How will you be repaying this favor?" Dord notices the fodder Knobby started.

My brow wrinkles with the reminder of owing my fraternal brothers a "favor" with hours of cleaning trucks with a toothbrush, followed by their bathroom floors. "I'm not sure yet."

"We know how desperate you are to have us help," Dord says.

"And we're going to need some interest built over time on this, or a large deposit up-front," Knobby adds.

"You're gangsters now? You're asking for a vig? You want juice? Interest?"

"Well, if it were just me, I'd do it." He chews the cut of bacon steak. "But it's all three of us, and we have families to look out for," Knobby jokes.

Pike, putting down his juice, says, "Let him ask for the favor."

"My dad—"

"P2," Knobby cuts in.

"Yes, my dad, P2, is going to lose his house in the next fifteen days. So his wife—"

"P6," Knobby cuts in again. "The one your brother dated in high school."

"Yes, his wife, P6—Midge—the twins, Jason and Jenna, and my dad are going to move into my place until we can sort things out."

"Holy shit! You're not going to fit," Dord says.

Knobby agrees. "Won't fit."

"Hear him out," says Pike, the elder statesman.

"You each drive a truck." Groans follow as my friends realize where this is going. "The big favor is to help me move his stuff into storage."

"Yeah, we'll do it. We already knew from the girls, and we were just giving you shit," Pike says, closing out any question of doubt or continued taunts.

"Thank you. I really appreciate it, guys."

"After all the years, this is not a big ask," Knobby says plainly.

"Is he going to keep everything?" Dord asks before drawing from his coffee cup.

"I'm not sure."

"You should see if he wants to sell things, do a garage sale or an online auction. You said he has lots of tools. Hell, I am happy to make a good offer on some items." Dord wipes his mouth with the white cotton napkin.

"Yeah, I am in need of good tools," Knobby says. "And from what you've told us, they're unused, right?"

"They aren't fresh from the box, but he never used them much. I will ask if he'll sell. It might help in a lot of ways to sell some of his stuff."

"You know, we're looking for some new appliances," Pike says. "Michelle and I would be happy to look them over."

"I didn't think of that. They're losing the house; I guess he still can take whatever isn't part of it with him."

"Do you know if he used copper?" Dord says.

"I don't."

"Because if he did, and not that plastic alternative, what's it called, Pike?" He looks to Pike, nearly snapping his fingers in search of the word.

"Well," Pike says with a sigh in explaining it. "You've got your CPVC, but that is not flexible or easy to use, so you might as well go copper at that point. Or the brand-name PEX tubing, much easier to put in and replace, and it's cost effective."

"So if it's copper," Knobby agrees, "we can pull it and add it to the dad fund. If it's PEX, we can reuse that as well. I mean, he's not leaving it for the next homeowner. It's the bank, and they are going to come in and do the same, but P2 won't see that credit to his bill."

Dord clears his throat before saying, "They're going to look at bankruptcy, I assume?"

"Yes," I say.

Knobby does a dull scratch to the side of his face. "I know a guy in Plymouth who is good at this. Small law firm, but good work, reasonable price."

I shake my head. "I don't have any idea how this works."

Knobby pats my back like a good friend. "Hank Hanson, you're looking at being close to Dad for a couple of years while he reorganizes his debt. Very close."

"You ever get an offer to sell that little business of yours?" Pike asks.

I try not to react to the question with more than the answer. "I get inquiries from time to time."

Pike picks up on this, having known me for years. "Unless you have a real burning passion for this venture, it might be time to consider."

"You think creditors would come after me?"

"You never know. They tend to follow the money, and he would be at your place," Knobby explains.

"I don't have any money. You've seen the car I drive. I walk everywhere, I never vacation, and I am frugal."

"I don't know your bank account, Hank, but I know you, saving for a rainy day." Knobby smiles.

I say succinctly, "I am not paying off my father's debt with my life savings."

"And you shouldn't," Pike agrees.

"You know what pisses me off?" Knobby puts his napkin down with fake outrage.

"What?" Dord plays along.

Knobby straightens his back as if this were the most important thing he has ever debated. "RV City over at the high school. The football fans for Saturday's game are already taking over Ann Arbor with the mega RVs they live in for football tailgating."

"Good God." Dord rolls his eyes. "Those RVs are annoying. There were hundreds of them in the high school lot when I drove by. The game isn't until tomorrow."

Pike softly says, "It would be kind of cool to do that, be with all the other fans, get away for a couple days, all the football and beer you want without the worry of driving home."

"That would be kind of fun, with the right people," I say.

Knobby, who loves the game of football, gives in. "Oh yeah, well, with the right people, I guess it would be OK."

Dord puts a real question to the table. "Do you think they own those? Or rent those?"

Pike thinks for moment and says, "I bet they rent them. Where would you keep something like that when you only use it at football games in the fall?"

"Who could afford to own one?" Knobby asks, looking down to his lap for inspection of a quickly devoured breakfast.

"Whoa," I say, stopping them cold. "You guys went from hating them to loving them in, like, ten seconds."

"Shut up, or we won't help you," Knobby threatens.

"I'm going to ask around on renting one, for next season, maybe get some tickets," Pike says.

"That sounds good." Knobby finishes his coffee.

"But you're within walking distance of the Big House. Why would you—"

I start to speak, but stop because of the look I get. I don't want to put their assistance in jeopardy or wash trucks with a toothbrush again.

The server arrives with a small glass, the paper bill for the breakfast rolled inside of it. Knobby pokes his pointer finger in my direction and says, "He's got this one." She smiles and puts the glass down on my quarter of the table before leaving.

THE DAYS BETWEEN

9

"*Sheng nu*, or leftover ladies," Dord says in my dad's basement. I place the unused tool back into its original box. "There are different levels of society that a woman must consider before she can marry."

"So you're saying there are leagues?" I ask.

"There are no leagues; he is going to tell you about cultural difference," Jean says. "If there were leagues in America, I would not be married to Dord; he's way too handsome for a small-town girl like me."

"There are leagues, and Jean is way too pretty for a farm boy like me. I am nowhere in her league," Dord says, opening another of my father's boxes of tools in the basement. "But in China, women do have to consider their place."

I sit on the unfinished stairs watching the two move from one box to the next. "I'm confused. There are leagues in China?"

"Yes. More women are going to school, having careers, and enjoying independence. So say you are a woman of high status. You are educated and have a job, your goal is to marry someone of higher status, but because you're already of high status, you can only find someone of equal status," explains Dord. "Or maybe you think that marriage is only for the production of children."

"The production of children?" Jean asks. "Really, Dord? You are starting at the end. If you are a woman of low status, you want to marry up, and it's easy to find a man in the middle or upper status. If you are in the middle, you're really looking through that list of high and elite status families to meet. Women of high status are left alone past the age of China's normal age of marriage. If she's a professional, runs a business, well respected, she is likely to remain single her whole life, dedicated to work and other interests than the traditional role of wife and mother, which is bullshit anyway." She holds up a gray plastic box holding a set of deep ratchets. "This one?"

"So there are leagues in China, but not in the US?"

Dord turns to me. He adds the ratchet set Jean has discovered to the keeper pile on the steps and says, "Who cares? If you like Erin Contee, pursue it. There are leagues, but you are a desirable guy. You might be in her league."

"It's true," Jean agrees. "You are smart, successful, and not bad to look at. She might be a good match; plus, just because she is pretty, that doesn't mean that she's in a better league. Besides the fact that there are no leagues, she may have some dark past. She might have killed a guy, spent time in prison. You never know. Did you do a background check on her? You can do that on the Internet now, you know."

"I'm not going to do a background check." I dismiss the notion quickly.

"You might want to consider it," Dord says, inspecting the next tool in the unexamined pile. "What if she has bad credit?"

"What about romance, making a connection? What about love?" I ask.

Stooping in a new pile of Dad's treasure, Jean says, "Oh, Hank Hanson, you're too old for romance. Think of the practical nature of what life is. These are chemicals in your body telling you things. In practical terms you want to find someone genetically suitable that you can have children with. Then, my friend, you have fulfilled the design of life."

"And what about you two? You're saying you're not in love?"

Jean and Dord look to each other at the mention of children and love, and Jean says, "Oh no, we're in love. We were lucky to fall in love at a young age, but an old guy like you...I do not know. I guess Charlie Chaplin was still having kids when he was in his nineties and married to a teenager."

"We're the same age, Jean."

"We are?"

"Yes."

"The real issue is the one-child policy in China," Dord says. "Between the leftover ladies and the one-child policy, in twenty years we are going to see a population in China that is so full of males, and so desperate for women, they're going to resort to invading other nations for women or building an incentive program to import them."

Jean stands and with a wave of her hand like a game show hostess, says, "Ladies and gentlemen, my husband, who knows all about romance."

Upstairs I join Pike and Michelle in the kitchen looking at appliances with a tape measure. A great deal of silence is exchanged between the two as they take measurements, look inside, and check websites on their mobile phones for brand reviews.

"How are things here?" I ask.

"Fine," Michelle says.

"I think there is a storage freezer that matches this one in the garage if you're interested," I say.

"Yep." Pike smiles.

The three of us venture into the garage, where the inspection continues.

"So, Dord and Jean are telling me there are leagues when it comes to women—as in the phrase, she is out of my league."

"There are," Pike says. "You shouldn't worry about it. If you like this Erin Contee, you should pursue her."

"Follow your heart," Michelle says.

The silence returns, and the two look over the appliance.

"Good talk. Let me know if you need anything."

The backyard shed contains a riding lawn mower. Knobby attempts to convince Kate, in front of my father, that their yard needs this. While the mower is a great machine, they have a postage stamp of a yard, and Knobby is not winning.

"How are things out here, Dad?"

"Fine, just fine. Your friends are being very generous with their time and money. I certainly do appreciate it."

"Mr. Hanson, will you throw in the attachments with that price?" Knobby asks.

"Son, you can have the whole damn shed for that price, and everything in it." My Dad laughs.

Knobby looks to Kate with puppy dog eyes.

"If you can move it and keep it somewhere, go right ahead, honey," Kate says.

10

RedMitten Greetings is in an old three-story, red-brick structure in the shadow of two younger five-story buildings. The
first floor is seamless in its modern technology and design. It
faces the street, with tall windows, perfect for the nearly century-old
used bookstore it was constructed for. Today it allows loyal fans to
watch the staff at work. Three large monitors centered in the three
largest windows reveal recent updates about our company, flash im-
ages of top-ranked digital cards, and our latest creations. The building still emits the scent of aged paper that shoppers lingered in for
hours as they wandered through the stacks of books.

The second floor is for function over aesthetics, especially reminiscent of its history. My office overlooks the street. Our second floor
also hosts the conference room and the accounting and administra-
tive offices where teams run our daily operations.

Up another flight, on the third floor, is where I reside. Though my
loft is the entire third floor of RedMitten Greetings, it is by no means
provincial. The hardwood floors are scuffed and worn; spots where
others removed mildew and mold have left a speckling of bleached
blobs, like the melted remains of snowmen in spring.

Part of the reason for purchasing the building was to live on-site
and to not have to pay rent or a mortgage. Some who did not share
my vision found my loft to be dreary and dark.

After a few weekends when Pike, Dord, and Knobby pitched in, we added lighting and cleaned the place up. I am most proud of our work building solid shelves for the thousands of books left behind that were still in fair condition. Each six-foot-high shelf is on giant steel casters with rubber treads that lock, to allow the shelves movement and for me to form areas of privacy. I have a corner that has become my bedroom, one for the television, and another is a sitting area. The fourth sets a kitchen nook apart from everything else by my movable walls of books.

Books are amazing.

When I think about the advancements in technology—between "papaya" and "parchment" scrolls, the limitations of one-sided print and individual delivery, to more modern double-sided print and easy distribution, to mass production of media—I am humbled to know that RedMitten Greetings is a single snowflake in the avalanche of this history.

Paper itself is a relatively weak substance. Combining several pages of the cellulous structure, pulp from mighty trees, processed, and bound, these blocks of information are easy to distribute and reference and difficult to dispose of. The structure of paper is not symmetrical like a snowflake, looking more like flattened piles of hair sweepings from a barbershop; its bonds are stronger and break down over eons. Now these fibrous, bound bricks produced by publishing houses are the movable walls of what I call home.

My fraternity brothers helped over one weekend of male bonding and were able to turn the third-floor men's and women's bathrooms into one room that included a tub with shower, sink, and toilet. Michelle, Jean, and Kate reviewed our work and decided we had transformed it from "dark and dreary" to "functional and eclectic." Then they asked the boys to return to their honey-do lists and stop messing around at Hank's place.

The last of our working weekends was more about video games, March Madness, and beer than it was about painting, and I know it was the primary reason the wives asked the boys to return their focus back home. The single wall we painted still looks somewhat unfinished.

I was never able to convince the sorority sisters to allow my brothers to come back and help me make a kitchen, so I've settled into a bachelor life with a single counter that has two toaster ovens, sink with cold water, a microwave, and a hot plate. This small setup with an electric kettle was inexpensive at the Goodwill store and has gotten me through several years. All my furnishings are secondhand. The video game console is old school, with cartridges that were a quarter each at a garage sale. In a college town, it is easy to live well if you don't mind living in the past.

My Monday morning start is early in the new arrangement. The area for my bed has gotten compact, with the shelves now pressed against one side and the brick and windowed wall pressed against the other. On the other side of the shelves is a space for Dad and Midge. The sitting area now features a set of child-sized mattresses for the twins. I explained to my twin half-siblings that we are making them a fort to live in, which seemed to make the transition more palatable. The main shelf in their space is made up of all the leftover children and young adult books, ready for them to take and look through at whim.

I make some coffee in my three-dollar Mr. Coffee and leave the rest for the others when they wake before I jump in the bathroom for a shower and shave.

Down one flight of steps, I am back in my office to sort through e-mail before sunrise. Jennie, the account executive, arrives at her normal time. Elaine and Michelle in operations clock in next, and I can hear the water cooler conversations and catch-up continue for the next thirty minutes before finally settling into the normal routine.

My focus is on the letter of interest from Missouri. Phrases that jump out with each passing include "no binding obligation" and "conduct in ordinary course."

Interpretation: We would like to buy RedMitten Greetings, but do not hold us to it; we change our mind often, but maintain your profit margins; be risk averse. Our phone call kicking this process off was cordial. They seem like good Midwestern folks who have every interest in keeping my team happily employed. It is what they've done. It is what they do. They have had a long record.

It is a new process for me, never having been acquired before, and is a lot to take in. So much so that I have bothered my lawyer a great deal since the letter arrived. The good people of Missouri have a forward team of people who are very reliable about answering questions and talking about "the process."

"The process" is very dull conversation to me. I would rather be in a creative meeting or with the designers. Instead, I take on a persona, pretending to be the adult, putting on the facade of responsibility. On yet another conference call with them, the woman's voice on the phone says, "the process," and I start to chuckle at its ridiculous redundancy, quickly hitting the mute button so she will not hear.

As she drones on, I text Erin. "Hey, beautiful."

To which she replies, "Hey, handsome. Who is this?"

"Hank."

"Hank who?" Quickly followed by a separate, "Teasing—did you dream of me last night?"

She is direct and to the point. I love it. She must be genuinely interested in me, which is an enormous boost to my ego, but it is uncommon for a woman this beautiful to be interested in me.

"All night," I reply.

"You filled my dreams."

"Really?"

"Yes—you were marching in the parade. When I woke, I realized the cat had turned on the radio by mistake."

It makes me chuckle and realize that the woman on the phone in Missouri had asked a question.

"Sorry, could you repeat that? Bit of a racket in the hall on that question."

She repeats the question about quarterly profit trends, and I dig into the reports Elaine and Michelle put together last spring.

At noon I follow a daily ritual to go upstairs and make a sandwich for lunch. A loud reminder of the family I had forgotten about over the last few hours screams and stomps a greeting when I open the door.

"Hank, what kind of kitchen is this?" Midge asks. "I can't find a thing. How am I supposed to make anything?"

I step over to the kitchen nook and open the closet door, revealing a pantry of generic-branded canned goods, dry goods, packets of things that are close enough to what I love to eat. Handing her the bucket of peanut butter, I say, "You have to stir that kind before you serve it." In the door of the first of two dorm fridges, I remove the large strawberry preserve jar. I point to the cupboard under the counter. "Breads are in there." Loud noises subside when I return from the closet with Oreo-like cookies and plop them in the center of the table for Screamy and Stompy to dig into.

"Where's Dad?" I ask.

"In the corner, on the computer." She touches my shoulder and points to his location. She seems to always find an excuse to touch me.

Peering around the kitchen nook, I can see his two sandaled feet from under the bookshelf. With a few steps, I can see he has borrowed my secondhand noise-canceling headphones and is watching a movie.

"He's trying to figure out how to sell all that extra stuff," Midge says, stirring the oils back into the peanut butter. "In the summer this bucket will make a great beach toy," she says happily to the twins. Dark sugar-crumb smiles come across the faces of the twins, and one says, "beach," making the other giggle.

I can feel the buzz in my pocket. It is a text from Erin, a selfie of her smiling from her desk with a banana by her head like a phone and the question, "What's for lunch?"

Stepping from the closet again, I send her a photo of one of my fifty-ounce restaurant-size cans of tomato soup I've had yet to bottle and store for multiple servings.

"Hungry much?" she replies.

After lunch I am in the second-floor conference room. Each day we hold a 1:00 p.m. creative meeting that includes everyone in the company. Anyone can pitch ideas from that morning, not just writers and designers, anyone. Everyone has a good idea at least once a day, and we need to capture it and leverage it.

We spend most of our time on gossip in the media; however, we learned early on that only about 10 percent of these types of ideas really do well. There are only so many jokes about politicians and celebrities not repeated on late-night talk shows. Some of the people on this crew are philosophy majors or economists who've gone astray from their studies, providing the highest caliber of humor only duplicated in *The New Yorker*. A few choice members, who are very popular with content, always come up with the most crass and sophomoric humor such as last week's top Christmas card with tree and Santa on the front under the words, "Fuck the Haters!" Others are more cerebral, some are dark, and a few are very innocent. It's a nice mix of people. They produce content each day to share with the world for the small cost of advertising.

Another buzz in my pocket means a text from Erin. I restrain myself from checking after my recent plea with those in this room two weeks ago to refrain from outside messages at the meeting. Another buzz in my pocket, and I find my curiosity peak. A third buzz in my pocket, and now I feel compelled to know what it says. For the first time, as a good citizen of the new policy I've implemented, I stand in front of my team, remove a five-dollar bill from my pocket, and place it in the goldfish bowl, walking out the door while I check my messages. This gets a huge laugh from my team, as they have never seen me check a message on my phone. A few random claps of righteousness from the largest offenders follow as I exit.

It was worth the five dollars.

Her first text—"I've got a new outfit I look great in. You should take me out so I can show off"—was intriguing.

Thirty seconds later I receive, "My schedule is filling up, what's taking you so long," and the third, with just enough time to write it, "PAY ATTENTION TO ME!"

I know these are funny, delightful text messages. They make me happy to know that someone out there is thinking of me as much as, or more than, I am of them.

Another text arrives: "Too late to ask me out. I am now married and have three children. Things move fast in the age of Internet."

My reply back is a time and location for the next night at a nice restaurant.

"Are you sure? That's moving kind of fast for me," is her reply, but she follows immediately with "Yes."

11

It has been five days since I met Erin Contee. My cell phone reports thirty-three phone calls, eighty-five text messages, and seven new pictures. We "hung out" twice for coffee, which consisted of each of us being in a coffeehouse at the same time talking to each other on the phone. This has brought us to this moment. Now she sits across from me in the dimly lit fondue restaurant with a specially designed table for two in the corner out of the way of everything. The table is made with a large heating surface to keep the pots warm, and is an L-shaped booth, allowing for one way to get in and out. A point she emphasizes when saying, "You're trapped."

"I am?"

"Yes, your gentlemanly instinct to let me sit down first has given me the advantage."

"Really? The way I see it, you are between a wall and me, and you're not getting out. You, my dear, are trapped."

"*Au contraire, mon frère*, you are now stuck getting up and down, and at my whim. You have played your hand, and I have seen right through it. You are one of those men I heard about in mythical legends. I caught you, and you are my Sasquatch captured on a gray and grainy film. A unicorn in the tribe of singles' culture."

"You're right. You caught me." I play along.

Her form and shape captured in a houndstooth pencil skirt and white blouse reveal lovely lines from her ankles to her hem. She looks elegant, with her contrast of pale skin, blue eyes, and dark hair. One wild ribbon of hair, tucked behind her ear, gives a hint of something dangerous.

"I am happy my elaborate trap worked." She sips at her red wine. I worry that one stray drop on her blouse could spoil the evening.

"So how did the move go? What's it like to live with your dad and his, what do you call her, P6?"

"Margaret. I do call her P6, but her name is Margaret. Dad calls her Midge, and when she dated my brother, we all called her Mary."

"Oh my God, your relationships are so complicated; I think I need a chart to keep up. Something that helps me get through one story about your family when I don't get confused." She laughs.

It's a great laugh. It's a warm laugh. It's the sound of light and airy fun but carries a slight undertone of guttural reaction, something deeper, closer to her heart.

Pulling a thick paper coaster from under the wineglass at the empty table next to ours, and a pen from my inside blazer pocket, I begin a diagram.

"In the center we have P1, which is Mom, and P2, which is Dad." Erin watches intently.

"Mom was married three times before she died, and has the odd-numbered guys, P3, and P5. Dad is on his third marriage as well and gets the even numbers, P4, and P6, who is Margaret, Midge, or Mary."

"OK, that is easy enough," she says.

"The ring outside the center is the hard part; it is the kids. My parents had three kids together: my older brother, my younger sister, and me. My brother has two kids, and my sister has two kids. P3 has his own kid, and one shared with my mother. P5 has two of his own kids, but none with Mom. On my father's side, there is P4, who has her own kid, and then there is P6 with the twins. You will get to know it better once you've met them all."

"Oh, you think I am going to stay around that long? I get to meet them all?" she jokes, placing emphasis on the *all*. Picking up the newly made disk of information, she holds it up for closer examination. "It looks like a snowflake."

"It does, doesn't it?"

"A slightly unbalanced snowflake. It's just got this one part by your name that needs a little arm sticking out to make it balance out."

"Yeah, I never thought of that, balance by adding one part."

The server arrives with the appetizer of chopped bits of bread and fruit to dip just in time to interrupt our conversation. It's part of professional wait staff training, I've come to believe, to keep the food on hold and wait for a moment when the conversation seems to be going somewhere, then pounce in and wreck the moment. Forgiveness arrives quickly as the nibbles taste very good. Their arrival allows for the playful nature built into cooking your own food with sticks in a pot. It's the main reason I take all my dates here at least once.

"You were about to tell me about the move?" she says.

"It was about as good as one can expect, I suppose."

I stab the first bread wedge and dip it.

"My guys, Knobby, Pike, and Dord, came over with their wives, Michelle, Kate, and Jean, the day after and paid my dad a reasonable price for some of the major appliances. They put the washer and dryer in one of the trucks, disconnected the stove, and took that. One of them bought the refrigerator and freezer.

"Dord and Jean took the furnace and the furnace blower. Many tools went out the door split among them. Jean bought a nice sewing machine Midge had. In the end my dad may have gotten ten thousand dollars in cash from my friends coming right over. Sunday my guys came back with their trucks and put everything into a very large storage rental. Dad and Midge have been making trips back and forth between my place and the house the rest of the week on small items."

"What's it like to have them there?"

"Tough. It is not that big. I moved a few of my bookshelves to make a partition of their space and my space, and five of us squeeze around the table in my kitchen area."

"So I guess I am not getting invited back to your place tonight." She looks at me with a devilish grin.

I giggle at this unexpected proposal.

"I like you too much to put you through that."

Somewhere over salads she asks, "How did you meet your last girlfriend?"

"A few years ago, I tried to break from this—I'm not sure what to call it—holiday marathon."

"Tradition," she corrects me.

"Tradition, yes, break from this tradition. I thought I would try something different or new. I was invited to see a friend of mine in Doylestown, Pennsylvania, about an hour outside Philadelphia."

"Close friend?"

"Someone from college, someone I knew well for a time and wanted to see again."

"Sounds nice."

"I thought so." I set down the fork and watch her eat as I tell the story. "So I get in the car and start driving out there on the Wednesday night. Somewhere just over the border of Ohio, into Western Pennsylvania, the road goes black. I can't see the reflective yellow lines in the darkness anymore."

"Oh no."

"It's true." I take a sip of water and let out one of those unfortunate audible noises kids make taking a breath. She appears unfazed, so I continue. "I think my tires, all four, have gone flat, and just as I make it over this rise in the Allegheny when gravity is starting to help me downward, I start to pull over. The side of the road is filled with hundreds of other cars in a line with hazard lights flashing out of sync."

"How strange," she says.

"I know, hundreds of cars lining the side of the road with hazard lights flashing, people getting out looking at the tires, and here I am pulling over, just the next one in line of this mess."

She has stopped eating. "What was it?"

"This black tar, supersticky, thick, and warm. Each one of the cars in front of me, and the next hundred that followed me, did that same thing. Pulled over to stop and see what was wrong with their tires. The line was so long behind me that people ended up pulling off at the previous ramp and avoiding the whole mess."

"Where are the police?"

"The first three got stuck as well, trying to drive to the front of the mess. The third one was smart enough to figure it out after getting stuck and called out on the radio to avoid the stretch and close off the interstate."

"How did they remove it?"

"They sent these plow trucks, but they didn't get that far. It took three or four of these giant rigs full of sand and kitty litter to spread before they were able to get more plows on the road to scoop it up."

"What a mess. Wait, how does this tie into your last girlfriend?"

I smile at her curiosity at every detail. "After pulling over, while this whole mess with police and sand and scraping goo was taking place, the car that pulled up behind me in this whole ordeal was my last girlfriend and her parents."

"You met on the side of a freeway."

"We did," I say, pouring her more water from the vessel on the table.

"In the middle of Pennsylvania," she says.

"You have to remember that there were hundreds of these cars stuck on the side of the road with bad tires, bad wheels, and tar goo all over the undercarriage of the cars. Tow trucks couldn't come in, and even when they were able to, where do you take that many cars? How do you find enough tires that fit? Who will put them all on? Plus..."

"It's Thanksgiving," we say together.

I smile, wondering if she will say jinx.

"It's Thanksgiving."

I continue. "So, we were on the side of that road for at least forty-eight hours. I got to meet her, I got to make friends with her parents. I am in the station wagon, which is a great place to lie down and watch the whole show play out. I had a cooler filled with bottles of water, and they had baloney and olive loaves sandwiches. You have to admit, that it is a pretty interesting way to meet a semiattractive single person in your age bracket."

She nods. "Oh, I'm sure it seemed like the stars had aligned and brought the two of you together."

We watch as the server removes old plates and brings new ones. "It did, for a long while. The momentum of that whole event kept us together, maybe longer than it should. I told myself it was fate, or kismet, that brought two people together who lived twenty miles apart. For a while I thought we would stay together."

"But you didn't."

"No, we didn't. She's a very nice lady, she has a heart of gold, had spent a lot of time doing mission work overseas, but when it came down to it, I didn't love her. My grandmother loves her, loves to keep in touch with her. Still, she was not the right girl for me."

"You just knew?"

Before explaining, I give pause to the thought that it might be too much, too soon, and that may be too scary. Still, she is direct and seems honest. Our connection seems genuine, and so I take the chance.

"She lost a baby right before we met, something she may never get over. She is nice, but has this darkness floating over her. This happened while doing mission work. She got pregnant believing the pull-out method and God's will was stronger than the science God created as rules to play by. I never really trusted her after she told me this."

By the time the main course arrives, the spotlight has moved away from my life and family. Over our slices of wild game and fresh fish soaking in the bubbling cauldron of oils on our intimate table, she says, "I should tell you something. Something you may not like, but after hearing this, and knowing that I really like spending time with you, you should know."

Half laughing at the awful way it sounds and hoping this will be a good joke, I say, "This does not sound good."

"It's not good or bad, it's the truth." She smiles a firm and conflicted expression for a moment before fully deciding to commit. "It's something you want to think about, talk about, before you fall under my spell," she says, softening the moment.

"I'm both intrigued and concerned. Go on." My body language backs up this statement as I lean back from the table and slowly remove my hand from her leg where it had been stroking the smooth material of her stockings.

"You like me, right?"

"I do," I reassure her.

"You've said that we've connected, that I am easy to talk to, and you like that I don't play games."

"It's true." I smile, thinking of how happy our moments have been together, the capacity of my mind filling with her in my daily life, picturing her face, hearing her voice, and reminiscing her wit. "I think you're smart and funny and attractive. And as much as you put me at ease most of the time, I'm finding you can do the reverse quite quickly with conversations like this."

She adjusts her body to face me more directly. "I just want to talk to you about why my last relationship ended."

My mind starts to race to immature thoughts of gender reassignment, of *The Crying Game*, of some strange disease, but instead I say, "Oh. Yeah, sure, it's a fair topic."

"I was previously engaged, that's all. Some guys freak out thinking about that, knowing I was in a committed relationship that went sour."

Hearing this with much relief, I say, "I can understand that. How long were you seeing each other?"

"We knew each other in high school. We were friends, good friends. We went to the same college, and it was nice to, you know, have someone you knew for so long go through that with you."

"Totally, I totally get that. New people, new surroundings, it's good to have a friend you can trust."

"And I never went to school to get an MRS degree. I wasn't following him or looking for a guy. I went to school because I like the art world, and I thought I could enjoy doing that type of design work the rest of my life."

"Sure, that makes sense," I say, still satisfied with a situation we can move past.

"But"—the word rings out as she says it, implying there is much more information to come—"there are some things you think you want to do the rest of your life, but they get kind of old after a certain number of years."

My head nods, automatically conveying that I understand. "Like a boyfriend or a degree?"

"Yeah," she says with a pause, looking down at the wineglass that turns in her hand, rotating the liquid to release tannins. "Kind of like that. I think I could have married him still, spent the rest of my life loving him."

She is having trouble meeting my eyes, so to encourage her, I say, "I look back on episodes of my life, and I can't separate the things that happened from the person I was with at the time. They shared the same time and space, so it can be difficult. I think I get what you are saying."

"Well, there's more. You see, my senior year"—she drinks the glass of wine quickly, in one large gulp—"two things were happening with me. I had only been with him. I mean, he was the only guy I'd had sex with. Other girls I had talked to had these other experiences, things seemed more magical, more fulfilling in that sense. I'm this fairly protected suburban girl who is curious about life and stuff. Hell, I was indestructible at the time."

I offer an out. "So you cheated?"

At the end of her deep breath, the words roll so quickly from her mouth, I'm not sure I hear them correctly. "A little more than that. I put some pictures of myself online and set up some dates with strangers."

My mind has processed each word individually, but has not made the connection yet. "What? I didn't catch that last part."

"I would set up dates with anonymous guys and spend a few hours with them in hotel rooms. It helped me pay for school and fulfill some of the questions I had about other things."

I can feel the blood drain from my brain. A vision of her flashes in my head. I picture several "Adonises"—designed by gods—in pretzel positions, having the best sex ever, regarded throughout the ages as the best bacchanal to have ever occurred, giving her epic pleasures I would never be remotely capable of providing, even if I devoted a lifetime of training and practice.

The only sound I hear is the boiling cauldron of hot oils on the table for fondue, which starts to mix with the rush of blood I feel, as my ears turn red with emotion. I am not sure what to say. I am not sure what to do. I start jabbing the sliced cuts of food, removing them from the pot, removing them from the skewer, thinly parsing each chunk it into smaller bites, and dipping them into sauces. Each chew is a definite act not to say the wrong thing while my mind chews through what has been said. It is difficult to make eye contact, so I look at the pot on the table.

With a gulp of a masticated morsel and a sip of the warm wine, I ask, "You said there were two things?"

She is nervous and patient at the same time.

She waits quietly for my reaction, as if she has been in this very situation before, and tucks that wild bit of hair behind her ear.

"My debt, I didn't have money to pay for school. I didn't want to take out another loan I couldn't pay off, so I had to make some money."

Her voice began to trail off into a sad and soft hush. This was not the Erin Contee I met who was so full of confidence, energy, and fun.

This woman seemed uncertain and worried about the choices of her past. The dessert tray arrives in silence, replete with baked morsels and fresh fruit ready for dipping into a milk chocolate pot on the table.

She gently places her warm hand on mine, saying, "I really like you, Hank Hanson."

I look up to meet her eyes.

I believe her.

"I like you enough to trust you with this information. It's not something I tell everyone, but I also don't want to spend three or four great months with you, only to have you leave after finding out about my past."

Her eyes are kind and remind me of the single snowflake dangling on an eyelash days earlier. "I'm not saying you would do that, but it's happened before. It's why my last relationship ended, and it really, really sucks."

The wine does not taste as good as I thought it had at first; it is more bitter and gritty, having lost that sunny Napa feeling and regaining the cloudy microclimate by a brown-dirt farm road. This restaurant, this location, my special place reserved exclusively for women I am ready to move forward in a romantic relationship, is now moved to join a list of locations both toxic and not to be visited again until the next half-life of its cycle expires.

"I don't know what to say, Erin. I really like the woman I've been talking to. She is adorable, that woman I shared adult hot chocolate with during the parade. She is the one I want to get to know better. This, this, this is a lot to process."

"I understand," she mumbles pessimistically.

"What you're describing *is* prostitution, isn't it?" I ask innocently.

"...More like sexual exploration..."

The conversation moves forward again, but it is like a roller coaster at the apex. There is a sensation the thrill leaves behind, suggesting there could be more to come.

"I mean, my progressive side tells me there is no reason why a guy who might sleep with hundreds of women should hold a disdain for a woman who does the same," I say.

I try to keep eye contact with her as I think through the situation aloud.

"The guy is a stud, but the woman is a whore? That is not right. It is just sex. Right?"

"Yes." Hope returns to her voice. "Think of me as a stud."

"My conservative side is proud of your entrepreneurial spirit and break for independence, against laws from a government seeking to control you as an individual."

Her brow wrinkles at the comment. "OK," she replies with a wry smile. "I'm not sure what that means."

"Oh, but then, my heart, oh my heart. You tell me that you did this while engaged to a guy, and I am betting you didn't tell him you were doing this. I mean, you were engaged. Do you two still speak?"

"No," she says in a hushed tone. "No, he left when he found out and has nothing to do with me. The wedding was called off, his family disowned me. I don't dare think of talking to anyone from high school or get invitations for a class reunion. My sister is the only one left who still talks to me, and that's mostly reserved for major holidays." I can see in her a moment of isolation and need for connection. "I'm sure he told everyone I was a bitch and a slut."

"The money? You did this with enough frequency to pay at least eight thousand dollars a semester in my mind, and I don't want to work the backward math to the number of hours that is, because the more I think about that, the sicker to my stomach I get."

She sits upright.

"I'm sorry it makes you feel that way." She dabs the corner of her mouth with a napkin. Her attitude stiffens, as if preparing to protect herself from some sharp comments. "I'm not ashamed of this part of me. I'm rather proud of my adventurous spirit."

A bit more steel in her spine, she says, "It is the oldest profession, after all."

I see her defenses rise and distance increase.

I look down at my plate again. "Was it all these hot guys who were just amazing, who shook the foundation of your world, and whom I could never compare to?"

Her tone melts back to one of understanding, realizing I have not given up. "No, Lord no, it was just the opposite. These were guys, many not very attractive, mostly older, who just got off on talking to a college girl or trying new things. They were all types of guys, and most were successful enough to pay for my time. Some guys saved up. A lot of them were just alone. They were lonely guys who confused sex and intimacy, or just guys who really liked to have sex."

She stops, realizing her words are starting to ramble. Collecting her thoughts, she says, "Think of them as a series of dates with new people. That is what I do. I dated a lot looking for the right guy."

"Do you still see any of them? When was the last time you, I don't know, posted to your website? Is it still up?"

"No," she says with reassurance. "I haven't seen anyone. I was at the grocery store, and one of them bumped into me, but I am not doing that anymore. It's my past."

"There's no urge to experiment again?"

"Listen, I am not going to lie to you. There are people I meet whom I wonder what it would be like to have sex with, but I think that's pretty normal. I wouldn't have talked to you if it wasn't."

"What's that?"

"Yeah, first time I saw you, I was attracted to you. I would not have said anything otherwise. It wouldn't have been that memorable moment at the parade."

I poke at a baked good and dip it into the chocolate. Quickly it is out of the pot, cooling over my plate, and gulped into my mouth. A smile returns to her face as I make obnoxiously loud and orgasmic sounds of delight.

"Oh, oh my God, oh, you have to try this," I say.

"Really? That good?"

"Well, I don't want to oversell it, but this may be the one singular best dessert I have ever had in my life or has existed in the universe; but like I said, I don't want to oversell it."

She mirrors my action with a sweet, skewer, and chocolate, dipping it in and having the "world's greatest" orgasmic reaction.

The server arrives and in response to our overacting enthusiasm, says, "I see you are really enjoying the dessert. I'll just leave the check."

We are nearly under the table with laugher and joy at the strangeness of the conversation, the public embarrassment of discovery, the sheer joy of being together. As laughter subsides, I look into her blue eyes, seeking the return of the girl I like, the one with joy, confidence, the offer of spiked hot cocoa. My left hand brushes her wild ribbon of hair and firmly takes hold of the back of her neck. I draw her in close to me and kiss her, gently at first, then more passionately, hoping she understands that all is not lost.

12

"Well, did you get lucky?" Dad says crassly, sitting in the kitchen nook. He receives a good dope slap from P6, who is sitting next to him. "What? I was hoping one of us got lucky."

He receives an even harder smack.

"Did you have a nice evening, Hank?" Midge asks.

"Kind of? It was nice, but confusing, but thanks for asking," I say.

"The twins are asleep," Dad says.

"What's on?" I ask.

"Local news," he says.

"Anything going on?"

"I'm not sure if you're aware of this, but the city of Detroit is going to shit and there are no jobs," Dad says. "I prefer my news from Fox Channel Two in the morning with Deena Centofanti. She's something special."

Dad receives a painful pinch from Midge when he mentions another woman's name.

I smile at the thought of Deena's crossed legs on the couch. "How are things going with Craigslist?"

"Hey," he snips, "I'm doing the best I can."

"I know, I know; I was just seeing if you have any questions about posting things, opening an account, if you had a computer challenge."

I can tell he is angry, maybe not with me, but mad at the world, the Internet, or his wife. He takes it out on me because he knows I will take it.

"There's a shitload of stuff here," he says with an angry hush, an attempt not to wake the twins.

"I know."

"This isn't easy," he says.

"I know," I say.

"You have to take the photos, write up these descriptions, manage the account, converse with buyers…It's like a full-time job that pays shit."

"I know, Dad; you are doing what you can."

"People aren't even paying half of what I am asking; they always want to barter on this shit. And I'm like, it's in the original package, never used, what the fuck?"

"I know, Dad. I know."

There is no place for escape. The other side of the loft is not far enough away, and there is a chance of waking up the twins.

"Your father's doing a good job on this," Midge says to calm him. "He's been working all day posting to different sites and making calls. Plus, I'm withholding sex from him. Just kidding."

"I am glad to hear that. Good. Dad, if I can help, or if you have a computer question, let me know. I have some great guys on my team who are experts with computers."

The bathroom is the only place I am alone now. With the fan on, there is a little privacy. It is nice just to spend a few extra minutes in here doing nothing. Eventually I emerge and head straight to my bed by the window with its bookshelf partition.

My mind replays favorite moments from my dinner with Erin. Her hair, just right, her smile so inviting, and eyes that melt my heart. She looked great. Still, it sounds as if she looked this great to many guys. With a quick search on the Internet to some local websites that offer a similar service, it becomes apparent that Erin Contee is much better looking than nearly all these women. Taking the best of five, and the average top rates they charge as a base, she may have listed services for $350 to $500 an hour. If it's me, an hour is not enough. If a semester is eight thousand dollars, she was with maybe five to eight guys. That is not too bad. I knew girls in college who did that in a semester, didn't I? Maybe. Mostly with the same guy, though. A semester is sixteen weeks, so is that one guy every other week? No, that can't be, there would have to be four weeks removed, or a whole month from that equation. I might not be able to fall asleep tonight. Why am I doing this to myself? It serves no good purpose.

Buzz. My phone has a message. "Thank you for a wonderful night. Can't wait 2CU again!"

So what if she whored it up a bit? It is not as if I haven't been with my share of women. Although eighteen is my lifetime number of different women, I have had sex with each of them—well, most. Actually, a couple of them were on a semiregular basis.

Sandy enjoyed sex with me, something I hope she never told Grandma. She was interested in getting together a few times a week. It may have been the best streak of physical intimacy I've ever had. While the frequency was high, the quality was never what I thought it might be. It was very pedestrian. We would hold hands, cuddle, and stroke each other for a bit in front of the television. This always went to kissing, followed by helping her warm up with my hand. Eventually we were both naked. With my head between her legs, I could hear her moans get to a certain point, and when everything seemed wet enough, I would slip on a condom, and I would enjoy the next five to eight minutes.

On the few occasions that we might break from this routine, the results were poor. Maybe I am to blame for our relationship falling apart, as I should have been more patient with her. I should have done something fun and sexy. I had thought about sending her to a class on how to change it up in the bedroom, or leaving the computer open on techniques for the proper hand job or oral favors, but she would have taken it as an insult. She had two girlfriends who were rather devout to the faith who still talked to her. Most of the people from her past world had shunned her after she became pregnant in Europe. I couldn't really go to them and drop the hint on improved behavior modification.

When it comes down to it, I am not sure that many women appreciate that men do not always want to be the initiator of every single physical encounter. It's nice to be wanted and desired by your woman. I am not saying every night, but maybe once a month, she could start things. Reach out first. Whisper something dirty in my ear and take me to another room. It wouldn't always have to be the bedroom.

It wasn't the unfortunate nickname my friends called Sandy that broke us up, although calling her the Pepper Grinder did not help. She started to talk about not needing a condom, which only planted a seed of mistrust in my mind. She may have been on the pill, but I never really trusted her about taking it after finding out about the pregnancy in Europe.

There is rarely a single reason people separate. Instead, it's an amalgam of things over time that you could accept, or compartmentalize, growing into a final moment when you know things are just not right. The effort you put in is no longer worth it.

Perry Winkelberry, the Wonder Cat, hops on the bed to join me as I consider Erin Contee's disclosures. Perry Winkelberry head butts my hand until I show affection with a head rub. He moves to the pillow and begins to lick my hair. It reminds me that this situation must be tough on Perry Winkelberry as well. New little sticky hands have been grabbing for him, his attention, and his tail. He and Midge seem to get along, and Dad has not thrown a sandal at him yet.

When Perry Winkelberry and I first moved into this loft above RedMitten Greetings, I made him a safe and untouchable place of his own. Two twelve-foot poles secured to the floor and ceiling hold his circular steps up to the semienclosed perch. At this height he can see the entire place, look out to the world beyond the windows, and keep away from nearly anything that might harm him. Each night since our new guests have moved in, he has made it a habit to make his way down and spend time with me in bed before his nightly rounds in the building watching for mice.

"Who are these strangers, and why have you brought them into our home?" he might say if he could talk. "You snore, but the older one shakes the building with snoring."

Perry Winkelberry reminds me there is a chance I might be capable of truly loving someone in this life. He gives me hope for Erin Contee.

13

Spirits are high leaving Ford Field. The Lions of Detroit have won a game. Yes, it was beating the Green Bay Packers in a very off year, and we did have the home-field advantage, but still, we won a game in a season filled with loss. Erin Contee and I took full advantage of the luxury suites P5 so generously invited us to with his business associates.

We are in a glow in the late autumn darkness as snow tries to spoil our walk past the home of the Detroit Tigers, beyond the loud dance clubs, multistory party complexes, and straight on to Cliff Bell's, the historic live jazz club, before things start to heat up. It is still too early for jazz, so we sit at the bar for drinks. She orders a greyhound, which is grapefruit and vodka, and I order a gin gimlet, gin and lime juice. The wonderful thing about Cliff Bell's is the highly trained staff. There is a culture of excellence and detail provided that adds to the elegance of the hand-cut starburst walls on the stage and copper ceiling tiles. It's an experience.

"I'm so impressed by the way you carry yourself, Erin."

"Thank you," she says.

"The thing is, many people may have gotten lost in meeting a room full of people they don't know, or shy away, but you took it right on."

"It's not my first rodeo, Hank."

"I know, but still, you were so delightful to P5, and his kids made mention of how nice you are. They never say those kind of things... well, to me at least."

"They're nice people. It sounds like they really liked your mother. She was important to them."

"Yeah, she was, especially to P5."

"They invited me to a New Year's party, with or without you."

"Oh really?" I take a sip of my drink and let the piney, lime delight linger.

"Yes, I think the words from P5 were, if Hank is foolish enough to lose you, you should come anyway."

"That sounds like him...opens the door to all the strays in the neighborhood, lets any pretty face come over."

We laugh and tease each other more. People start to trickle into the club talking about the game and how loud other bars are. We notice but ignore it, safe in our little bubble.

"Oh," Erin says with a troubled voice, looking up.

"What?"

Looking straight into the mirror behind the bar, she watches a gray-haired man in his fifties approach. He is doughy, with a slouch, and carries a slightly confused expression on his face and a beer in his hand when starting to talk to Erin on the side away from me.

"No, no, I am with someone. Go away," she says, swatting away this fly.

"This guy?" he asks, looking at me.

I rise and say, "Leave the lady alone."

"Fuck you," he says.

"Please, we are just trying to have a nice time here."

"Fuck that," he says.

"Leave—" I hear the thud of the beer bottle hitting my head before feeling its sting. With a weakness in my knees, I start to lose my footing. My last vision is a large older figure jumping over the bar and driving his fist into the face of the instigator.

As I regain consciousness, the large figure comes into focus before me. He is in his late fifties, early sixties, black, with a jagged white scar that starts below the right ear and charts a mountain range of misshaped tissue across the cheek.

"You're all right, son."

"Where am I?"

"You're in the back office. Here, put this on your head." He hands me a white towel filled with ice.

"Where's..."

"Your lady friend? She will be back. She just wanted to get one more kick in before the boys took him out."

"Oh." I apply the white towel and ice tenderly with a few attempts.

"You know where you are?"

"The back office at Bell's?"

"Yes sir," he says proudly.

"Do you see much of that kind of thing?"

"No." He steps back over to a desk with closed-circuit monitors looking over the bar behind it. "Not for some time. Most folks around here are just in for a good time. Bell's is a good place to be. Don't worry; we nipped that trouble in the bud."

"I like Bell's," I say, still discombobulated.

"You should keep coming here. It's a good place," he says with confidence.

"Where did you come from? You were right on top of that guy, came from nowhere."

"I was just stepping out when I saw that bottle in his hand. I couldn't get to him fast enough."

"Thank you, thank you very much." I extend my hand, "I'm Hank Hanson."

He steps back over to me, hand extended. "It's nice to meet you, Hank, I'm Ruben Jefferson." The differences in our hands are considerable. My soft and pale little sausages have not witnessed a day of hard work in their life. Most of the mileage has been over computer keys and mouse clicks. His hand is large, each finger the size of a Chiquita, rough, cracked, and rugged from making a life.

"It's good to meet you, Ruben. I feel bad for the other guy. Look at the size of those mitts you have."

Ruben smiles. "He went down in the first."

"Thank you." I pause, deciding how rude it would be to ask, but take my only chance. "Do you mind if I ask where you got that scar on your face?"

His laugh is deep and expressive, as if to say, "You have some balls, kid."

With a worried smile, I say, "I don't think you got that from a guy like me."

"No, Hank." He sits at the desk. "I got this in 1967 on the corner of Twelfth and Clairmount Avenue. That bar is gone, but the memory isn't."

"The riots?"

"Riots," he says dismissively, as if the word described the wrong side of history. "There was one tough pig who liked to beat the shit out of teenagers with his nightstick. I happened to get in the way that night. Ended up spending ninety days in the Washtenaw County Jail with thirty other guys those cops liked to pick on that night. Had to take us to the next county over so we wouldn't accidentally slip and fall on something in the city cell."

"Wow, I've never heard that part of the story. I always hear about the tanks, the governor, and LBJ calling in troops."

"Hank, you're a lily-white suburbanite. I don't expect you know shit about what really happened. Hell, this city went down after that night. You never think the little things will turn out big, but then one night you are out drinking late with friends, and everything changes." He reaches over to a tumbler with brown liquid on ice sitting on his desk and takes a swig. "It was hot, and there were five of us living in a shitty little apartment. I was just trying to cool off, relax, and have some fun. We hear about this party a few blocks over for some guys coming back from the war. Well, it's like I said. These couple of pigs try to break it up. One of them really likes taking swings on me."

Adjusting the towel, I lose an ice cube. "I'm sorry to hear that you had to go through that."

"Sorry don't mean shit, Hank. It is what it is."

"Thank you."

"No problem. No need to call anyone. That guy was taken care of."

"We're cool, thanks," I say.

Erin pops her head in to see us talking. "Everything OK in here?"

"Yeah, Hank and I were talking."

"Erin, this is Ruben Jefferson."

"Ruben, thank you, it's good to meet you."

"Erin."

"Hank, you feel like you can make it to the car?"

"Yeah, sure, I can do that." Ruben helps me off the couch as I speak.

"You can keep the towel."

"Thanks, Ruben. Thanks for everything."

"You folks have a good night."

Slowly we make our way back to the parking garage on the other side of Grand Circus Park. The cool night air feels good in my lungs, and Erin's arm wrapped tightly around mine feels great.

Her first few minutes driving Paris the station wagon are shaky. The footprint takes the entire parking space. Fortunately, we are the only car on the level still around. Her delicate hands on the substantial steering wheel force her to complete several revolutions to test the short turning radius. Once on the road, free of most obstacles, her confidence returns.

"Why are we here?" I ask on arrival at her apartment.

"You're staying over," she says, disengaging her seatbelt.

"I am?"

She reaches over to disengage mine. "You are."

"I have to work in the morning."

"That's OK. I want to keep an eye on you, Lumpy. I want to make sure you are all right. And you're not ready to drive."

I am in no state to argue. "OK."

Her apartment is clean. Her apartment has a sense of design. Erin Contee is cool.

"Make yourself comfortable," she says, stepping away.

"Your apartment smells nice, like flowers. My loft smells like diapers and feet."

"I can't wait to visit," she says from the other room.

"Your furniture is comfortable and looks nice."

"Thank you. I made it."

I can't tell if it's the blow to my head, or that it is simply impressive information. "You made the furniture?"

"Yep, I took a class on modern design and made nearly everything in here."

"Wow. You really are a girl who has it all. You might be the coolest girl I know."

She comes back in the room wearing only a white T-shirt a size too large for her, with a faded logo, "May the Force be with you." It looks very comfortable. Thin from age, it reveals that she is wearing red panties and this nearly transparent tee.

"I'm a woman, my dear Hank, not a girl."

"I can see that."

"Let the cool girl look at your head, Lumpy." She turns on a light. "It's not getting any bigger, but it's going to hurt for a while." She steps away to what sounds like the kitchen and returns. "Take these, drink this." I am handed aspirin and a glass of water with these orders and comply.

"Done," I say.

"Let's get you to bed." She takes my hand.

"Are we going to have sex?" I ask.

"Do you want to have sex?"

Excited at the prospect. "Always."

"Do you feel like you're up to having sex?"

Sadly, I say, "No."

She starts to pull in me in the direction of her room. "Well, let's get to bed and see what happens."

The mattress is deep and soft, and I can feel one side is hers and the other has been mostly unused. The cool fresh air leaves when we crawl under the covers, and that nice homey feeling of toasty warmth starts to build. Her skin is soft to the touch and responsive to my movement. She puts her arms around me in an embrace. I can feel that soft wonderful flesh of her inner thigh wrap around my leg. It is the best sensation of comfort and togetherness. I feel cared about.

"Why did that happen at the bar tonight?" I ask.

"He was someone who knew me from my past. He wanted to be with me again. I told him to leave me alone."

"He hit me with a bottle."

She sighs. "I know."

She looks at me through the darkness. "Should we go to a hospital? Do you have a concussion?"

"No. Why make a fuss about the little things?"

"OK, but let's stay up a bit and talk, not fall right to sleep." She lies down, and I can feel her hair, light, delicate, dance across my chest as she pulls it away from her face.

"I didn't do anything to him, but he hit me with a bottle."

"I know. He's an odd man."

"Did you help beat him up?"

"I kicked him really hard in the balls for you."

I chuckle. "Thank you."

"Lumpy, the way you talk about your friends, Pike, Knobby, and Dord—the way you talk about their wives, it's the way most people talk about their families. Did you ever realize that?"

"No. Not really. We're close, but I never knew I talked any way in particular."

"Those boys are more than fraternity to you. They are family."

"Yeah, I guess that's true."

"You remember when you drew that snowflake on the coaster to describe your family?"

"I do."

"That made me think about your friends. You have six friends, like a snowflake has six sides, like your extended family, six parental units."

"I never noticed."

"All your talk of snowflakes made me think about it. It made me want to have friends as close and tight as yours."

"I'll introduce you. I bet you'll all get along together well."

"Sometimes it's hard to be a part of a group. They might not take me in."

"These are good people, they are pretty accepting of others. Let's not put too much pressure on things. You may not like them."

"I hope I do. I would like to have more friends in my life. I'd like to be part of something bigger, like a family again. My sister is great and all, but that's only special occasions."

Although I'm hardly able to keep my eyes open, she tries to keep me awake longer. "Ruben's friends who work the door at the bar held that guy down, and I kicked him as hard as I could."

"That's great, thank you," I say, drifting into early slumber.

"Hank," she says with a soft hush, "don't hate me for my past."

This wakes me back up. I stroke her hair and kiss her gently on the mouth. "I don't hate you at all, Erin."

"When I was young, in Sunday school, at church, they used to build up that I had this thing that was precious, special, saved for only one person. That if I gave it away to the wrong person or too much, something inside me would be lost. My value in small bites would be eaten up by the things of the world," she says in the hush of her dark bedroom.

"That sounds familiar."

"But they were wrong. I have value. Doing it more often made me better at it. I still have value. I still have love to give."

"You are very valuable. I see great things in you."

"Don't hate me for taking so long to learn that about myself," she says.

"I don't hate you, Erin." I kiss her forehead. "I don't hate you at all."

"When you put pain in perspective"—she pauses to find the right words to articulate the sentiment—"it isn't that we experience it in the moment. It's that we are always going to have it, always going to carry it with us. It's the weight we carry with aging."

Arriving at the loft late that next morning, with as much stealth as possible going up the stairwell at RedMitten Greetings, I find Dad silent in front of the computer. The place is a mess. I head to the bathroom. Stepping out of the shower, I realize where the mess came from. Someone in a rush has grabbed a bunch of stuff.

"Where are Midge, Jason, and Jenna, Dad?" I ask, putting on my shirt.

"She left." There is no emotion.

"Left for the day? Took the kids for a walk?" I ask, buckling my belt.

"No, no, she left. She left me."

"Has this happened before? Will she come back?"

"Well, she's left the room before and I don't freak out. She gets emotional, things happen," he says with little inflection. Then he answers the question, "I don't think she will. She took the kids and the car and went to her mother's."

"Oh." Not entirely sure what to say. "Are you all right?"

"Hank, I'm about as good as a guy who's lost his third wife can be. It doesn't get easier. There's not a lot I can do about it." He keeps his back to me, focused on the computer.

I find my shoes and put them on. "What are you doing online?"

"I am trying to sell all that shit I don't need in storage," he barks.

"OK."

His hostility bubbles around the edges of his tone. "It's kind of freeing, you know. She's off to her mother's, no more kids for me to chase after or wake up for; I can do whatever I want now."

Looking for a packet of oatmeal. "All right."

"I'm going to sell all this crap and just go somewhere. Drive out to the desert, or up north to the woods. Just get away from here."

Bowl, spoon, and oatmeal in hand, I say, "Well, I am going downstairs to work, say good-bye before you go." Then I add with a touch of sarcasm, knowing he hasn't looked up once, "This giant bump on my head? I am fine, don't worry. Nearly died in a bar fight, but I'm alive, thanks to a brave black man."

"All right, see you later," he says, unmoved.

14

"I called her," I say. "She's not coming back. A blessing and a curse; she won't stop touching me all the time, but dad needs her. I can't blame her really. I love my dad, but he can be kind of self-absorbed."

"Your dad is an interesting guy," Knobby says.

"I know the six of you have great parents, and this kind of oddity for you to hear must be crazy," I say.

"No, no, we understand, Hank," Jean says.

"So there I was," Dord starts. "Standing in line at Whole Foods."

Erin is not here yet, and I am starting to worry. It is a tough first encounter. All my lifelong friends at the same time in our little Irish pub can be a daunting engagement. The snow is really starting to come down. The parking can be tricky. My directions could have been wrong.

"And there is shit coming out of the baby's diaper dripping down on the belt." Dord is partway through his story.

I check my phone, and the last text from her was from an hour ago. "See you soon."

My concern has to be natural. It must be normal to want her to do well here. She has been a real charmer so far in these situations. Maybe it's too much to ask for the woman you really like to be friends with your friends. I would hate her not to be accepted. Would I even know? My friends politely put up with Sandy for what had seemed like a long stretch of crazy.

"And that's when Lloyd Carr says—'I don't think that's melted chocolate.'" Dord's conclusion gets the whole table in an uproar of laughter.

"Hey, is this seat taken?" I hear the sweet sounds of Erin's voice and feel the press of her hand on my shoulder. I stand, and our eyes meet. I kiss her on the lips with a welcome and help her with her jacket.

"Pike, Knobby, Dord, Michelle, Kate, Jean." I point to each of them around the table. "I would like you to meet Erin Contee. Erin, this is Pike, Knobby, Dord, Michelle, Kate, and Jean." I make another round of pointing and names at the table.

"It's a pleasure to meet you all." She smiles and sits.

"Dord? I don't have any idea what that means. Pike and Knobby, I can see. Dord? What's the story behind that?" she asks.

"Dord is an error," Jean says.

"An error?" Erin asks.

"Dord is a ghost word," Dord starts writing on a napkin. "It's an error from the past. One of the editors at *Merriam-Webster's Dictionary* wrote this," he shows her the napkin that reads *D or d, cont. /density*. "It was part of a communication; but it was lost, or mixed up somewhere in the process. Someone found it and put it into the dictionary as 'Dord' without spaces. It got past the proofreaders and stayed in the dictionary for thirteen years, meaning 'density.'"

"Interesting," Erin says.

"Yes," Jean says, making that pretend yawn motion. "He is very *interesting*. Dord here is dense, full of interesting facts and stories and tales. He is full of density." Jean smiles and kisses him.

"When Dord tried to sell us this fifty-cent word to show off how smart he was, it stuck," Knobby added.

"We've called him Dord ever since," Kate says, smiling and turning to her best friend's husband. "I don't think I even know your real name."

"Dord, it's Dord," Dord says with a smile.

"Your bump is going away, Lumpy," Erin says, shifting the hair I have moved over the bruise on my forehead.

"*Lumpy!*" the group says in unison.

"Oh, that's perfect," Kate says.

"Lumpy, I love it," Jean adds.

"Oh shit," I say.

"So, Lumpy, what's up with that bump on your head? What's the story on that? Tell us more about that thing you're obviously trying to hide that your girlfriend has named," Dord says, shifting focus away from himself.

Erin smiles and says, "So there I was—having drinks at Bell's after the Lions game."

"Oh, you are going to fit in nicely here," Michelle says.

"Yeah, not like the Pepper Grinder," Kate says.

"Who's the Pepper Grinder?" Erin says.

"I told you about Sandy. This group called her the Pepper Grinder."

"Really? Why's that?" Erin says.

"Let's just say the poor girl was inexperienced at which direction her hands should move when trying to please her man," Michelle says.

Erin bursts into laughter, followed by the rest of my friends at the table. I am immune to the comment. I bask in delight that Erin is welcomed into this circle quickly.

Pike follows me to the men's room and stands next to me at the urinal.

"What's up, Pike?" I ask as he looms over me.

"How much do you know about Erin?" Pike says.

"A good deal. We've been close since Thanksgiving."

"There's something you should know about her past."

I flush, zip, and walk to the sink.

"Pike, I know about her past."

Our eyes lock in the mirror as I wash my hands.

I pause. "How do you know about her past?"

He says with an awkward voice, "You know about her past?"

"I do," I say.

"You're OK with this?"

I start to dry my hands.

"I am. Is this going to be a problem?" He doesn't answer.

"Does Michelle know?" He doesn't answer.

"Did this happen a few years ago?" I ask. "Before you got married?"

"Are you sure you're OK with it?"

"Is this going to be a problem for you, Pike? Are you going to be able to keep this to yourself?"

Suddenly the men's room gets smaller as two other patrons enter. We leave the bathroom and step out the back exit by the kitchen into the snow-covered alley. Pike had been my roommate starting freshman year and lasting until I moved into the loft at RedMitten Greetings. He invented the term "bunk thump" in reference to the solitary love of a lonely young man in the dorms. He selflessly shared in cleanup efforts after the Great Jägermeister Experiment of our sophomore year, even though he had no part in it. He judged our forty-ounce Mickey's Big Mouth Speed Competition in our junior year. He counseled a myriad of college crushes, complex decisions, and navigations on choices made in life. If there was one person in this group I knew best and trusted most, it was Pike. Tall, discreet, intelligent Pike.

"Talk, Pike. Let's work through this."

"It was before the wedding. I had some doubts. I found this website, and she had…well, she's an attractive woman."

"Yeah, I get it," I say.

"We met at a hotel. It lasted about an hour. It was fun, but it was not what Michelle and I have. After that I was certain Michelle was the right woman for me. Erin may not even recognize me. It was years ago, I may just be one of hundreds, thousands…"

My hurt and angry look stops him from finishing the sentence. Flashes of the time we took him to the hospital to get his stomach pumped and helping him get home naked after his debacle with Michelle at the sorority house fill my mind.

How many mistakes has Pike made? I only knew the two. Is it more surprising to discover that Pike did something I wasn't aware of? Was it that he was part of Erin's "experimental stage"?

Pike tries to recover.

"Dozens of other men."

"I'm surprised, Pike. I thought there would eventually be someone who knew about her past, but not you."

"I'm human, Hank. I make mistakes."

"Yeah, I know, it's just that I had this image in my head where you and Michelle seemed above these kinds of things. You were the first to fall in love and get married out of school; you've been together the longest."

These emotions are not anger, not rage.

I feel confused by the honesty of life.

I have looked behind the curtain of love. It feels like the Wizard of Oz, where behind that curtain is nothing more than the illusion of something great and powerful. Maybe this is what my father was talking about, the reality of life and how relationships were complex, real, and so, so not "love."

"Are you OK, Hank?"

"I am. I don't know what to say or do."

"Let's wait here for a little bit, regain our composure, and then go back in."

My phone buzzes from a text message. It is from Erin. "U OK? Been in there long."

I type back, "Talking w/Pike."

It buzzes back in seconds. "Don't let him pull a Pepper Grinder."

I chuckle. "She is so fucking awesome, Pike. So fucking cool. I don't know what a girl this good-looking, this smart, this funny, is doing with a guy like me. And there is this one thing in her past, this one thing that I think I can get over."

"It has to be tough; but you have to see some balance to this—a girl this great has a flaw, and she needs a great guy who understands that one thing about her and is OK with it."

"Yeah, I guess. I kind of want a cigarette out here."

He turns to me until we are facing each other and has my full attention. "I've been able to keep this from Michelle for years. I don't want to tell anyone. I wanted to warn you. I wanted to make certain you weren't going to get hurt again. I thought it was the right thing to do, tell you."

"I know, Pike. That is what makes you such a great friend. You were looking out for me. It would be nice if no one else were to know."

"So what if I know? It is me. No one else."

"OK. You are right. It's just you and me." We shake our secret handshake on it, binding us to a high level of commitment and understanding.

We're greeted at the table with a round of "Lumpy!"

I put on a smile. Here I have a beautiful girl, great friends, a business, and a family, so why do I feel so badly?

15

"Get up, Dad," I say sternly as if I were a parent and he were a teenager sleeping in.

"Why?" he whines from the bookshelf-constructed area of his bedroom.

Mr. Coffee gurgles and spits into its pot.

"Get up. I'm taking you shopping for Christmas presents."

"I don't want any," he moans.

"They're for you to give to your other children."

He groans and I hear him slowly get out of bed.

"Take a shower; we are going to be in public," I say, hearing him shuffle his sandals.

He groans some inaudible curses under his breath like Popeye the Sailor before I hear him search for clean clothing. I stand in the kitchen sipping coffee when he flashes his tighty-whities on his way to the bathroom. I suspect this moment played out twenty years earlier, but with roles reversed.

We are walking between the shops of Briarwood Mall. There is a slow shuffle of masses here between the windows of what is new and on display. Few are here to purchase goods. Most are looking at what they might order online.

"Do you recall when we did this when I was a kid?" I ask.

"Kind of...Your brother and sister were there too."

THE SYMMETRY OF SNOWFLAKES

"Yeah, but it was at the Oakland Mall. We kept asking to go on the hippo that was there."

"Oh yeah, I remember that. The concrete hippo you kids would climb up and slide down. We used to call that the tooth chipper."

"Really?"

"Oh yeah, that thing was dangerous. We were never there more than ten minutes when some kid climbed up and fell to the concrete. It must have been donated by some dentist to stay in business."

"They moved it. It's not there anymore; it's at the Detroit Zoo now, near the entrance."

Indifferent to my nudge at sentimental discussion, he asks, "What are we shopping for?"

"You're going to pick out some things for the twins and a nice gesture for my brother and sister. It would also be good to get something for your mother and father."

Humbled, he says, "You know I can't afford it."

"I know. We're not going big, just something thoughtful. You have some bridges to build."

He is melancholy.

"She's not coming back, Hank. I'm lost without her."

Instinctively I add, "I know. I spoke with Midge. She isn't coming back." I quickly realize I should not have said it.

His attention perks up. "You did? Did she say that?"

Regretfully, I say, "Yeah."

"She actually said that?"

"Yes. That's what you told me she would say."

"Yeah, but I didn't really believe it." He returns to a wistful state. "It, well, it's starting to sink in."

As I let him walk ahead of me, that same beaten shuffle he had at Thanksgiving came back—the aged boxer coming to the realization that there are some fights he will never win. Bouts that may play in his mind hoping to change the past—just move and bob and weave a little faster, the jab that didn't connect, or the blow he couldn't duck.

"Dad." I take his arm. "Dad, are you all right?"

"Yeah, let's get this over with."

The twins are simple to please with identical plush, white, baby seal stuffed animals with nearly natural, big, black, loving eyes made from glass. It's important, I've learned in the last week, that the twins receive identical toys. They are at an age when the need to have something to play with has arrived. Whatever one has in hand is what the other wants at that moment. By providing a redundant toy, there is nothing to argue over, and each is equal in the other's eyes.

Grandparents are more difficult to shop for as they have everything they have ever needed at hand, and are looking to have as few items as possible in a limited space, or to get rid of later. Grandpa has a box of cigars he can sneak outside to enjoy, while Grandma has a box of her favorite peanut brittle that she always enjoyed, but never was able to afford, as a little girl.

Gift cards inside a thoughtfully written holiday card seemed to be the easiest to deliver, the most thoughtful and least intrusive way for Father to express to my brother and sister that he wishes them well during this time of year and hopes to connect with them again soon. If they are returned in the next seven to ten business days, we will know if they worked or not.

With Dad looking tired and a bit gray by the end of shopping, I take him to get something to eat at a local chain restaurant he enjoys. My sensible salad is not interesting to him, but the large plate of chili-cheese french fries with the mountainous greasy cheeseburger and chocolate milkshake seems to go down quickly. His outlook improves slightly on the ride home.

After arriving back at the loft, parking the wagon, and getting up the three flights of stairs, all he wants to do is take a nap. In a variety of ways, he repeats "perfect napping weather today," "days like this are perfect for a nap," and "shopping like a woman makes me want to sleep."

Allowing him to sneak off to slumberland is my opportunity to go downstairs to the office and get through e-mail. Our revenue is on the up for the holidays. Inventory of our physical products is well stocked, and our ability to fill orders is steady. My primary line of business, the eCards and advertising, is on the rise. Revenue from our automated sign-up and renewal website sales looks solid. We are doing more than making payroll this year. There looks to be a solid profit and a nice holiday bonus for each member of the team. The good folks in Missouri who are about to purchase us would be happy with this news. I am lucky to get such talented people to work for me...I mean, work with me.

Monday morning I have a call with the good people in Missouri. I tell myself that as it's a phone call, not a personal visit there or here, it means they are going to pass on making me an offer for RedMitten Greetings. If this were a serious offer, they would have flown here or asked me to be there. With these positive numbers, my nature of being averse to risk, keeping the business is just fine for me. I like what I do. It's profitable. It's good to have a team of smart and talented people to work with. My dad and I could live together, Erin would be my girl, my friends would keep me entertained.

A few hours later, back in the loft, Dad is awake in front of the computer wearing his comfortable wine-colored robe in his pajama bottoms, T-shirt and sandals, gray ponytail down his back, ready for Perry to pounce on it when he moves.

"Hey, Hank, I think I've got a buyer," he says with rare enthusiasm.

"That's great," I say, closing the door. "For what?"

"For everything," he says with delight. "Everything in storage."

"That's great!" My excitement for him builds.

"It's low, but I'll take it."

"How low?"

"Lower than retail, but not rock bottom. We both see something on the deal, little meat on the bone for us both."

"Well, good. All is not lost."

"Can you drive me there?"

I was a bit surprised at the request. "Now?"

"Yes," he says as if I should already know.

"Sure."

"We're going to give the buyer the key and give the storage place a thirty-day notice on the lockers."

"That sounds pretty easy," I say, putting my coat on.

He starts to put on the outfit he wore to the mall. "That's what we were looking for. An easy way out."

"Will you be able to pay off the house? Or the credit cards?"

"God, no." He chortles. "There will still need to be a bankruptcy. But there is enough for Midge and the kids."

I watch him buckle the brown, worn-out belt that prevents his saggy old jeans, which are a size too big, from falling off in public. "You're not going to drive away and find a new life?"

"No, Hank," he says with seriousness. "You can't run away from some things." His slight sense of responsibility is surprising to me.

When we arrive at the storage unit, there are two large white box trucks and a team of five entrepreneurs in their early twenties wearing matching Carhartts. The leader of the bunch is the shortest of the group, with the strut of a bulldog. He is the one with a thick envelope that Dad takes, opens, and steps back into the wagon to count.

"Kind of snowy today," I say to make small talk.

"Yeah, that won't slow us down. Keeps my guys focused on moving fast."

"You're going to remove everything today?"

"That's the plan." He grunts. "We have a storefront on Carpenter Road, by US 23. We'll fill it up and start to price it to move out the door."

"Solid plan. Buy low, sell high. Little meat on the bone for everybody," I say, mimicking every cable-based reality show focused on dealers of this caliber.

"Yeah, tough times for others unfortunately mean good times for me and my crew." He wipes his nose with a straight pointer finger, leaving a damp line on his dark glove.

"We're good here," Dad says from the passenger seat.

"Let me get that lock for you," I say, taking the key from my pocket.

"All right, boys, load her up," he barks.

We sit in the wagon watching. After about five minutes, the coats are off and the young men are starting to fill the first truck.

"All those years," Dad mumbles.

There is nothing I can say to quell the burning feeling of lost pride.

"You want to stay?" I ask. "Or you want to go?"

"Let's go. It's only stuff. It's only things."

16

"Get up, Dad. You are going to meet Erin Contee for Sunday brunch. You've got to get moving," I say as the stern parent rousing his teenager for church.

"I'm going to pass," he mumbles from his sleeping area.

I lean in on the bookshelf that mimics a wall of his room to see him in bed. "Your chance to meet a beautiful woman, and you're going to pass? That's not like you, Dad."

"Well, I'm not going," he says loudly. I can hear the video he is watching through my secondhand noise-canceling headphones, which are plugged into the laptop on the dresser next to his bed. It's a recent habit he's taken on.

"OK, you can stay here and stew away your Sunday morning from under the covers if you like. But you're going to have to change the litter for Perry Winkelberry if you're staying."

Begrudgingly he says, "Fine."

"That means you have to throw out the old litter, rinse out the tray, put new litter in. It's not just scooping."

"Fine." He moans like a teenager and focuses back to his movie.

Minutes later, I am at the Zingerman's Roadhouse looking into the beautiful blue eyes of Erin Contee, ready for a great meal.

"He's acting like a teenager," I say.

"It sounds like it."

"But it's been nice to spend time with him. I haven't seen him this much since I was young."

"It's good of you to take him in like this."

"I just think that Midge leaving him is harder than he's letting on. He sold the storage units for way less than he wanted."

"He's desperate," she says.

"Yeah, but we could've waited a few months. So now he has this wad of cash. I hope he won't blow it on weed, or run off with it, or God knows what."

"You think he might?"

I shrug. "He's got this reputation of not following through on things."

"All you can do is love and support him. Be there for him," she says, sipping her coffee.

"Yeah, you're right. I know, you're right."

"You've got great friends. I had so much fun the other night at the pub." Her smile at the memory gets big.

I am so happy it went well. "Yeah, they're good people."

"Some of the stories they tell." She reels back in the thought.

Leaning in a bit, I say, "I wish they weren't all about me once you arrived. Most times they are talking about themselves and their adventures."

She starts to laugh loudly. "Oh, that poor girl, Sandy, the Pepper Grinder?"

I consider another sip of coffee. "I can't believe they told you that."

"You really are a saint for going out with her. Do you take in strays too?"

"Just the one cat now."

She says firmly, "I think they are a good group. The girls invited me to their weekly euchre game."

"Really? That's very cool. I am glad you like them." I notice that her hair is worn back today, and she's wearing glasses instead of contacts, looking like a very sexy schoolteacher.

"What was going on outside with Pike?" she asks.

Honesty in a relationship is very important. So my decision at this moment is: (a) Am I being more honest to Pike not to say anything, since we agreed that only the two of us would know; or (b) Am I being more honest telling Erin something she may already know, but if she doesn't, will alter her perception of the new friends she has just made?

The easy answer is "nothing," "stuff," or "sports." The hard answer, the one that spoils the day, is the truth. My short-term goals are having a great day with her. But the reality we face, the one that she trusted me with on a night full of fondue and fidelity, is the one I must confess.

"Nothing much, some stuff." I have become my father. I hate myself for it.

"Nothing?" she says, knowing it is less than true.

"Guy stuff." I try to buy time. "You know, stuff guys talk about, and stuff."

"So there was lots of stuff to talk about?"

"There was this thingy too."

"Stuff and things."

"A thingy."

"I see." She looks at me, waiting for the truth.

"It's not an easy thing. It's a hard thing."

"OK, you're making full sentences, that's a good start." She smiles. I can see that she is trying to encourage me to trust her.

"The stuff we talked about over fondue, that night. The website, the gentlemen callers, paying for college."

"Gentlemen callers?" She giggles at the notion.

"Pike was part of that past sex work."

Astonished, she says, "Oh. I was a companion for Pike?"

"Yeah, companion, so you see that it's kind of complicated. I think Michelle is under the impression that the two of them are the only ones the other has been with."

"But he spent some time with me?" she asks, thinking back over the span of entanglements. "I just don't remember it specifically."

"He spent an hour with you at a moment of his own—how nicely do I say this—doubt and exploration."

"Ah, I see." She nods.

"But then he went back to Michelle."

She softly says, nearly under her breath, "I'm so glad to find out that his time with me was so good, he went running back to his wife."

"Fiancée," I correct her. "They were engaged at the time."

With a sigh she says, "Even better."

I try to be optimistic. "So they did get married. That's a good thing. You like the way things turned out."

"I do. They are nice people. Good people."

"Nice, good people. Good people with happy lives of ignorance about this specific topic that we should never ever speak of again," I say firmly.

"I know." Her face cringes a little as the words come out. "It's going to make it a little weird being friends with Michelle, knowing this."

"I don't think so. I think that if I had not just told you this, you would not have remembered Pike."

She thinks back a moment. "But he remembered me. What if he came out and said something? What if instead of telling you, he came right to me, tried to use this information to get me to do stuff, blackmail me, or split us up?"

I hadn't thought in those terms. This was Pike after all. My mind didn't go down that darker path, I doubted his would. "Pike doesn't think like that."

"No?" she challenges.

"No," I defend. "He is so logical, cautious, and conservative; I am really surprised that he was able to spend that hour with you."

"Some guys are not like that. Some guys would do just that, turn it into something."

"I don't think we have to worry about that. Not with Pike." I sip at my coffee again.

"OK, that's good. I really do like this group."

I put my hand on hers and say, "Let's do this. Let's keep this close to the vest, you and me, a team. Enjoy their friendship; let them get to know you for a while. Once they know you well enough, you'll be able to tell them basically anything, and they won't *hate* you for it."

"Really?"

As if it were obvious to everyone, I say, "Isn't that what friendship is?"

"I guess."

A shiver starts in my reptilian brain and travels straight to my neck, pushing each hair on end at the sound of the voice. It's an early warning of an unexpected presence.

"Hank Hanson?"

I turn to see Sandy. Her lanky arms and spindly fingers reach out to me for a kind and friendly embrace. I stand and try to be quick and polite about the situation. She's got me locked in her embrace, making the moment inappropriate. I can smell the familiar fruitiness of her shampoo. My chin finds that old place, tucking into that space where her shoulders turn into neck, and I feel the palm of her hand press against my occipital bone just above the top of my neck. It's too much, too intimate, too fast to stop from happening.

"Hey, Sandy. Here for brunch?"

I pull away with a little more effort than expected.

"Yeah, here with Mom and Dad. We're just here on the other side of the partition. I thought I heard your voice and had to see."

Humble, I say, "Yep, it's me."

"And who's this?" She turns to Erin.

"Sandy, this is my girlfriend, Erin Contee. Erin, this—"

"Girlfriend?" Sandy asks in feigned shock.

"Yeah." I look to Erin for confirmation. She gives me a positive nod. "Girlfriend."

"Grandma didn't say you had a girlfriend."

"My grandmother has not yet met Miss Contee," I say, firmly defining the moment.

"So you're not telling your own grandmother about your new girlfriend? It is as if it hasn't happened unless you tell her. What's there to hide?"

Her last question is spirited.

"No, that's not what I am saying. It's just that they haven't met, so you shouldn't be surprised or upset that my grandmother didn't tell you about her."

She turns on a type of baby talk to speak down to me.

"Hank, so silly, keeping secrets. Typical Hank."

She turns it off and coldly says to Erin, "It's nice to meet you, Erin."

"It's nice to meet you too, Sandy."

Erin reaches out to shake hands.

Sandy leaves Erin's alone by grabbing hold of me in another clench, saying, "It's good to see you, Hank."

Her parents hear their cue. They stand and smile slightly to acknowledge me as they leave.

The moment is uneasy. It is over before I can really think, so I sit.

"That was Sandy," I say, dumbfounded.

"Yeah, Sandy, your ex, the Pepper Grinder," she says in a similar stunned state. "Interesting lady."

I finish my coffee and replay the moment in my head.

"You don't think she was listening to us talk the whole time, do you?"

"I don't know."

"I'm going to try something," I say, moving to the table behind us, where Sandy and her parents were sitting. "Can you hear me?"

"Oh shit," Erin says. "Perfectly. They were listening to every word."

Returning to my seat with Erin, I say, "Well, that's not going to bite us in the ass later. I think you're going to need to meet my grandmother. Are you OK with older people?"

She laughs. "Yes, I will meet more of your family."

"Yes, Grandma, I would be happy to come over for dinner this week," I say into my cell phone.

"Why don't you bring your father with you?" she asks.

"I will ask him to come, but can't promise he will."

"It's very good of you to let him live with you in this tough time." She is sympathetic and emotionally rewarding with kindness.

"That's what family is for."

"He really is a good person. He's just always had this problem staying focused."

"I understand, Grandma. How is Grandpa?" I ask, changing topics to one less emotional.

"He's fine, doing his crossword, watching John Wayne."

Avoiding the emotional topic again. "How is your bowling on the Wii?"

"Oh, terrific. We've decided to make some shirts for our team. We're the Osteoporo-splits," she says, waiting for a laugh.

"I get that. That's very funny, Grandma," I say with a dry tone.

"You know who thought that was hilarious? Sandy." She brings it back to the topic she's interested in most. "I just spoke to her a few hours ago. She said she bumped into you this morning with a new girlfriend?"

After the emotional reward comes the emotional guilt. The news should have come from me directly, not Sandy. Who knows what information was actually conveyed through Sandy?

"It's true, Grandma. I've been seeing a new girl for a few weeks now. It was a little awkward to see Sandy. I hope she's all right."

"She's fine. A little sad that you are moving on, but she's a pretty girl. She'll find a new boy. I told her that very thing."

It may be too far to push as a topic, but I want to get a better sense of what Sandy may have said. "Did she cry?"

Grandma has years of experience in turning the most turbulent discussions to delicate topic. "A little. She is an emotional girl, you know. You're a hard person to get over, Hank Hanson, a hard person to forget."

It is difficult to interpret without specifically asking or telling her more than she already knows.

"That's very kind of you to say. I hope Sandy finds the right person soon. What day should I bring Dad over?"

"Any day, we're always here. Just call ahead," Grandma says as if she were always alone.

"Let's plan for Wednesday. It takes a few hours to get there, and I have to plan ahead to be there before you go to bed."

"OK, Wednesday it is."

"See you then."

"Bye, Grandma."

I walk over to Dad, still in bed with the laptop, watching a movie with headphones on.

"Dad."

He looks up.

"We are going to your parents for dinner on Wednesday. Be ready at three o'clock. OK?" He nods his head.

"How are you feeling?"

Annoyed with the question, he removes the headphones. "I'm fine."

"You don't look fine. You've been inside all day. You look pale. Have you eaten anything? There are vitamins above the sink in the bathroom. Take some."

"I'm fine, Hank." He puts his headphones back on.

He's not. I can see that he is losing weight. His skin is pasty. There is a slight bead of sweat on his forehead. Maybe I interrupted bunk thump time. Maybe it's just a phase.

17

"Dad, get up," I say in my parental voice again.

It's Monday, the day for my big call with Missouri, and I focus on the phone call. I am up early and have been in mental preparations. During my shower I answer each question elegantly and intelligently in my head. If it's disappointing news, I'll keep my broken pride and pain hidden, assuring them that there are other opportunities. If they ask the tough questions about the sales for this season, I have data points to back it up. I need to go over the financials again in the office.

My fast pace and parental chime starts again. "Dad, I've got an important call this morning, but I'll be back up for lunch. Time to get up."

I pet Perry Winkelberry while taking a last bite of my toast.

"Dad, time to get up. Do some cleaning today. The place smells like shit and gross feet, literally, Dad, and it smells like shit. Clean up *today*."

Across the street the bank sign alternates between "9:58" and "22°." Two minutes until the conference call. A cold chill of nerves runs up my back. My attorney sits across the table and seems nervous.

"It's just a phone call," I say.

His skills have become suspect as the dialogue with Missouri has played out over the last few weeks. I am not sure if it's the new experience or if it may be the complexity of the situation.

The phone rings three times before I hit the little speaker icon. The anticipation causes a look of pain on the lawyer's face. It begins with introductions of each team on the phone. There are a few dry corporate attempts at humor. Dry comments about weather and holidays make me want to yell out "balls" or "scrotum" to see what happens. I refrain from the influence Knobby has had on me. They explain that they have completed the assessment valuation with some additional analysis on the future maintainable earnings assessment of RedMitten Greetings and are very optimistic. They have completed the letter of intent and are currently faxing over a letter of opinion. A hard copy should arrive this morning via express delivery. They are also including an offer for a cash acquisition of $14.2 million. All I hear is "cash" and "14.2 million."

My lawyer's face is flabbergasted. I was hoping for more from him.

"That is positive news," I say in the plainest voice I can muster. "Once the documents arrive, my team will review them and respond accordingly."

"Don't wait too long, Mr. Hanson. We need to know by week's end. The stipulations are detailed in the work we sent over."

We have to reload the paper tray twice on the fax machine before the entire feed is complete. Twenty minutes after fully printed documents are in hand, our delivery arrives in a substantial box. We now have a duplicate set of the documents and a real appreciation for the number of trees the legal department of a corporation must churn through each year. An e-mail comes through with a set of matching PDFs that provide us a third copy, "just in case."

"My God, Hank, they must think we are going to lose one of these," my lawyer exclaims. "They must really want this place."

We sit. We read. He circles things, makes noises, and adds an occasional, "Oh, I see what they did here." Six times he borrows my computer to look up a legal term.

My assessment of the documents is its weight, the number of pages, and the terms and conditions of payment.

After an hour of staring at the things with little sense of their true nature, I inform my lawyer that he can stay as long as needed; I am going to go upstairs for a few minutes.

"Dad! It still smells like shit in here," I yell on entering the loft. "What have you been doing all morning? It's noon, and you're still in bed."

He is ashen gray when I find him. He is barely breathing. The white sheets are soaked in yellow urine and brown fecal matter smeared where he attempted to move. I rush to him when I realize what has happened.

"Hank," he gasps. "Thank you. I love you."

He is slurring his words.

My ear nearly against his mouth. "I'm sorry. Tell Midge I'm sorry."

I cannot dial 911 fast enough. The emergency operator cannot take my instructions fast enough. I repeat the address many times. The siren finally sounds after what seems like hours.

The confusion in the RedMitten office is unnecessary. Paramedics stomp up the stairs too slowly and deliver oxygen, finally. The stretcher arrives, and we are in the back of an ambulance. I hold his hand. There is a push through emergency-room doors, and a nurse stops me from following.

The wait. The weight.

Midge is my first call. Mark is next, followed by Lisa. I explain details; I give instructions; I list the relatives to contact. I call Grandma, asking her to put Grandpa on the phone. He understands. Out of courtesy, P4 is the last call.

The distance between me and my grandparents is like that from the Great Depression to the Great Recession. The connection between years past and years present are linked only by family lineage and the proximity of nearly shared experiences. Just as I remember shuttling between parents in the car, my father stoned, listening to Bob Seger, fighting in the backseat over which song to play next, everyone else in the car remembers these moments through his own lenses.

Years from now, the twins will ask about the time their father nearly died, and their minds will remember a story that each thinks is truth. They will carry that truth with them, but the truth is that they were not present, and anything they know is an illusion, told to them.

They will not know the smell of an overcrowded university hospital in winter, with its mix of body odor, vinegar, urine, and blood. They will only have whatever memory is imparted to them. Just as I do not know the true tales of my grandparents' struggles in raising my father, or a time when the opinion that Europeans themselves should resolve a Great War in Europe, I have heard tales. I have thought I knew truth.

Midge is the first to arrive. Her arms shoot underneath mine, wrapping around me tightly. Her voice warbles as she struggles to maintain her composure. Finally, she can hold it no longer, and the emotional dam breaks, spilling tears that seep through my shirt as I maintain a strong silence taught to me by generations of Hanson men who abide by such a silly notion.

Our embrace is too long.

I am starting to get tired.

She is so close that her hair begins to get trapped in my mouth.

"How is he?" She sniffles.

"Not good. But stable."

"What happened?"

"Some type of blood clot."

This term seemed nondescript to me, as if I should know the ramifications that come with having a blood clot. I do not know how clots are created, avoided, or resolved. In simple terms, blood clot equals "bad," just as cancer equals "death."

"Oh no, no," she mumbles.

I try to explain that it wasn't my fault, without saying it directly. "It happened sometime in the night, and I didn't see him again until lunchtime. He hadn't been able to move or get my attention for hours."

Her face is red from tears, smudged in running makeup. "How horrible."

"I know, just awful. He's resting now, but if you want to see him, you can. He's in and out."

"Thank you." She kisses me on the lips and smiles as she draws back. "Thank you for being here."

It is both a kind and generous moment of affection and a stirring of creepiness, to know she has been with both my brother and my dad. I suddenly wonder if I may be her next target, but I disregard it as a silly notion.

The battery on my phone has expired from the dozens upon dozens of people calling for updates. My brother and sister did not execute the phone-tree structure explained earlier very well.

In theory, they should be the two calling me for information to share with others. My poor phone has suffered the consequences of this failed attempt. There are two pay phones on the campus of this hospital. I have found both the one in need of service and the operational one. I change my voice mail to give an update to the state of Dad and explain that I will update this again if anything changes.

There are fifty-eight messages I must delete from a cavalcade of family, distant relatives, and acquaintances of my father. Many of the messages state, "You know we are praying for you and the family," which I find comforting, but redundant after a while. Other messages are fumbled attempts to clarify that this is the right number.

It's dark when I arrive back at the loft. In winter it seems to be dark all the time. It feels as if there were a one-hour window of daylight that I forget to enjoy. It still smells like shit. My hope that one of my brilliant workers downstairs would take pity on the situation and call a maid or come dispose of these items was wishful at best.

Under the sink I find the big black garbage bags, the unbreakable kind. There are also these yellow gloves for dishes still in the box. I slip them on with care to make certain they fully cover my skin and approach the sleeping nook created by bookshelves. The fecal matter and urine-soaked sheets greet me, along with Perry Winkelberry, who now needs to be cleaned from the unspeakable sin committed in my absence that covers his face.

"No, Perry, no" is all I can muster through the private tears I share with him. Every time he attempts to lick me with affection, in the future this moment of dread and sadness will be summarized in one word: unclean.

Everything goes in the garbage bag. Everything. Sheets, comforter, spread, items left behind by the paramedics, the towels I wipe Perry with, all go in black plastic garbage bags, with the yellow gloves last. In two trips, I am able to move the bags, followed by the mattress, to the Dumpster in back.

Perry's yowl is penetrating. "No, no, no. I hate baths" is what he would scream. "Why are you doing this to me?" His butt is all he shows me after a good rubdown with the towel and a few minutes with the hair dryer Midge left behind.

I go through the area one last time and remove all the filth, and then I go to Dad's dresser. While packing a few personal items to take him in the morning, I discover thick yellow envelopes. There are six in total. Inside each are banded stacks of hundred dollar bills. These are added to the overnight bag.

Once I am in bed, exhausted from the day, Perry forgives me for the water torture by providing head butts and nuzzles and his first attempt at an unclean lick. I shun him by rolling over and trying not to think of the ugliness committed.

The alarm rings too early for the rest required. It all comes back in an instant. The internal drive to get up, get clean, get moving, and back to the hospital. With my phone fully recharged, it is activated to show over eighty more voice-mail messages have come in overnight. There are three texts from Erin. I had forgotten about her. Neglected to include her in my life.

♫

"You can't do that!" Midge says loudly.

"I'm sorry, Mrs. Hanson. Once the doctors clear him as stable, it is part of the process."

"But he's sick, this is a hospital. You've got to let him stay."

"We have to treat people, and we've treated him. He is stable. He can be released." The administrator speaks calmly.

"Hello, I'm Hank Hanson, Mr. Hanson's son. What seems to be the trouble?" I extend my hand to shake.

"I was just explaining to Mrs. Hanson that Mr. Hanson is being released. He is stable. We need this bed for other patients," she says with professional certitude.

"OK, let's have this conversation in a private room. Is there somewhere away from the patient we can go? Let him rest while we work this out."

"Certainly," she replies.

"Dad." I kiss him on the forehead and put my hand on his head. Under my breath I say, "I found the envelopes from the sales you made online. They should help us here."

"No," he whispers in a sloppy lisp. "For Midge. For twins."

"Dad, I've got this covered. Trust me."

I rise and follow the woman to an office.

"Thank you for listening, Mr. Hanson," she says, "I didn't mean to cause a stir earlier with your wife."

"Actually, that's my stepmother. She can be a little dramatic."

"My apologies for the confusion."

"It's not a problem; we get that in our family at times," I say with my charming business smile engaged.

She removes a multipage document from Dad's folder and slides it across the desk to me. "This is the bill your father has accrued since he was admitted."

I look over each line and make assumptions about each step of the process.

"If you need to go on a payment plan, or break this out over a fixed period of time, we can work with you. The doctor's release of a patient, once he is stable, out of danger, it's out of my hand, you see."

"I think I understand."

I continue to look at each page and let her fill the uncomfortable silence. It is a tactic I've used successfully before, acknowledge without acceptance or denial.

"There is another facility we can recommend that often works with follow-up treatments for patients who are uninsured," she says from behind her desk. "Mostly it is a student-training center for medical students, but they are some of the best and brightest."

Removing the thick yellow envelopes from the overnight bag and placing them on her desk, I say, "Would cash be all right? I would take this to the cashier, but feel rather unsafe with this much in hand. Is it OK if we count it out here together? Then we can see where we need to go as a next step."

Her eyes get big after opening the first envelope. "Well, I have to say, this is a first." She looks at me and back at the cash.

I can only wonder what she is thinking. Drug money? Prostitution? Life savings? Where do her preconceived notions of this large bundle of cash take her? "I had to check under the old man's mattress before coming over."

After counting the full amount, she says, "Well, Mr. Hanson, I would consider us settled. Let me print out a receipt for you. You'll want a receipt."

"Yes, a receipt would be best, I think."

Sheepishly she says, "Mr. Hanson, we will need to open that bed up by three o'clock this afternoon."

I smile politely and professionally. "Thank you for your time. I'll start to work on arrangements."

"Mr. Hanson," she says after the whir of the printer starts and the receipts begin to arrive in the tray, "I am going to send Sara, our top nurse, over when her shift starts. She can talk you and Mrs. Hanson through the care he requires. She knows how to optimize the medical process. You should listen to her."

"Thank you, thank you very much." I shake her hand and take the freshly printed pages, still warm.

People come and go with regularity in this shared hospital room. It is a gentle knock at the door, and the pleasant voice of an angel who introduces herself as Sara, that stands out.

She says there are "many notes" to go over. There are many instructions detailed in this folder she has assembled. Pamphlets, phone numbers, names of contacts, e-mail addresses, and diagrams. Sara wrote out a ninety-day, detailed, regimented plan to follow Midge would have to carry out, in specified details, to get him well. Deviations from this plan could be problematic.

18

From my bed I can hear the new ritual begin. Midge wakes Dad and begins to wash him. She moves his arms and legs to improve circulation. There are pills to take. A small meal is prepared. He must improve his strength by stretching these giant rubber band things, squeezing a ball, and trying to stand up with assistance.

Perry Winkelberry attempts to lick me with his unclean tongue, forcing me to flee from the bed to the bathroom. The loft is full again this Thursday morning. It has been an unexpected week. My decision for Missouri is due at the end of the next day. My father, his wife, and their twins are taking up my time and space again. I have not corresponded with Erin since Sunday. Her last text to me, still unanswered, was just an unhappy face.

The cell phone buzzes on the bathroom shelf. Sixty-five new messages since last night.

In the shower my thoughts drift back to that night in bed with Erin. How we held each other close, the feeling of comfort and of being home. It is difficult to interpret the reasons for not calling her back, not texting the state of things, or to start the tales of adventure from that week. It would take too much time to explain. There are so many layers of history, relationships, financial dealings that it would take too much time away from the focus of this deal. She would ask follow-up questions. She would want to know why these things were this way, how they got there, and why no one had planned better.

"Nice, I can help you with that if you ever need," Midge says, watching from the bathroom door unannounced.

"Hey, get out of here. Do I have to put a better lock on the door?"

"You need to go to the store later, I'll make a list," she says. Before closing the door I see her take a long look at me.

Absent are the texts and calls from my friends. On any normal day, there would have been a few about corn prices, ethanol subsidiaries, the M Super Line of tractor, or an interesting and fun fact from *Farmer's Almanac*. There are no emotional checkpoints on P2, no flowers, no cards, and no well wishes whatsoever.

My lawyer highlighted twenty-eight points from the offer. He sits across from me in my office talking from his notes and occasionally referring back to the original offering. There are details about the ownership of intellectual properties, staffing, creative services, code from the website, exchange of copyright, and things I do not understand. He does his best to explain to me the intention of the offer in terms I can understand.

A new message arrives on my cell phone, and I place it in my pocket.

"Why do you think they are this interested in RedMitten Greetings?" he asks.

"My impression is that they're an old company, the internal processes they have in place don't allow for innovation, and they need to jump ahead in the market or fall behind and close doors. Purchasing a small company like this one means it is ready out of the box, so to say. They don't have to invest or hire or push the current teams. They just add it to what they have and try to scale it up to produce larger results."

"Oh. Well, that makes sense."

In contemplative terms normally reserved for my inner voice, I ask, "Did they mention anything about the building?"

"The building?" he asks with a bit of surprise.

I start to spitball the idea. "Do they intend to stay here? Do they want to rent the space? Are they going to relocate office locations?"

Flipping back a section, he says, "No, they don't mention it."

"They want to keep the staff. They are interested in keeping the talent. That is clear, is that right?"

"Yes," he says. "Those are well spelled out."

"They don't want me, they want the team." I can feel the cell phone vibrate in my pocket. I try to keep focus in the moment.

"That's accurate," he says.

"They want all the back stock, all the rights, all the intellectual stuff," I say.

"Correct."

"But they don't mention the building, the rent, the location where it all takes place."

"Correct."

"So they're going to offer everyone a job in Missouri? Or they're going to move offices to a local branch they already own?"

"Maybe they didn't think to include it," he says.

I say innocently, "Let's just call and ask."

He puts his hand out like a traffic cop to signal stop. "Wait, why don't you and I talk through this first?"

"What do you mean?"

"Let's not show our hand until we've considered the options here. If they forgot, what do we want to ask them for in return? If they didn't, that means they have other plans. What are those plans?"

"Good point."

"We want clarity. We want to call them with the right question. Ask a question that will provide an answer we really want to know—did they forget, or are they up to something else?"

"What question do we ask them? That's the hardest part."

"So we call and ask for a point of clarification."

"OK." I take a deep breath as the cell phone wiggles again. "Could you please clarify the intention of property?"

"That's too much," he says.

"Could you clarify the new address for business?"

"Interesting." He tilts his head.

"Where does the contract take place?"

"They have written in that all disputes and resolutions will be taken up in the judgment in the courts of Missouri," he says.

"Typical."

"I would have written it for Michigan; you have to ask for home-court advantage," he says, chuckling at his little lawyer joke.

After an hour of discussion, my attorney calls the low-level attorney on their side and simply says, "I have the document in front of me and wanted to clarify the forwarding address for the new business."

The reply is, "There will be no change."

I update my outgoing voice mail without reviewing any of the messages. It assures people that Dad is home with me, stable, and I will reach out to everyone when things change.

"Hank Hanson, thanks for taking my call," the senior attorney says twenty minutes later. "I wanted to follow up on a clarification from your legal team earlier, about that forwarding address."

"Sure, he said there would be no change," I say.

"That's right. We're not looking to relocate the business," he says with an open-ended nature, leaving me to believe he is searching.

"I am glad to hear that. I'm sure if the offer goes forward, my staff will be happy to know they can be just as productive and creative without major changes to their lives."

"We are too. It's been our experience that uprooting talent, or changing that type of successful chemistry, isn't good for anyone," he says.

"That's good news. So you've contacted the landlord about staying at this property?"

"I would have to check on that," he says.

"Or maybe you were planning to continue the current lease, which makes sense, and then extend or negotiate that?" As I say this, the buzz in my pocket goes off again.

"You know, I don't have that in front of me at the moment." I can hear the shuffle of papers from his end. "I would have to check on that."

"When you are ready to discuss the location, please feel free to call me. I think I can help."

"You have a good relationship with the property owner?"

"I am the property owner. I guess the bank owns part of it, but the loan is in my name."

The sound of his realization is a simple "Oh."

"So if you are looking to rent, or take over the location in a separate call, ring me back. Or we can talk about an addendum that rolls it into a bundle."

"Say that we wanted to own everything outright, the company, the building, everything, and all at once?"

"Knowing what I owe, what the local values are for something downtown Ann Arbor, I would ballpark the whole offer at seventeen million."

"Well, that is a different number than what's on the table. I would have to go back and look over the details for something like that."

"I'll be available all afternoon for your call. I am interested in doing business; we just have to find the right package." A new buzz from my pocket distracts me.

"Yes sir, I can respect a man who sees the details that aren't in the contract. I will call you later, Hank."

"I look forward to hearing from you later."

"All right, good-bye." The speakerphone clicks off.

"So?" my lawyer asks.

I take the cell phone from my pocket and turn it off. "They're going to call us back. I think they missed this part altogether. Someone on their team missed a lot of money to consider."

"Maybe we should have let them figure that out later. We could have gotten a better number out of them."

"I'm not looking to be greedy here. If they come back with a fair price, I am way ahead of the game."

My lawyer smiles and says, "Did you think this was going to happen when you started this business?"

"I didn't." I think back for a moment and say, "I just thought it was an interesting little project to do between classes. When it got big enough to hire a few other people, then when I made enough money to get this building, hire a few more people, no way. I guess I was pretty lucky."

"What's up?" I ask.

"Can you run to the store?" Midge asks.

"Sure, what do you need and when do you need it?"

"The list is on the counter, and now."

I look over the list and realize this is going to be more than an hour. The parallel from the top of the list and bottom are not lost on me. The top part, "Things for the twins," includes pull-up diapers, wipes, talc, types of food they like, crackers, and juice. "Things for Dad" at the bottom of the list includes adult diapers, prescription, XL wipes, medicated powder, types of comfort snacks he likes that are approved, and juice.

In my rush to the store, I forget to turn the phone back on. My focus is on getting to the store for the kids' list and most of Dad's, then finding things on Dad's list I've never had to purchase or look for. As I suspect, one store does not carry everything. The store that would have all the items under one roof, our regional grocer called Meijer, is an extra ten minutes out of my way. I make a note to myself: an extra ten minutes to get to one store is better than seeing multiple stores in closer proximity.

After finding parking, sneaking past the office downstairs so I do not find myself answering all kinds of work questions with a variety of diapers in tow, and dropping everything off with Midge, I can now get back to my office.

There is a message from the Missouri senior attorney. I return his call. He finds the seventeen million number acceptable and "something his team can offer as an addendum."

There are stacks of pink slips on my desk that say, "While You Were Out." Each of them is from a relative now calling my office phone since my cell phone is off.

I take a deep breath, call my attorney down the street, and ask him to get back here to review the addendum coming over the fax and e-mail. We need to sign this and get it out the door tonight, with scanned digital copies to go as well.

Seventeen million. The number tumbles in my head.

Pay off the loan and hand the building over to them. *Sixteen million.*

After taxes, that is somewhere around eight million, and then legal fees, so $7.5 million. What to do with that? First, make sure to share part of this as a bonus with the rest of the team.

My lawyer walks in with two large coffees in hand and the fax in his mouth. Our clean copy is printed, and we review. Satisfied with all this, I begin the process of putting my initials, HH, on dozens of pages, with a signature on six different spots over three different pages. He then signs pages as a witness. A new face, a female face, is at my office door, and she states she is the notary. She presses things with a seal, signs things, and asks for my signature as well. Next, she scans them to a set of files live on my desktop. All fresh copies are put into an overnight box and labeled. I proudly hit the send key, and walk with the box to the corner to personally deliver this shipment, overnight. I feel a weight lifted. On our walk back to the office, new snow falls.

Snowflakes are frozen water droplets bonded with an air particle. That particle is a weight that causes it to fall to earth. Water particles act like a tiny prism that refracts light waves. Today, on a sunny day, when it snows lighter crystals, they dance in the atmosphere at high levels, and sometimes you can see rainbows. When the balance between water and weight is just right, the particles fall to earth, and they refract certain waves of light. Waves are measured in the distance between peaks, and blue is shorter than many of the other colors we can see. Today's flakes are showing us the spectacle that causes deep-blue skies with blue flakes, refracting the short but enjoyable distances.

In the loft I find Midge with a look of frustration and despair. The twins are asleep in their bed. Dad is in bed with the small television, wearing headphones, in his nook, content.

I go to her and say, "Get out of here for a few hours. See a movie, go to the mall, and eat alone. Go be alone for a while." She takes the offer without hesitation and slinks away. I find a pad of paper and pencil and sit in the kitchen area doing what I've dreaded for most of the day, turning my cell phone back on.

There are 232 voice-mail messages and 28 text messages. Many of the calls are from my aunts and uncles. There are three from my grandparents offering a thank-you for taking care of Dad, and to reach out if anything changes. Some of the calls are from friends who have recently found out about his illness and who want to wish him well. P4, his second wife, leaves a thank-you for the update.

The most surprising of these calls is from P5, Mother's third husband. He is in tears. He is crying like a child, sniffling with sensitivity and repeating, "Why haven't we talked in two weeks? Did I do something wrong? Are you mad at me?" This grown powerful man, captain of industry, trustee to blooming businesses, board member of multiple organizations, takes me aback with his cry for attention. He is like a frustrated four-year-old who cannot convey his emotions properly to describe what it is he wants. Am I too much of a reminder of my mother, his last love? Is he lonely and in need of a friend? Who can I find to replace me as a focal point for his attention?

Finally, there is Erin. "I don't know what's going on." I can hear the honesty and tenderness in her voice. "If you are in trouble, if I can help, please let me know. I played euchre with the girls this week, and I do not know what they told you, but I'm sorry about the whole thing. Call me."

Sorry? Sorry for what? I wonder.

"Hello?" Dad calls out. "Midge?"

"Hey, Dad." I walk over to him. The television lights flicker, and the little bits of sound from the show he is watching slip out of the headphones. "Are you all right?"

"Where's Midge?" he asks with a slurp.

"She went out for a few hours."

"Oh."

"What do you need?"

"Nothing. Nothing." He is dismissive.

"Are you sure?"

"Yeah, yeah, it can wait until she gets back."

"OK, I'm just in the kitchen, so if you need something, let me know."

"Yeah, yeah, sure." He puts his headphones back on.

Back in the kitchen nook, I start to return phone calls to aunts and uncles. It's too late to call the grandparents, who can wait until morning.

"Hank," Dad calls out about twenty minutes later.

I scurry over. "What's up, Dad?"

"When is Midge getting back?"

Tenderly, sympathetically, I reply, "I don't know. A while. She needed some time alone."

"Oh," he says with letdown.

"Dad, you should just tell me what's going on so we can address it right now."

"I need"—he is self-conscious—"I need to be changed."

Surprised by the reality of the situation, I say, "What's that?"

"I need to be changed. I fell asleep and, well—"

"OK, let me get the wipes."

I find the XL wipes and pull out several; I prepare a fresh adult diaper and grab the kids' bottle of talc. The wiggling in bed makes a new sound of rolling and wrinkling plastic under the sheets. Removing the top covers, I find that it's a number two problem, not a number one. He looks like a wet plucked chicken with sagging skin over the bones. I help him prop up his legs, remove the soiled remnants, wipe and powder the area.

"It's just like working on the twins," I say.

"See anything familiar?" he jokes.

"How's that?"

"When you were a kid, I did this for you. You were pretty interested in your pecker. Always wanted to touch it, grab it, play with it."

"Thank you for not popping a boner while I'm down here, Dad."

"I'm just saying that I bet our dicks are pretty similar. It's genetic, like looking at your own."

I groan in disgust. "You know, it didn't really enter my mind."

"Thanks for doing this," he says quickly.

"You're welcome."

His embarrassment forces a certain type of genuineness he has not shown before. "A son shouldn't have to do this kind of a thing for his father."

"Dad, I am trying to make it so that I won't need to do this for you, that Midge won't need to do this for you. I will find you a hot young nurse who will do this for you."

"Oh, too expensive, don't pay for something like that."

"Dad, you let me worry about that kind of stuff." I finish and cover him up. The soiled diaper goes in the bin, and I sit on the edge of the newly purchased mattress with him. "If you had told me about this a year ago, I could have added you to my coverage. I could have helped you get out of this situation better."

"Not..." He tries to explain.

"You don't have to say anything, Dad. I love you. You are my dad. I do not like some of the things you do or you have done, but I love you. And I am going to look out for you."

"Thank you."

"All your brothers and sisters are interested in being here for Christmas. They want to come see you. They've been calling me non-stop over the last forty-eight hours, wanting to reach out to you."

"What about Mark and Lisa?"

"Dad, they are not too happy with you. They're worried about you, but I don't think we should expect them to show up."

"Don't blame them," he says.

"They had a hard time getting over things."

"Midge?" he asks.

"Yeah, I don't think my brother got over you marrying and having kids with his high school sweetheart, and the girl he lost his virginity to."

"No, I guess not."

"As great as she is, it's a hard thing to get over."

"Yeah." He lets out a deep sigh.

"And Lisa, well, Midge was her babysitter, Dad. She didn't understand all the intricacies of an adult relationship that were shared between your second wife for years until the divorce. She didn't know what to say and stopped talking completely that one summer." I stop myself when I can see the pang of guilt in his eyes. "It's in the past, Dad. It's all in the past."

"But they can't get over it."

"It's going to be tough. Maybe that's a reason to get stronger. Maybe part of you getting better is rebuilding relationships."

"You're a lot like your mother."

"I don't want to hear this, Dad; I get it from other people all the time."

"No, listen, she had her faults. She was human, but you got her best parts. She was kind and forgiving like you are. Thank you."

"You're welcome, Dad." Moments of honesty are rare between the two of us. So I feel compelled to press the opportunity to find out more, answer questions that have long lingered in my brain. "I know I was never your favorite, but I'm here for you now."

"Parents don't have favorites; they love all their kids equally."

"That's a line parents feel they have to tell their kids. It is a line I know is untrue. Mark was your first, your favorite, your everything."

"He was certainly the first. I don't know about favorite."

"He knows things. You spoke with him openly when we were younger. I know that you and Mom trusted and confided in him things that you tried to keep from me."

"It wasn't that he was a favorite, just that he understood things earlier, was more mature."

"It's OK. You can admit it now that we're all adults, and you have a special place in your heart for him."

Reluctantly, in a moment of needing to be honest or wanting to go back to his movie, he finally admits, "Well."

"Oh—I knew it." I am happy to have caught him finally admitting it. "I knew he was your favorite."

Worn down, he says, "He was so special. He was our first. As tough as it is to admit, Hank, and maybe tougher to hear, we didn't plan for you. You were unexpected, likely after a night of drinking."

"Oh." It is all I can muster. I hadn't thought to be that honest.

"It isn't about loving one more than another, it's just different. When you were a kid, you were annoying as fuck, never leaving your mother's side, stuck to her like glue, scared of your own shadow. And if you weren't by her side in public, you squirreled away in your room reading all those books or working on that computer shit. I just didn't understand you. Mark, on the other hand, he and I were friends; he was funny and brave and social. Our friends were impressed by such a smart kid."

It was quiet for a moment while he searched his memories for the parts that were still vibrant, the times not clouded by a haze of weed or an intoxicated drowning of sorrows. "But now, Mark is nowhere to be found. He won't return my calls, not interested in me at all, while you are here, taking care of me."

Not many parents would say something like this to one of their children. In this moment of clarity, in the opportunity of being open and honest for once, I ask, "Were you jealous of Mark?"

"What? What does that mean?" he asks.

"Were you jealous of Mark and Midge? Is that why, why you started seeing her?" I ask.

"Oh, you don't know, you weren't there," he blusters. "That's just bullshit."

"I'm just asking, since we're being all honest and shit. You were, weren't you? Jealous of your son, attracted to her. You saw her, watched her with him, and you wanted to have that, you wanted to be with her."

"Hank, you're just saying shit now, you don't understand what happened."

"Help me understand," I say. "Honesty is the price you pay for wiping your ass."

"Let me get some rest, Hank. Let's try and not think about these things. They're all in the past."

"Fine. Watch your show. Get some rest. If you need to pee, let me know, and I'll get the container," I say, leaving him to his entertainment.

"Will do."

19

"Hey, Erin, I am really sorry I didn't call or text. Let me tell you what's happened this week."

Panicked, she says, "Oh, Hank, thank God you called. I thought the worst."

"I should have called earlier, I know."

She rushes to get her words in first. "I am so sorry about your friends. I shouldn't have said anything."

Surprised by what she says, I need more details. "What did you do?"

"You haven't talked to Michelle, Kate, or Jean?"

Again, more details are required. "No. What did you do?"

"Hank."

The one-syllable response, the inflection, it leads me to think the worst. "What did you do?"

"We were playing euchre."

"What did you do, Erin?"

"Shut up and let me tell you." She silences me. "Sandy has Michelle's e-mail address. She sent her an e-mail detailing the conversation you and I had over brunch. Everything." She takes a breath. "She found out about my past, she figured out Pike's indiscretion. She put it all out there to Michelle in an e-mail." Her voice had a tremble to it that sounded erratic. "So when I go to the house to play cards, Michelle confronts me. I told her the truth. I told her the truth." She starts to whimper.

I do not know what to say. No wonder my friends have not talked to me this week, no e-mail, no text, no funny photos.

"Hank? Are you still there?"

"I am."

"Tell me you've talked to them. Tell me you explained things and were able to work things out with them. Tell me you aren't mad at me."

Evenly, plainly, taking in the facts, I say, "I'm not mad at you."

"I was just…I told them the truth. I didn't want to lie to them."

My mind starts to decipher details, and the details go straight to my heart. My emotions churn. I find myself angry.

"I'm mad at Sandy. Why would she do this?"

"I don't know. She hasn't gotten over you?"

In silence we remain on the phone, connected through wireless waves, but miles apart.

"All your guy did was hit me with a bottle at a bar," I mutter. "My past had to go and wreck people's lives."

A few more moments pass; then, Erin finally says, "What are we going to do, Hank?"

"I'm not sure."

"Come over. Talk to me face-to-face. I want to look you in the eyes to know you are not mad. That you aren't just saying things."

"I can't come over. I'm with my dad and the twins."

"Can't he look after them?"

"No. He had a major medical episode on Monday. We took him to the emergency room, and he almost did not make it. That's why I haven't been available this week."

"Oh, Hank, you should've called. You should have let me know. I could have been there for you. I could have been your girl…brought you soup. You should've called."

I smile at the notion that soup solves problems, although the generosity of bringing something nutritious does speak to me.

"I know, I know, just—things happened so fast. Then I was over-whelmed, and I had a decision I had to make about work."

"Work. How important could that be?"

"It was a major decision. I should've called. I'm sorry." It was true. It was honest. There were so *many* things in my life I had done wrong, by accident, by malice, by oversight. I could have called, despite all the activity that week.

"You should've called," she says, breaking the silence once again. "I do not think your friends know. They don't know about your dad, and if they did, they would have been there for you."

"You think so?"

"I know so," she says, resolved in her answer. "You're so much more to them than just a friend. You're family. They look at you so fondly. You're an important part of their lives. You underestimate them."

"Was Michelle upset?"

"I don't know her as well as you do, but all three girls seemed upset at first."

"Did they call you names? Treat you badly? Throw punches? I need details, Erin."

"There was a printout of the e-mail on the card table when I got there. All three read it, and Michelle asked me if it was true. I told her it was; I told her about bumping into Sandy at brunch, about the reasons I did what I did, and the time, and the problems it caused."

I cannot help but ask, "Was there yelling, scratching, fighting?"

"No. They understood. They did not like it. Kate said she understood not everyone had the same options as she had in school. Jean hugged me and laughed. She told me not to sleep with anyone but you."

I chuckled. "That is so Jean. That is good advice, you know. You should follow it."

"I think Michelle needs you to call her. She and Pike are going to have a hard time with this."

I agree. "They all will."

20

"Hi, Michelle, thanks for taking my call."

Her voice is soft, distant. "I was hoping to hear from you earlier."

"A few things have happened this week. I've been out of the loop since Sunday and only moments ago spoke to Erin for the first time since card night."

I sucked in and just spilled it. "I am really sorry that you found out about this whole situation this way. I'm not sure where to begin with apologies—for introducing you to Sandy, for not telling you once I found out about Erin, or for not telling you more about Pike when I found out."

"What could be more important than this?"

She was shrill.

"What would possibly keep you from calling me earlier?"

"Michelle—let me get to that. I do not want to distract from the importance of this one thing—I am very sorry for hurting you, for being a part of this deception. You must feel betrayed, and I am so sorry to be at the center of this." I try to be specific in my descriptions.

I can hear her begin to cry over the phone line. "It hurts, Hank."

"I know, Michelle, it hurts."

She sniffles. "Pike is in the doghouse. He should have been honest with me back then. I like to think I would have understood if he had told me. I'm progressive. He should have told me the night we met Erin at the bar. I should have gotten news like this from him. I am most hurt by that."

"I understand."

"I don't hate Erin, I really like her. In school, girls are so hard on one another. They are sometimes mean about the most superficial things. There was one girl at our school, Ally, who had a reputation for being promiscuous."

"Did you use the word *promiscuous?*"

She chuckles. "No, no, we didn't. It was middle school. We called her slut and whore and other things, worse things. Ally ended up sitting by herself in the cafeteria. She did not have many friends. I always felt bad for her. I felt awful for hanging with people who would say those things, so I went and made friends with her. I started to sit with her every day and talk with her. She was pretty, got top grades, super smart, but alone."

"Alone?" I ask.

"She had a tough life. Her parents did not treat her well, and she had a creepy uncle who lived in the basement who was always trying to pay the wrong type of attention to her...You can imagine."

"I can."

"It wasn't a happy story. Ally became one of my best friends before going to college. We still keep in touch. She's doing very well today, but it could have just as easily gone the other way. She could have run away from that awful life. She talked about it often. Without friends, without a home, where do you run? Where will a thirteen-year-old end up? So my mom and I always made sure to invite her over on weekends for sleepovers, nearly every night for dinner."

I commiserate. "I can't imagine where she would have ended up without you." She takes a double breath, the kind little kids take when crying so hard, in need of extra oxygen.

She continues. "It's one of those things growing up that you have to realize: not everyone has it as good as you. Not everyone has a home and loved ones; so it is important to do the Christian thing, watch out for one another. I do not hate Erin, not at all. I thought she was the perfect girl for you, that we could all be great friends together."

Wishing there was more to say, I simply reply, "I know."

"What Erin did, what she did, it was her own choice. I don't see life like some beautiful bay window overlooking an ocean of events. It is a broken window. There are shards, imperfections. They shatter between adolescence and adulthood. You have to put that window back together over a lifetime. Each person who works at that is a good person."

"That's just so cool what you've said. Do you really think of life that way?"

"I do. There are little reflections, reflections in the glass. Family, friends, lovers, memories, and they are all a different color, creating a design. They refract the light in our lives a little bit differently and at different times."

In her pause I wonder if she's completed a thought, or if she's making a decision to open up. "I just thought you were one of those perfect pieces that let just the right amount of light through."

It is touching to hear her say this.

"Michelle, I am very sorry—"

She stops me. "You didn't do anything but follow your heart. Pike made a rotten choice. Pike hurt me, and Erin was the way that he did it. Fine, she has a speckled past. I will get over it. I do not love Pike any less. I don't love you any less."

Surprised at the notion, I say, "You love me?"

"Of course I do, Hank. You don't think we spend this much time together because I put up with you, do you?"

It is rare and refreshing to hear this. My only reply is, "No, no, I suppose not."

"You're a very important part of my life. You are an important part of all our lives. This is a bump in the road, not a split."

"I'm glad to hear that."

"Now, what was so important that you didn't call me for three days?"

21

"Do you open presents on Christmas Eve, or Christmas morning?" I ask Erin as we walk from her car to RedMitten Greetings.

"Christmas morning. Doesn't everyone?"

"I've always been surprised by little things in life, this one different variation between families, and tried to figure it out," I say.

"What do you think it's about?"

"Don't know. For a while I thought it was that part of the reformation. Protestants were looking to represent the gift of the magi, while Catholics were doing mass. The more I have asked others about this, the less true it was. Both have a service on Christmas Eve."

"Maybe it's socioeconomic," she says.

"Maybe."

"Like, people of one group had to work on Christmas, while others didn't, so they had to do it on Christmas Eve instead," she says, carefully stepping around a suspicious-looking slick on the sidewalk, grabbing my arm tightly. "I know in my family, we had time in the morning with my family, then went to my aunt's and saw my cousins and grandparents."

"I could see that, rooted in a long family tradition. So it may not have been the immediate family, it could have been something from a generation or two before."

"Christmas has gotten out of hand with all this spending. Starting to promote it right after Halloween," she says, stepping in rhythm with me again.

"Families are funny things. You can take a small family of four, mom, dad, son, daughter, and each has his own perspective. As perspectives change and mold and shape, future interactions to outsiders do as well." I feel a pull from her and turn, thinking she may have slipped.

She stops and she looks me in the eyes to say, "Thank you for inviting me over."

I smile. "You're welcome. I'm glad you could come."

"No, really, thank you. I'm happy to be a part of something again. People get together for all types of reasons. There is the basic chemistry of physical passion; some just click and feel connected. I've known people who laugh all the time with each other. And there are those who complement each other—she feels needed and sexy around him, while he feels smart and important."

"What kind are we?" I ask.

"I don't know. I get this sense that you get me. You understand something that no one else does."

"Yeah, I can see that."

She smiles. "Plus, you've got a nice ass."

"Thanks." I watch her hips sway as she starts up the steps of RedMitten Greetings. "Now, keep in mind that there are several of us living in the loft, and the place is a bit of a mess. I'm glad you're going to meet my dad and Midge."

"Why so excited?"

"To prove that I'm not making all this up."

"Ha." She laughs. "Of course I believe you. Why wouldn't I?"

"Erin, I've got to tell you, I'm in the middle of it, and sometimes *I* still don't believe it's true."

"Um, you know I am expecting the little shack from *Willy Wonka and the Chocolate Factory* when we get up there."

"The one with Gene Wilder, and they live in the UK as expatriated Americans?"

"Yeah, that one."

"I can assure you we have electricity and don't all sleep in the same bed as Grandpa Joe."

I open the door to the loft to find that Midge has been making something to provide a nice, warm, friendly welcome for the senses.

"Hello," I say to Midge.

"Hello, Hank." Midge greets me with a kiss at the door. She has on an apron, her hair done, and is wearing a dress like a "good homemaker."

A little surprised at the kiss, I hold out my hand and say, "And this is Erin. Erin, this is Midge. Midge this is my girlfriend, Erin Contee."

The two exchange pleasantries, and Erin is quick to compliment her dress.

"Hank's said so many nice things about you," Midge says.

"That's so sweet," Erin says.

"Would you like a glass of wine?" Midge asks.

"Yes, please," Erin says.

"Hank has this stash of Frog's Leap here. I opened one. I hope that's OK, Hank."

"Sure, sure, it's there to drink. I got that one on Thanksgiving."

Dad calls out from his bookshelf nook, "Hank, bring your lady friend over here and introduce me."

"Sorry, Dad."

I whisper to Erin, "Not too bad so far. Let's go meet Dad."

Two steps ahead of her, I take her to the part of the loft Dad is calling from, behind the books, where he is clean and things are tidy. "Dad, this is Erin Contee. Erin this is my dad."

Erin steps forward to see him in a better light and shake his hand. "It's nice to meet you, Mr. Hanson."

As the words leave her mouth, I can see my father's expression of happiness and joy at meeting his son's new girlfriend melt into one of shocked recognition. In an instant I can see that my father already knows Erin. When he looks to me, I look to Erin, who shares the same expression.

"Well, shit," I say. "This isn't going to work, is it?"

"Hank," Dad says.

"No, Dad, I already know. You don't have to say a thing." My blood begins to boil. It is hard to breathe. My jaw tightens, and I find it difficult not to yell obscenities and to keep my indoor voice.

"Here you go, Erin." Midge hands her one of my seventy-five-cent, almost matching wineglasses.

"Thank you," Erin replies kindly.

"What did I miss?" Midge asks. "What happened? You three look like something happened."

Between my gritted teeth, I say, "Erin forgot something at home; she's going to go home now and get it."

"Oh no, it can't be that important," Midge says. "You just got here."

I speak for her. "Yeah, I know, it's…She has to go now. I'll walk her back to her car."

"Oh," Erin says with disappointment. "I can get to my car. I'll be all right."

"No," I say, "I insist. I will walk you to your car. There's ice on the walks."

"It was so nice to meet you, Erin," Midge says.

"It was very nice to meet you too, Midge," Erin says, turning quickly for the door. I catch a tear run down her face and see her quickly brush it away.

I help her with her coat, walk her down the steps and out the door. The silence is uncomfortable. I can hear the fresh layer of snow crunch beneath our feet as we make our way to her car.

"Aren't you going to say anything to me, Hank?"

I can feel my nostrils flare and my voice rise. "I am trying really hard to say the right thing, Erin."

"Hank." She stops. "Don't hold it in. You do this, you keep it down, you act like a good soldier, a tough guy, and I need to know what you're thinking, feeling, at this moment. Talk to me!"

"I'm pissed off," I yell for the first time in ages. "Who the hell didn't you fuck?"

She looks surprised at the volume and shudders. "I was honest with you right from the start."

"I'm not doubting your honesty. You told me. I knew, I knew." I try to bring it down a level. "I like you more than that knowledge should bother me, but it seems that the men in my life have these hidden secrets, these dark little episodes, and they all seem to involve them putting their dick into you." Uncontrolled, my voice gets loud again.

Erin starts to tear up. Her voice is very soft as she says, "I really like you, Hank. I have this crappy past. I cannot change that past. I hope you can still like me for who I am, what you've liked about me these past few weeks."

I take her by her arm and walk her toward the car. My hope is that I can convert the rage I am feeling into energy by fast, long strides. It is a relief valve for my adrenaline.

"Slow down!"

"Oh!"

"Wait!" she says as I drag her along.

"Erin, I..." I cannot complete a thought.

She wraps her arms around me. Her hair is sweet and floral. Her body is warm, and I can feel it press against me in arousing ways. I remember how much I like her, how much fun we've had together. I remember the times we're apart and how I long to be with her again. I remember the happiness I feel when I know she is thinking of me.

She whispers in my ear, "Hank, I'm crazy about you. I do not want this to be over. Not like this. Not because of this. We can get past this."

I sigh deeply and say, "I'm going to need some time." I kiss her on the cheek, but she will not leave it at that.

She begins a full, deep, passionate kiss with her warm lips. Her hands make my neck and ears tingle, and I am fully aroused in the moment. She looks in my eyes with an expression that makes me feel connected, tied together with her. As wonderful as this moment is, I remember that I am but one man she has not fucked, and these physical triggers are manipulated to get a desired outcome. She is a woman who can control men.

"I'll still need some time," I say.

"OK," she says in a hushed voice. "OK, I understand."

I reach into my jacket pocket and feel a box. My finger tickles the ribbon at its top, and I recognize what it is in an instant. "I don't know if I will see you before Christmas, but I got you this."

Tears trickle down onto the Tiffany blue box. "My God, Hank, what did you get me?"

She opens it to find a necklace that took me hours and the help of a sales associate to select.

"It's beautiful Hank. It is…it is too much."

She holds the pendant, and it sparkles with diamonds, emeralds, and sapphires.

My rage has transformed all right, changed into an immeasurable sadness that rocks me to the bottom of my soul when it hits. It begins to fill with the tears I cannot shed in front of her. I say nothing; she says nothing. We stand in silence.

I look into her eyes and know it is time to go. I give her one last quick kiss and can feel her pulling, wanting more. I turn. I walk away.

The farther I walk, the less I can hear her sobs.

Heading back to the loft at this moment is an option filled with lies or explanations to Midge I cannot invent. My friends are a tender spot. They need time to heal.

I cannot go to Erin. I have left Erin.

I get in my station wagon, point her north, and drive with no destination in mind.

Driving is my remedy, especially long distances, over several hours at a time. I have my mix tapes from years past, and this allows me to gain perspective. The choice for my first hour is "UK's Most Recent Invasion" from a girl named Amy in high school. She is a reminder that my emotions over someone I was once crazy about eventually, one day, will subside. Today she is married to a veterinarian, with three kids and a wonderful life. Her name is still my password. She is a distant reminder of just how women can make me feel.

I fill the next forty-five minutes with side B of a ninety-minute tape, "We Will Rock You like a Hurricane." It's a reminder to another girl from my past. I completely embarrassed her with a hickey, or love bite, so deep, so large, that it looked like someone had taken one of those miniature bats from Tiger Stadium on Bat Day and struck her in the neck. Her whereabouts are unknown, but the tape reminds me of how poorly I've treated others.

After this, the time slips with each mile as I switch to my plug-in adapter and turn on my iPod to a playlist from the few last weeks. It's nothing I've selected on purpose, just things that have been playing. Van Morrison comes on, reminding me of the call on Thanksgiving with Erin, when she turned a phrase about playing cards into something dirty.

She is such a smart person. The furniture she designed is elegant, comfortable, and simple in the way it holds together. She is so talented. I was fortunate to have spent time with her.

An orange light on the dashboard begins to flicker. I realize I have no idea where I am, or the last time I saw civilization. My best guess is that I am somewhere north of the state's capitol, Lansing, and south of Mackinaw City, as I haven't crossed five miles of suspension bridge.

There are hundreds of red flashing lights on towers across the horizon. These must be wind turbines. I must be outside Alma, Michigan, home of America's Highland games. At the bottom of the off-ramp is a choice of east or west, but no indication of east or west what. I choose east and find more farms, more wind turbines, no service stations. After a few minutes, I pull over on what seems a side road or entrance to the plot of land, to find some privacy.

It is a clear sky, brilliant with stars, reminding me of a Van Gogh painting. It is a cold sky, which might challenge Admiral Byrd, and reveals my every breath. The hood of the station wagon is warm, and I wrap a blanket from the back tightly around the areas my jacket doesn't reach. The silence is welcome. No stomping, no screaming, no bickering or asking for help, no requests for vacation, no errors on a spreadsheet, no whining about not using an idea. Just silence.

Snowflakes have that effect on the world. They hold strange acoustic properties. Air trapped in the crystal structures between fallen flakes. A fresh snow does this best. Once the sun hardens it or wind blows, the softened sounds are lost and the noise returns.

My cell phone rings. It is Midge.

Torn between things I might have to say and things I might make up, I decide to answer it.

"What are you wearing?" she asks.

"What?"

"Tell me what you're wearing, describe it in detail?" she says in a sexy voice.

"Midge?'

"I was just kidding. You OK?" she asks.

"Yeah. I guess."

"Where are you? With Erin?"

"No, I don't know where I am. I went for a drive to figure things out."

"She seemed like a nice girl. I hope you two can work out whatever it is that happened."

"I hope so too."

Her speech is slow and thoughtful.

"You know, your father and I, when we first started seeing each other, it was all about passion, desire. After the kids it seems like we stopped talking. A fire went out, but we were still committed to each other. It's why I came back to care for him. It's why I understand he has a mixed past. I knew that about him, and I still married him."

She is trying very hard to be kind.

Her words are encouraging, but her perspective is unclear. She goes on. "It wasn't until we started to argue, talk, communicate, that I realized that I still needed him."

"When did you figure this out?"

"A few days ago, in the hospital. All those hours together, forced into a small space where he couldn't get away from me, I talked some sense into him."

"So this was recent."

"Very recent."

"I'm glad you figured that out. He is lost without you, Midge."

"He also told me about Erin tonight. He told me that he used to see her, that he was frustrated with me after I got pregnant with the twins, but couldn't tell me," she says with a twinge of bitterness in her voice.

"Oh."

"Yeah."

Her reply hangs in the dark and cold sky for a moment. The thought of her leaving him now would make things very problematic at this moment.

"Are you staying with him?" I ask.

"I am," she says.

"I love my dad, just not what he does. I think that's how most people feel about him. What is it about him that makes us feel that way?"

"He's your dad. You cannot give up on your dad. He's my husband; I have to give my marriage a chance to work."

Sitting on the warm hood of the engine under an unspoiled night sky, I have to take the opportunity to ask on behalf of loving siblings, "Have you tried to make amends with my brother? Do you think my dad ever will?"

"Oh, Hank, I don't know," she laments. "He won't take our calls. I think about your brother very often. All the Hanson men are great, but let's face it: some things just aren't meant to be."

"Thank you for calling."

"Take care. Call and let me know where you land."

"Will do," I say.

I am told there are steps, or stages, to get over anything.

I don't know if there is something to get over or figure out, but I can say that I am not mad at Erin. I am hurt and don't want to be hurt again. Yet I can see this one thing, this small thing that I don't care that much about, coming back time and again when I introduce her to old friends or new acquaintances. What will it matter what they think?

It is less fun sleeping in the station wagon than as a kid. That may be true of many things in life. With daylight, I now look over the Pontiac 403 V8. Unlatching the hood makes a distinct sound. When I look at her engine, I can see what is slightly amiss. It is the comfort of knowing something, the familiarity of having worked on it repeatedly, that I find rewarding. From the back I pull out a ratchet set and tighten the number four sparkplug a quarter turn, then reattach the wire. Three pumps on the gas pedal, and she roars to life. In no time heat is coming from the vents. I can fix the wagon. I can keep her running.

Why can't I do this in life?

Why not with Erin?

Why not with Dad?

CHRISTMAS EVE

22

"You sold RedMitten Greetings?" Dad asks.

"Yes, and they're now the owners of the building. So we're going to have to move."

"Wow, I didn't know you were seriously considering an offer," Midge said.

"Well, it started as a conversation a few months ago. Then right before Thanksgiving, it got serious. They gave me some documents and dollars, and I couldn't turn it down."

"But it's your passion," Dad says.

"I'll find another."

"When do we have to move?" Midge asks.

"We need to be out by the new year. So I have started looking at furnished places we could stay in until we get a permanent place. Something on the ground floor, without steps." I smile and look at Dad. "I've also hired a caregiver to come take care of you, Dad. She will be here in about an hour. Her name is Trish. That will mean Midge can have some more time to herself and the twins. It's still a team play here. She won't be here twenty-four hours a day, just days for now, ten a.m. to seven p.m. with breaks."

"Oh good, I get a babysitter," he says grumpily.

"She is actually specializing in physical rehab. She's going to get you strong and healthy."

"I like that idea," Midge says.

"How much did you sell the company for?" Dad pushes.

"Enough."

"Oh, that much," he says sarcastically.

"It's a private company and a private matter. So, enough. I'd appreciate you not asking again, Dad." I try to set him straight from the start.

"OK," he bemoans. "I was just trying to be happy for you."

"Really? I can see you spending it in your head already. Here is the deal. I am going to make certain you and your wife and kids are going to be OK. Nothing crazy over-the-top, like dancing robots, giant televisions, McMansions that no one needs or can afford. Nice little place in a nice school system. Got it?"

"Yeah. I got it," Dad says meekly.

Midge leans over and gives me a big kiss; I can feel the lipstick saturating every pore on my lips. "You are wonderful, Hank. Thank you very much. This is more than we deserve. We are very grateful. Don't listen to sourpuss over here."

I smile and nod my head politely, wipe the thick lacquer from my lips, and wonder what has sparked this deluge of kissing and affection from Midge.

Trish is everything Dad loves and Midge hates. She is a twenty-something spitfire with lots of energy. She is athletic, wears tight clothing, and is very attractive. I think Dad wants to please her because he is a man, and at the core of every man is this desire for every beautiful woman somehow, someday, to have sex with him. The thing is, Trish is also demanding. She pushes Dad to do more than he wants to do, makes him stretch and move in ways that appear difficult for him. She is in control.

I can only stay for the first hours they have for introductions. My father and Trish toil through a workbook of tracking activities, what the routine will be each week, a proper diet, the removal of any alcohol or cigars he has been known to sneak.

Before leaving, Midge catches my attention with a few words at the door.

"I'm not so sure about Trish," she says.

"What do you mean? She's great with dad."

"Well, I am worried she is pushing him too hard. She might hurt him," she says.

Again, with the touching my arm, standing too close. I can hear the fabric covering her breasts rub against the skin of my jacket.

"She is a professional, highly recommended; we are going to try things out for a while."

"Fine," Midge huffs. She raises her voice and sneers in the direction of Trish, "But if we notice anything stolen we are calling the cops."

"Uncalled for," I say.

Knobby and Kate are having the gang over to their house for lunch to celebrate Christmas a bit early, before we go our own ways for family. It's the first time we have been together as a group since card night, so I'm not sure of the mood. The station wagon fills the distance between the two driveways of their house and the neighbors. I love their home. It's older, well kept, the perfect place to host. It has a new interior living room, kitchen, and backyard deck. I am last to arrive.

"Come on in, Hanson. Good to see you."

"Thanks for having me over, Knobby."

"Wouldn't be the same without you, you know that."

I turn the corner to find all my good friends in the kitchen, listening to Christmas music in front of the fire. Wrapped presents are piled in the center of the room, and a real Christmas tree sits by a glass sliding door.

New snow is falling; it is perfect.

"Hanson" rings out, with the exception of Dord, who slyly calls, "Lumpy." This gets a huge laugh out of the room. I cannot help but laugh myself. The ice is broken, and any awkwardness subsides; the group is reset to normal.

Knobby begins to serve champagne around the room and makes certain everyone has a glass.

"I'd like to make a toast," he calls, gathering attention.

"An afternoon toast?" Jeans asks.

"It's more of an announcement. Kate is going to be the world's greatest mom!"

Knobby's announcement finds cheers and hugs.

"To my best friend and greatest first wife, Kate."

We all raise our glasses. "To Kate!"

Dord clears his throat. "I don't want to steal your thunder, but we had planned to tell you this today as well—Jean and I are expecting. Two months and three weeks today!"

"To Jean and Dord!" Knobby raises his glass.

We all raise our glasses and toast, and more hugs follow. The typical jibber jabber about parenting follows. Michelle, Kate, and Jean head into the kitchen to talk and finish the lunch Kate has cooked.

Dord, Pike, Knobby, and I gather by the fireplace. Knobby, fearless, at times tactless, blurts, "So were you dating a hooker?"

"I always think of hookers as women on a corner," Dord says. "A more accurate description would be escort."

"They like to be called courtesans," Pike says softly.

"Really?" Dord replies.

"Prostitutes, escorts, hookers, sex workers, they all have their own professionalism, their own structure," Pike says. "Courtesans are supposed to be the most sophisticated and respected of them."

"So which was this one?" Knobby asks.

"The way I understand it," I say softly, so no one in the kitchen will hear, "she was 'exploring new things, and trying to pay for college.' I think that's called being young and desperate."

"I don't know what Erin and the girls talked about after they found out, but Jean was interested in trying some new things we hadn't done before," Dord says.

"Kate too," Knobby says. "I thought it was being pregnant and all, but she was all, 'Let's try this thing,' and 'I've heard about this.'"

We look to Pike.

"I'm still in the guest room," he says quietly.

"Well, I'm happy for you fellas," I say. "I'm glad to hear Erin Contee was good for you."

"Are you talking about Erin?" Michelle asks loudly from the kitchen. "Will she be coming over? There's plenty of food."

"Well, no," I say. "We're on hold at the moment."

"I'm sorry to hear that. I like her, she's so nice."

Kate nods, followed by the other two.

"That's good to hear."

That is about all I can muster, without going into the strangeness. I am certain the whole take will come out in full detail one day.

I really want to be with Erin. I like Erin.

If it were just Pike, she might be right here with us now, but with Dad involved, I appreciate why my brother hasn't talked to Dad and Midge since the wedding.

"You won't mind if we still invite her to card night, will you?" asks Michelle, the one person I thought would be uninterested in being her friend.

Surprised at the offer, I say, "No, I don't mind at all. Call her, write her; I'm glad you're all getting along so well."

We eat some great food, exchange presents, some of which are functional and some funny. Everyone gets a copy of a group photo we took earlier this year. Overall, it's a pleasant afternoon with lifelong friends.

Back in the loft, Trish is just finishing her day and helping Dad to clean up. Midge has been cleaning the loft, and with the help of Trish earlier, she was able to move the rolling bookshelves, allowing for a pathway and space. Perry Winkelberry watches from his perch as Midge prepares for the first volley of visitors she is expecting— Dad's sister from out West. The group from Chicago is flying in after

Christmas Day, along with the one from DC, and we will all meet with my grandparents for a day. I've reserved a private little room on the back of a restaurant I know and like, where we will all fit for the day in fellowship.

"Thank you for coming, Trish." I shake her hand.

"It's a pleasure; your dad is a pleasure to work with."

"What are your thoughts on his state? How he can progress?"

"Hank, it's one day at a time. Each day we'll do the best that it allows."

"That's a good philosophy. We will see you in two days. Happy holidays."

Trish gets my attention just outside the door as she departs, asking in a concealed voice, "Is Midge always going to be here?"

"Yeah, I think so."

"She is kind of protective of your father," she says.

"I understand. I'll see what I can do."

She smiles, turns, and speeds down the steps.

I turn to my father. "That was pretty good, eh, Dad?"

"I'm pretty tired," he says, fatigued. "If it's OK with you, I'm just going to sleep."

"Sure, busy day, I get it. Midge and I will be quiet, keep an eye on the twins. You rest. I'll wake you when your sister gets here."

Midge does her best with what is in the kitchen. I can't help but notice that she is an attractive woman. The freckles on her breasts dance in the low v-cut top as she vigorously wipes off the table in front of me. I can see what the men in my family find so appealing about her. Her curves are in all the right places; she works very hard to pay attention to details and cares about others. She is kind and she smells great. She also catches me watching her and looking down her rather loose blouse while bending over to set the cookies on the table to cool. Our eyes meet, and she knows I have been studying her movements. I'm a little embarrassed to have her catch me in the act. I find myself a little stimulated.

"You want to rip my dress off and take me on the table?" she asks in all seriousness. Then follows it in an airy, soft voice, "Just kidding."

I gulp. "What?"

"Oh, it's OK, silly," she says. "It's bound to happen. I won't deny I've caught a quick glimpse of you getting ready for work in the morning and running out of the shower."

"I know."

"You don't need to say anything, we're both adults. It is actually somewhat nice to have someone look at me that way. I'm human, you know. I need to be desired."

"It's been a tough time, for us all."

"It has."

The front bell rings. It is my aunt. In our hug at the front step of RedMitten Greetings, the smell of cigarettes rubs on to me in ways I will never be able to clean. It trails her wherever she walks: up the stairs, through the loft, over Dad's bed. It lingers in the air for a good twenty minutes after her several-hour visit until I open the windows and spray fresh scent. The first act drops the temperature rapidly, the second sending Perry Winkelberry up to his loft to save his sensitive snout from the overwhelming chemicals.

23

In the first minutes of the new morning, I think the pressure against my lips is Perry Winkelberry's paw attempting to wake me for attention or food, but the scent of fingernail polish in the darkness tells me it is not the cat clawing for my attention.

Her fingertips cover my mouth gently in an effort to keep my silence and to stir me awake. Eyes now open, I see Midge in her white nightgown. She floats over me as if a ghostly apparition. The alternating light from the bank across the street reveals that for her, the time is now. Her nails graze over my chin delicately, then dance and drag across my chest. She leans in and kisses me. Her leg swings over my core. She is now straddling me. She takes control of my wrists, holding them out of the way, limiting my resistance.

I whisper in warning, "Dad."

She covers my lips again. "Headphones, sleeping pills, out," she says.

"Kids."

She presses her finger firmly over my mouth. "Stop thinking."

Her kiss turns deeper, more passionate. Her movements become more rhythmic and determined. I can feel nothing between us as she moves.

My hands begin to explore her legs, soft skin under my palms, working up her sides, to her breasts, unchained from the constricting bra I studied so carefully in the kitchen. Natural, comforting, breasts. With the brush of my fingers, her nipples become engorged and responsive. She starts to moan and breathe deeply.

I feel myself start to rise. It does not take much to get me physically aroused. It has been quite some time since my last close physical encounter. I have pure, physical needs. She seems neglected, ignored, finding no satisfaction from her husband. Is this revenge for having been wronged too many times?

Whatever the catalyst, it brought her to my bed, separated from her husband by only volumes of books and noise-canceling headphones.

"Oh!" she cries out as I take her firmly by the hips and lower her to the bed. I am in command and begin to lick her neck softly, following with small kisses. She wiggles and moans beneath me. I grab her knees and pull them into position, to open her and bury my head in her. Rubbing with my nose, I lick with a narrow tongue and then go deeper. My hands work their way back to her chest.

I wish this were Erin.

I want to do this for Erin, to Erin.

I want to hear Erin call out my name, writhe with passion, moan for me. It is wishful thinking, I know, to have moments with Erin, like this. In the darkness all things are possible, wishful thinking or not. A surrogate sensation easily impersonates Erin. Her fingers in my hair could easily be Erin's fingers touching me. My focus and attention is on her pleasure, her relief, but my thoughts are selfish, all about my own desires.

I feel her pull at the elastic waistband of my boxers, pull them down, and then off. I can feel her attempts to find a good position. Instead, I pull back and reach for the drawer near my bed, feeling for foil in the darkness. She pulls at me again, harder, demanding. In a fumbled placement of the packet's content, I respond to her, grabbing with a small smack at her hand, which brings rise to vocal satisfaction. She likes it rough, enjoys being taken.

My grip is firm.

I thrust into her.

We start our rhythm, slowly at first, until we find and increase the right tempo, a strong and steady beat. Her voice is light; her sounds are full pleasure. My mind diverts to darkness. The thought of my father intertwined with Erin changes my mood rapidly to wrath. He is a thief in time, having stolen my happiness, depriving me of the joy I could have had with her.

Involuntarily, my muscles begin to tighten, movements become harsh, and her moans turn from whimpers to gasps. She is unable to hold on, and unbridled sounds pour out. Her noises nourish my cravings, feeding into a cycle of anticipation between the two of us, until we reach our zenith. Panting, gasping for air, I collapse at her side, depleted.

"Oh my God, Hank. That was…just what I needed."

CHRISTMAS

24

I am not proud of what transpired overnight. Midge, who had been sleeping on the couch since Dad's new medical bed arrived, woke up in my bed when the twins started stirring.

Maybe I am more like my father and brother than I'm willing to admit. The things that one likes may be the same types of things we all like, or the things the men in my family especially find pleasurable. Whatever that might be, Midge is very familiar with them.

The need for silence is even more enthralling, the knowledge of how wrong it was be damned. It heightened the thrill and made the event all the more exciting. In darkness it was wrong in all the right ways the flesh enjoys. In light of the new morning, it was just wrong.

The twins, after waking up, went right for the small plastic tree to sort out presents. Midge was in the bathroom like a flash. Dad, still sound asleep with his headphones on, snored away, unknowing, unaware that I now considered the two of us even.

Midge jumps out of her quick shower, starts coffee, and opens a box of coffee cake. Walking to the bathroom for a quick shower of my own, I receive a nice hard smack on the ass as I pass her.

"You're a sexy devil, aren't you?"

It makes me smile. It gets my heart racing. I am wide-awake and strangely still aroused by just how wrong last night was, and awful, and disgusted by myself, all at the same time, these thoughts and feelings swirling around the drain in the shower.

By the time I am out and fully dressed, Midge has gotten Father up and moving.

"I'm so sore from yesterday. I didn't realize just how much work we were doing." He groans. "That's the best night's sleep I've had since moving in here."

I smile, knowing. "I'm glad to hear that, Dad."

"Help me get to the toilet," he says. I comply.

His legs are still shaky, but he is out of bed and in better control of his bladder. These are two giant steps forward, in my book—a true Christmas miracle.

While Dad enjoys his first bit of privacy, Midge snuggles up to me in the kitchen and with her hot, sexy breath tickling my ear, she whispers, "Hank, you're amazing."

It brings a smile to my face, but I have no reply.

"I mean it. You were just amazing. You are so much bigger, and you just kept going and let me finish. Oh God, you let me finish. You're such a kind lover to take care of me."

She nearly starts things up again.

Stopping her, I say, "We can't do that. That was one time."

"I know, I know, but it was a good time. I needed that so bad."

"One time," I say.

She bites her lower lip, tilts her head, and says, "That's too bad. You know, if you ever need to, feel the urge to, you let me know. Anytime."

"Thank you," I say politely, uncertain how to reply to such an offer. My friends and I had agreed earlier that when your father's second wife's father dies, flowers with a thoughtful card are the appropriate action. What is the proper etiquette after sex with your brother's first love, your father's third wife, and the mother of your stepsiblings? A thoughtful card and flowers just do not seem to send the right message. If I still owned RedMitten, I bet I could make a card to cover that. I wonder what kind of sales numbers I could get on that card.

She hands me a full cup of coffee. "Thank you."

I can see the desire in her eyes, that small leap to joy starting to fade at my lack of enthusiasm for our newly shared passion. She can see my face in the light of this new day, and it is not what she had imagined in the darkness of our sins.

Leaning in, too close, an intimate distance, I whisper in her ear, "I thought last night was amazing. You rocked my world. You knew just what to do and how to move, and the moment between us was like nothing else."

I continue.

"You are still P5, Midge, Margaret, Mary—my father's wife—and I am still Hank Hanson. There are three other people in this loft we have to protect and care for."

"I know." She takes a deep sigh. "Last night was a beautiful dream, and you have to wake up from dreams at some point."

"It would be great if I could dream like that every night, Midge— but I don't know that we can repeat that dream, and if we ever tried, it might spoil what we had. We should just enjoy what it was, hold on, and remember it for what it was."

"That would be nice."

"It would."

Dad calls out, "I'm done, a little help here."

I plant one last kiss straight on her lips to feel that pressed flesh burn once more. I pull back, tasting her, and carry that delight on my tongue as I open the door to the reality of the bathroom.

After presents with the twins, I am back in the station wagon for brunch and presents with P3. Again, downriver for lunch and presents with P4, out to Bloomfield Hills with P5 for drinks and gift exchange, and then back to tuck my grandparents into bed in St. Clair. I get white socks, and they get a new afghan, peanut brittle, and a box of favorite cigars.

During my ninety-minute drive home from my grandparents Erin weighs heavily on my mind. I should not have been with Midge. Being even does not feel as good as I thought it might.

The symmetry of this situation feels unbalanced, overly complex, a weighted burden. There is no being even with Dad. There is no being even with Erin. I can no more abandon my feelings for her than I would be able to disown my father.

I sneak into the building, up the stairs, and into my bed. I pass the twins cuddling on a mattress. My father's snore rumbles and drowns, and Midge rolls over on the couch. After I'm undressed and under my sheets, Perry Winkelberry jumps on me and kneads my belly until it's comfortable enough to curl up.

"What the fuck were you thinking last night?" I imagine Perry saying to me. "I watched the whole thing. You're an idiot."

THE DAYS BETWEEN

25

Dad is sick. It could have been from an open window to let out the smoky smell and to allow cool fresh air to enter. It may have been the germs latched on to one of the relatives, shared with family members on first embrace, during the holiday visit in the restaurant. It could have been from the time spent with Trish after her shift in the hospital, then touching him for hours. Or maybe it was anything my grandparents may have carried from the retirement home. All of it or some of it has latched onto Dad and arrested his momentum of getting well.

A simple cold to anyone else is worse for someone in this weakened state.

The twins have returned to their grandparents for the rest of the week. It's just Dad, Midge, and me in the loft. While she is dutifully by his bedside, I search for a residence that is open for us to move into by week's end. There is nowhere in Ann Arbor that meets our requirements, so I look east to Canton, near where Erin Contee is in Plymouth, and north of her, to Livonia, Farmington. Anything the right size and furnished is unavailable until the next month. Some take pets, others will not.

Instead of finding a place for all of us, I decide that staying together is less important. It is too limiting. After that stupid rendezvous, it is too uncomfortable. I find a place for them, with two bedrooms, no pets. It is furnished, so they can move in right away.

Knobby helps, and in four hours and two trips with the station wagon and Knobby's truck, I have moved all their personal belongings to a month-to-month arrangement at an extended-stay corporate housing complex. They are on the first floor in a handicap-accessible location.

Knobby and I are able to buy a slightly used wheelchair and move Dad down the steps from the third-floor loft to the car. We follow Midge, Dad, and the twins as they drive to the new place. Dad's move to the wheelchair, up the ramp, and into his new bed is much easier than it was getting him out of the loft at RedMitten. I call Trish on the way to dropping off Knobby to let her know about the new location, the new arrangements, and that the cell phones numbers are still the right ones to dial.

Alone in the loft for the first time in recent memory, I remember what I love about this place. It is walking distance to every neighborhood I've loved since school. The greatest coffee in the world is nearby, my favorite bar only a few blocks, the faces that smile on the street each day are familiar, and I, the "mayor of Ann Arbor," am preparing to leave all this behind.

The soft pads of Perry Winkelberry's paws press against my belly, and he kneads its doughy softness. "It's OK," he might say. "As long as we're together, we're home."

Finding a second wind, I start to pack my things. Kitchen stuff fits into three boxes, bathroom stuff and linens into two. The other things, the things that I wear or that I have carried with me over the years, fit into four more boxes. Which leaves the big stuff such as bed, couch, chairs, tables, stuff I do not have room for, cannot carry or bring with me.

These things I question. Do I need them? Do I want them? Are they going to make it to the next stage of this journey? These things just seem like things. Sentimentality was something I saw my father struggle with in the self-storage facility. The things he had earned, had worked for, had spent years to achieve, in the end were just things. He had faced this before with each separation, unable to keep much after each divorce. A life of rebuilding, reinvention, and reinvestment all wasted in the end.

As much as I do not like the things he does, I find myself on a similar path—unable to keep a real relationship, homeless, and without course or direction ahead of me. With the first of three wire transfers deposited from the acquisition, I do not feel rich. My savings account, while fat, does not match the places available listed on the Internet I would like to call home. Anything in walking distance of my neighborhood is expensive. My plans to save and reinvest what I have earned are only the spark of an idea for the moment. There is no additional cash flow coming in. Now that I am cash-rich, investment-poor, I have to think of things in a new light. After thirty minutes on the web, I find a hotel with weekly rates that will allow me to bring Perry Winkelberry. Still, the location is off my map.

First thing in the morning is the knock from the donation van drivers. They remove all my boxes and furniture in under an hour. Gone are the three-dollar coffee maker, quarter plates, twelve-dollar range, and mini fridges. I say so long to the secondhand furniture, gaming system, and television set. I'm handed an extensive receipt for my tax return as they are all carried out the door in minutes, ready for the next person in need to use.

Perry Winkelberry, who has been skittish and shy all morning, hides in the one remaining item in the loft aside from my luggage, his private perch. We watch each other, knowing that something will eventually have to happen. I know his weakness for boxes. He has proven it repeatedly all week by inspecting every one as I pack. This box is different. It's smaller, for one large cat, and has a handle on top strong enough to carry.

"OK, Perry. It's time."

His meow is one of acceptance that the box is where he will go. I open the box and make a little scratch sound on the side. "Say goodbye to the perch."

He turns and rubs against the perch, then finds his way down the spiral path.

"Merow." Perry rubs against my leg and pokes his head in the box. He jumps in without complaint or concern, and I close the lid, folding it into the handle.

Perry is silent as we traverse the steps with my carry-on bag. I set things down at the bottom of the steps and activate the security code. It sounds three beeps, and sixty seconds count down until we say good-bye. With a clicking of the tumblers, the key is turned, and I am the last one out of the office as RedMitten Greetings, a privately owned company by Hank Hanson, vanishes into the past.

NEW YEAR'S EVE

26

"I love my iPad," Knobby says.

"He does," Kate says. She puts down a card. "He's been playing with it all week. He's touching it instead of me."

"Hey." Knobby feigns a hurt tone before reengaging with his device.

"It's true," Kate replies.

Dord adds, "I guess it's no surprise that the technology leader of the me generation has created a legacy of products starting with *I*."

"Blech," smacks out of my lips. "Don't get me started on the boomers."

"Not a *Big Chill* fan, Hank Hanson?" Jean asks.

"I've got enough boomer problems; the evidence is a growing stack of bills they can't pay," I say.

"You certainly have been generous, no one would ever say differently," Michelle says.

"Lumpy," Jean starts, "I think I've figured you out."

"You have?" I say, mouth full of a freshly dipped vegetable from the tray.

"Yes, I was reading a book on parenting and have come to the realization...well, I always knew, maybe it's more of an epiphany..."

Dord interrupts her story to advance game play. "Just tell them, honey."

Jean smiles at his impatience and lays down her card. "I came to the epiphany, Hank Hanson, that you are a middle child." Her smile beams with the expectation that others will share in her enlightenment.

I smile in good faith and factuality. "Yes, I am, and?"

"Don't you see? It's birth order." As if that were suddenly something we should all know about. "You are basking in the attention from your father you've wanted all your life, but your brother always got instead. You are diplomatic. You're always pleasing people, and let's face it, some of these family members don't deserve to be pleased."

"Hmm. Interesting, Jean. I never thought of it in those terms," I say politely.

"How is your dad?" Pike asks.

I can see that Jean is frustrated by the lack of interest in her epiphany when she shakes her head at Pike's question.

"He's sick; we've had to put his physical therapy from the original incident on hold. He has a private nurse now. Someone Midge knew, or knows. I'm not sure who she is. The one good thing about the change in our situation is we're no longer piled on top of each other in the loft. Man, I loved that loft."

"I loved that loft too," Knobby says from behind his new device.

"Me too," says Pike.

"What's it like living in a nice clean hotel, rather than a dark and spooky book depository?" Jean asks.

"Kind of the same as visiting a hotel, but Perry Winkelberry is there. The staff likes him. Mostly they see dogs, one told me. So a cat is a nice change."

"How are Midge and the twins?" Knobby asks.

The question sends a shudder through me. I know he is not trying to touch a nerve, like he normally would, because he doesn't know. Nobody knows. No one should ever know what happened between Midge and me. He must have some instinctual ability to find weakness in others. "They're fine."

"The sandwich generation," Pike says softly, playing another card.

"What's that, honey?" Michelle plays her hand.

"It's called the sandwich generation, although our good friend Hank Hanson has a slight twist on it," Pike says, picking up two cards. "You're taking care of the older generation and the younger generation at the same time while being in the middle. In Japan it is an honor, it is a tradition, it is the reason people have children; but you, my friend, are not Japanese. So as an American, it's an oddity and burden, that someone from the boomer generation can't care for himself or the second, or third, round of offspring."

"Mmm, sandwich, I like sandwich," Knobby says.

"You're a club sandwich," Pike says.

"Thanks, Pike. I feel like a club sandwich," I say, standing up from the table. "But it's time for me to go make an appearance at the P5 party."

"Uno. You're leaving?" Michelle asks.

"Yeah, I'll be back before midnight to be with all of you. I promised P5 I'd go to his New Year's party a month ago, and he seems fragile these days."

"So you're going to drive forty-five minutes out there to hang out for an hour, then drive forty-five minutes back here?" Dord asks.

"Yeah, I am," I say.

Dord's expression is judgmental, as if to say I am a fool. He says with a wry tone, "I want you back in time to kiss me for the New Year."

I smile. "I will, Dord. Put on the lip balm."

The circle drive at P5's estate is full once again. I park the wagon on the street. My walk to the house fills my lungs with brisk, refreshing, cold air that helps to steady my mind from a drive filled with the thoughts of suppressing my oedipal mistake.

P5 welcomes me at the door with a fresh glass of wine. He talks about Frog's Leap, just as he did at Thanksgiving. I explain that I enjoyed the bottle he gave me, and he offers to give me another, but I decline. He walks me through the house, introducing me as the "man who just sold RedMitten Greetings" to friends, coworkers, and other members of influence from the area. I recognize one of the women serving food, wearing her white shirt and black bow tie, as the same who ran the kitchen during Thanksgiving. She has raven-black hair with cut bangs that square off her pale-skinned face. Her bright red lipstick is a beacon that flashes a smile with each utterance of, "Would you like an appetizer?"

"You like her?" P5 nudges my arm.

In a certain light, she reminds me of Erin. Not as toned, less spirited, but she might fill the gap I am still feeling in the hollow of my heart. Nothing I have done has helped with the way I feel about Erin. No other person, not millions of dollars, not the kindness of friendship. Maybe it just needs time.

"She was from Thanksgiving, wasn't she?" I ask.

"Yeah, good memory. Her name is Leslie; you want me to introduce you? She is one of the top party planners in the area."

"No, thanks, I'm good. No need to."

"Where is Erin Contee? You two seemed perfect together at the football game."

"I think we broke up. We're over."

"Oh, she's a terrific lady; I hope things work out for you. I really like her."

"I really like her too, but sometimes that's not enough."

After a tour and introductions to everyone in the house, I look at my cell phone to find that this one walkthrough has taken about fifty minutes. It is time to start to say good-bye and make my way back out. P5 is disappointed, which is his normal state with me whenever I'm leaving, but says he understands. Before I make it out the door, he hands me another bottle of Frog's Leap and wishes me a happy New Year.

Stepping off the hand-cut quarry marble porch, I think about the small fact that I was the only offspring to show up to this event. If he were to be disappointed in anyone, he may want to consider looking closer to his gene pool for a target. I am not interested in an ambush on voice mail whenever he has a bad day, feels lonely or sad. He is responsible for his own life and happiness. Here I am, and my biggest concern is someone being too nice to me.

"Hank?" I hear a honeyed voice in the darkness ahead of me. Her shape comes into focus as my eyes begin to adjust to the light.

"Yes," I say.

"Hank, it's good to see you," Erin Contee says.

"Erin? What are you doing here?" I am surprised to see her. In a flash I think the worst. Another person in my circle will be subject to her siren call, manipulated by her wiles like Pike, Dad, and me. My heart is a marionette and she its master, pulling each string until it collapses.

"P5 invited me at the football game, remember? I told you this weeks ago," she says. When she is standing before me, I see beneath the hem of her coat those same patterned tights from the night of fondue, with the houndstooth pencil skirt I've imagined peeling off her several times while I'm alone in bed.

"Oh yeah, now I remember." She was invited weeks ago, which felt like a lifetime ago. It was a time when I remember happiness, health, and hearth, things that have all been twisted since. "You came. That's really nice of you to visit with P5."

"I suppose. To be honest," she says, reminding me that she was always honest. All the problems we had were not because of lies she fostered, but secrets others harbored deep inside. Erin may be the most honest person I know. "I was really hoping to see you here. So I took a chance."

Her eyes are more blue than I could remember, and I see that smile that penetrated my heart, "You wanted to see me?"

"Yes. Yes, I came here at the chance I might see you. Driving over, I was still conflicted, but when I saw the station wagon, I knew I had to go in and maybe…"

"Maybe?"

"Maybe, just maybe."

"Just maybe." I walk to her and close the distance. "Just maybe might be the best thing I've ever heard." I take her hand.

"P5 called me; he insisted I come out tonight. He was worried I would be home alone. Which was my alternative." The words ramble from her mouth quickly in an attempt to explain.

I take her in my arms and squeeze as she says these things. "I am sorry, I should've called," I say. "I should not have gotten mad. I shouldn't have said those things."

She looks at me with her big blue eyes, that wonderful smile, and kisses me gently on the lips. It is soft, wonderful, and feels like home.

"I should've called you," I repeat.

"It's OK. We're here, now, together," she says.

"Do you want to go bring in the New Year with my friends? It will not be some crazy drunken party. It's just the group of us playing games all evening with the television on in the background. But we kiss at midnight."

"I would really like to do that. I would really like to kiss you at midnight."

"Dord called dibs, but you can go right after him, I promise," I say, and laugh.

She laughs. We laugh. Laughing turns to kissing, long and passionate kisses to make up for the distance and the mistakes and time apart. I agree to follow her to her apartment, where we drop off her car. She jumps in the wagon to head back to my friends. I enjoy every mile and moment with her, drinking in our time together.

"Erin Contee, how the hell are you?" Michelle hugs her at the door. "It's good to see you."

"It's good to see you too, Michelle," Erin says.

"Come on in, we're just about to start Cards Against Humanity," Michelle says. "You'll love this game."

"I've never heard of it," Erin says.

"Oh, you'll love it," Michelle repeats.

On entering not much has changed—people in the same seats, game at the table, *New Year's Rockin' Eve* on the television. The only thing that is different is the number of empties on the counter and the dwindling number of fresh snacks. I recognize a glow of friendship in the room immediately. It is captivating and quickly lures Erin over to the table. I imagine that she has missed many close friendships. All the people who knew her before might not talk with her much now or are no longer available. There is so little I know about her, her family, her life. I know this: she needs support, she needs love, she needs companionship. These are all things I can provide. Seeing her at that circle drive an hour ago, I recognized it in an instant. I love her. I want to be with her. I want to be there for her.

Cards Against Humanity has whipped my friends into a frenzy of laughter and drunken joy to ring in the New Year. As we watch the ball drop in Times Square and count down from ten, I pull Erin in close to me and squeeze her lovingly, holding her tenderly. As we get closer in the count to one, Dord makes an overt movement to try to kiss me, but he only feels the palm of my hand hold him at bay while Erin's lips press against mine in the most delightful way. I can feel her chest rise and fall with each breath as our kissing lingers and we are caught in an orbit around each other.

"OK, happy new year, everyone," I hear Kate say blandly.

I turn to realize that this grand and magnificent moment is only between Erin and me. My friends have been watching us make out like teenagers left home alone without supervision.

"Good technique, Hank," Knobby says. "I like the way you cradle her ass."

"Thanks," I say.

"He really does nice work," Erin adds. "His tongue was in there."

Oh, friendship. It allows us to laugh at the most intimate moments of life. Friends provide perspective to view the honesty of life.

"I was checking for cavities," I say. "You can never be too careful about good hygiene."

We laugh for a while and return to our game, cold drinks, and salty snacks.

Another hour, and everyone is tired.

Kate and Jean are sober, so they drive, taking their husbands home. Michelle offers the guest room to Erin Contee and me, but we decline. The beer over the last three hours had little impact on my sobriety.

Without asking, I drive to the hotel and walk her inside. Perry Winkelberry is waiting at the door to rub our legs and meow about the hours he watched out the window over the parking lot below. Perry takes an immediate liking to Erin, with small head butts and loud purring. We make ourselves comfortable on the bed; I wrap my arm around her.

"The last time we did this, you called me Lumpy," I say.

"That was a good night," she says.

"It was," I say. "We missed too many good nights; I don't want to miss any more."

"Me too." She sighs deeply in the comfort of my arms.

I can feel her head start to drift into sleep and roll into slumber. She springs from the bed with some autonomic reaction and into the bathroom. The fan turns on. I can hear some water run for a bit. With a click of the light, she joins me in bed, wearing only a T-shirt, and crawls under the covers. I undress and meet her there. I can smell the freshly applied soap and the dampness from a wet cloth across her face. I kiss her good night as she falls asleep in my arms.

THE NEW YEAR

27

We wake up late. It is wonderful. No commitments, no responsibilities, and not a care in the world, we are free from any of the entanglements from the outside world. What a great way to start this New Year.

Our laziness dissolves by midmorning. I get in the shower to wash away all the smells and blemishes from the previous day. The hot water of the hotel provides several options from the showerhead, and I choose the pelting and powerful stream that shoots the grime away with a vengeance.

I am fully aroused at the thought of Erin Contee in my bed, with her white cotton T-shirt on. I could be a brute and go take her here and now, but instead I decide to make this day about her. Focus on the things she likes and enjoys. I owe her this from my time of confusion and silence.

"Hey, this is your day," I say, popping my head from the bath. "What would you say about going back to your place? You can freshen up, put on a new outfit."

"That sounds good," she says with the sleepy happiness of a cat in the sun.

I finish up and get dressed. We jump in the wagon. She picks through the cassette tapes, calling out titles to get answers.

"'Joy, Joy, Joy, Ahoy'?" she says.

"Christmas songs or nautically themed songs," I say.

"'Happy Fun Time Super Terrific Excellent'?"

"It's a bootleg of a band I saw in Las Vegas years ago. All seven band members are Elvis impersonators, but each is a different Elvis. One is GI Elvis, another is fat Elvis, a Jailhouse Rock Elvis, and Hawaiian Elvis."

"Interesting."

"The best part is that they're all Japanese, and English is not their first language."

"'The Saddest Songs That Make Me Cry'? Why would you have a tape like that?"

"To build up my immunity to them. I do not want to be at some party or wedding and get sad because of something from the past. I am reclaiming each of the songs on there."

"Here is the one, 'Best Songs for an Hour Drive.' That about says it all."

"Sounds good."

Her place is still cool. I will never be this cool. It still smells great. I don't think she even realizes this about herself. She must not know; it's just part of who she is, how she cleans the place up.

"I'm going to step in the shower, so make yourself at home," she instructs, leaving me alone.

I suspect at this moment most guys would find this the perfect opportunity to go through things, find out more about her past, maybe even get the inside scoop on details. I don't need to know more than I already do. If it's important, she will tell me. If she wants me to know, I will know.

I make my way slowly into her bedroom and lie on the queen-size mattress. I have been here before, the night of the knockout, but I did not enjoy just how soft and welcoming it is until now.

She steps out of the shower, towel over her head and one wrapped around her top, just under her arms. "Oh, you're in here."

"Is that OK?"

"Yeah, sure, I just thought you might be watching a football game or something."

"I'd much rather watch you."

"Pardon?"

"I'd rather watch you, if that's OK."

"You want to watch me get dressed in front of you?"

"Please."

"You think this is sexy?"

"Yes. Everything about you is sexy."

"OK," she says in a soft, teasing voice.

Slowly she rubs the towel on her head, drying her hair, and starts to bend over. Her damp hair is just slightly past her shoulders when she stands normally. This is the first time I have seen her without makeup, and she looks like an innocent girl I may have known in my youth.

She starts to saunter through the closet, knowing I am watching her every move. She is deciding what to wear, pointing to small outfits and special outfits, dresses and tops.

"I wonder what I should wear," she says coyly. "I think I am going to need some undies first."

She steps over to the dresser and begins to dig in the second-to-top drawer. "Black silky thing?" She looks to me. "Or white lacy?" She shakes her head no. "Hot pink?" Then puts it back. "Royal blue, I think." Her selection is a dark basic blue with little flower patterns surrounding the underwire and reaching back to the elastic sides. In the drawer below it, she finds the matching bottoms. Without removing the wrapped towel, she bends over, revealing the lines of her legs peeking through the gap, putting one toe in each of the openings and slowly drawing them up above her knees. She turns around and pulls the panties up the remainder of the way, showing me her curvaceous ass. The towel drops, revealing her V-shaped back, with the beautiful form women share from the hip to the shoulder. She teases by putting on her bra that clasps in front. With one nice last peek, she bends over and picks up both towels, making sure she looks back to watch me, watching her.

"OK, big boy, show's over. Time to put on the makeup." She steps into the bathroom again. She adjusts the mirror ever so slightly so she can see me watching her from the bed. From the reflection in the bathroom mirror, which is reflecting off the full-length mirror on her door, I see her smile. Realizing that I am careful to watch every detail, she applies eyeliner, lip liner, lipstick, and the other miraculous products that mystify the common man. I am aroused and very excited and can feel the fabric in my inseam become restricting.

With the preparation in the bathroom complete, she steps back into the bedroom and sits on the side of the bed to put on white socks. She finds a pair of comfortable jeans and slides them over that great ass of hers, leaving the zipper undone as she walks around the room looking for the right top. It drives me crazy to watch her parade around in her bra, and she knows it. Finally, she finds the dark top that is both warm and formfitting, which is perfect.

"You are so amazing. You're so beautiful," I tell her.

She smiles and says, "I know."

Walking to the coffeehouse from the car park, I let her get a few steps ahead of me and say, "I love to watch the rivets on your jeans move up and down."

She pivots to me, flush from the cold and the embarrassment of my loud comment, and says, "Hank. People can hear you."

"Who cares?" I then add a gruff caveman voice, "You my woman. Nice rivets."

This receives a playful slap on the arm as I hold open the door for her.

Over coffee she whispers to me, "That little show this morning was fun."

"It really got me going. The things I want to do to you…"

"I like that kind of control over you." She adds in a cavewoman voice, "You my man. Nice club."

Every once in a while, as we sit and watch people come and go, I'm certain to gently touch her, stroke her arm, or graze her leg in some way to keep her stimulated. So many naughty things that seem innocent enough, taking place in public, without being overt and calling attention. I can sense her excitement building.

Over the next two hours, we drive around the city like teenagers, looking for places that are open on New Year's Day. These do not include the Detroit Institute of Arts, Science Center, or the Detroit Zoo. I rub her upper leg, sometimes moving higher, and tickle that thick part of the seam where the pant legs meet. Her response of light moans and deep breathing says everything.

"Drive to my place," she finally moans. "Go there, now."

She leans over to kiss me while I drive, only making things difficult. No matter how large and comfortable the wagon may be, it still needs one steady hand to drive.

As I put the car in park, she is nearly on top of me with deep passionate kissing. We practically tumble out of the driver's side door to the concrete when I pull on the handle. It has been almost five hours since we have left her place, and she is now dragging me by my coat to get back inside.

Inside, our kissing takes on a more acrobatic approach as we attempt to keep pace with each other, undress, and move toward the bedroom in a smooth transition. Instead, I take her firmly in my hands and continue to hold her firmly by her hair as I remove her jeans. My hand cups her cheeks as the jeans fall to the ground. I stroke her hair and follow down the back of her neck as she turns and pushes her back into my groin. My fingers explore until I find that spot where the seams in her jeans tickled her earlier and she lets out a gasp of pleasure. Her panties are wet as I pull at the thin fabric, accidentally breaking them, and they drop to the ground.

"Now." She grunts.

"Wait," I say sternly.

I turn her toward me and begin to kiss her lips more, working down the area just south of her ear. My right hand makes its way down to the small of her back, following the curves, over her cheeks, and find that minute spot on her leg that made her go weak. She cries out, "Dear God" as I pull her leg up around my waist and lift her off the floor. She is light in my arms. We kiss, stroke, and touch each other as I carry her to the bedroom. Her sighs are deep.

I set her down on the edge of the bed, where she stands, her legs slightly spread. I take the opportunity to lift her top slightly, revealing her belly button, and kiss it. I can feel her quiver. I can see the goose bumps on her skin standing at attention. I work slowly down from the belly, lower, past her waist. My hands continue to caress the back of her legs, and my fingertips graze the bend in her legs again. Finally, deep within her, I began to lick and kiss. Her groans grow louder. Her legs bend, and she falls back to the bed, her face buried in fallen pillows.

Half on the bed, I continue to kiss her inner thigh in that little area, which makes her feel so good. Unhurriedly I work back up to the area of her delight and importance until her toes contract, her back arches, and her breathing becomes erratic.

"Oh dear God!" she calls out, surrounded by moans of delight and pleasure. "Oh God." I continue softly to caress and stroke the areas that provided similar results without overstimulation. There is no time limit, no rush; she is the only thing in the world that deserves my full attention.

I hear a new little pant or moan with each flick of my tongue. It's like playing the most beautiful instrument in the world.

"I want you inside me," she says.

"I need you inside me. Now. Look in the drawer."

Opening the drawer, I find several condoms. I grab one and remove my pants while she struggles to remove her top. After a moment's pause, I begin to kiss a new area deserving attention, a place neglected for far too long. Her button-sized nipples are firm and sensitive to the touch. My warm hands cup each breast, gently moving and caressing. A lick from my tongue, and her back arches again, fingers grab at the sheets. She is writhing and twisting with delight under my body.

She smiles and says, "I'm ready."

"I know," I tease, taking the tip of my manhood and slowly stroking it outside her fleshy folds and the tip of her clitoris.

She moans and moves, ready to accept. "You're such a tease." She calls out, "I want you inside me."

I continue to taunt her in the same motion, just holding back what she desires, taking full pleasure in the type of control she held over me dressing that morning.

"Oh please, fuck me. Fuck me, please," she shouts out.

Done with diversions, I thrust into her slowly, releasing the sounds of ecstasy. Our bodies begin to move as one, entangled in the rhythm of intemperate heat. Each thrust causes an uncontrolled opening of her mouth, a rush of blood flow, and a moan of "more" and "yes."

I can feel the well-lubricated movements begin to build again in her as she tightens the muscles that wrap around me. I provide a long and single thrust, pushing hard and deep, lifting her hip to one side. Her back arches once more. Her legs squeeze my torso. I can feel it build inside me, the distance from reality, a disconnect of my conscience, those first steps in front of the pearly gates. I call out her name, feeling this amazing sensation dance on my every nerve ending. I continue to move as reality returns, ever so slowly, allowing the momentum to ebb. I kiss her, lightly at first, as she is sensitive to the touch, then deeper, and stroke her hair, until I am unable to do so any longer. I am spent. I roll to her side and try to catch my breath. She curls up on my outstretched arm and tries to breathe normally. Breathing is the only sound as we reconnect to our civilized instincts, holding back the animal desires that have been on display.

My breathing now normal, I visit the bathroom. After washing my hands, I visit the kitchen, pouring two glasses of ice water, and return to her in bed, delivering the much-needed refreshment. She gulps down the water as I climb back into bed.

"Hank, it's never been like that, ever, with anyone before."

"So that's a good thing, right?"

"Oh hell, yes, Hank. That was amazing."

"Good, I was worried our first time together might be awkward, clumsy."

"No, it wasn't that at all."

"No, it wasn't, was it?"

"No, that was great," she says, finishing her drink.

"You want to try that three or four more times?"

"Yes, please. You up for it?"

"This whole day is about you, Erin. I'm here for you."

She smiles, she kisses me, and we start from the beginning.

28

Before going to Dad's, we stop at my hotel so I can shower and put on a fresh set of clothes. I am sore from using so many of my untapped muscles in the past twenty-four hours; still, it has been great to spend this much time alone with Erin. She seems in high spirits.

"I want to watch you get dressed," she says from the bed as I leave the bathroom, a towel wrapped around my waist.

"I've got to tell you, Erin, it's nowhere near as sexy as when you do it." We both laugh as I step into the bathroom and return with an added towel on my head to the one already wrapped around my waist and slowly start to go through my drawer.

The twins, full of energy, greet us at Dad's front door. They do not act like four-year-olds. They seem older to me somehow, and I realize they are nearly five. Old enough to answer the door, the phone, or master any mobile device put in front of them. What type of childhood will they remember? P6, Midge, Margaret, Mary, seductress, or Mother—pick a name that fits—is only a few steps behind them in the hall.

"Your dad has been asking for you all morning," she says with mild concern. "We haven't seen you in a few days. Thank you for *finally* coming over," Midge says, her last word trailing when she sees Erin.

"We took some time for ourselves over New Year's," I explain.

"Well," Midge says with a crackle of discomfort in her voice. "It's good to see the two of you together again."

Erin smiles politely. "It's good to see you too, Midge. I'm sorry the last time we met ended so poorly."

"The important thing is to see us all together again," Midge says with the strained smile of politeness.

I take Erin's hand and step through the doorway. "Let's go see Dad."

He's worse than last time. His skin is ashen. Breathing shallow. A gurgle followed by a wheeze repeats from his chest with each exhale. His nurse sits in the corner, playing with a tablet.

"Dad, how are you?" I ask.

He stirs and tries to rise. "Hank, Hank, good to see you." He gives a ghastly pulmonary gasp to clear his throat.

"Dad, do you want to go to the hospital?" I ask.

"No, no, the nurse is looking after me." He turns his head and smiles in her direction.

She does not respond. She is fully engaged in the glow of her game, book, web browsing, tapping at whatever it may be.

He begins to cough again, less violently, closer to something normal. I catch the spattering of pink foamy mucus that speckles and soils the tissue he is hiding in his hand. When our eyes meet, he knows what I have witnessed. His expression turns to one of a guilty child caught hiding the truth.

"Nope—we are calling an ambulance and taking you to the hospital," I say with a certain finality that catches the nurse's attention. "Erin, use the landline and call an ambulance. We're taking Dad to the hospital."

Erin follows the instructions while Midge and the nurse watch in disbelief.

"It's just a cold, Hank," Midge says. "He's fine. There's no sense in all this fuss. Really." Her words fall empty to me, and I can hear Erin repeat the address and the phrase "transportation, nonemergency" to the person on the other end.

Twenty minutes later there is a rap at the door. It startles Midge midsentence. Two beefy men with a crash cart walk to the back room and begin a familiar scene from the original incident. They take vital signs, drop plastic coverings of medical items to the floor for later cleanup after use. With a final nod between the two men, they lift Dad and move him to the gurney.

"He's stable, Mr. Hanson," the one at the front of the cart says.

"We're taking him in," he says with a powerful nonstop momentum like a freight train on tracks. "He's dehydrated, and I'm worried about his breathing. You can join us in the ambulance; the others can meet us there."

I take my keys from my front right pant pocket and toss them to Erin. "Meet me there?" The throw connects perfectly.

"Sure," she says with a nod of a team player. "Meet you there."

"How could I pass up the chance to ride in an ambulance?" I say to Dad, holding his hand from the side bench, keeping out of the medic's way.

His voice is muffled under the clear plastic oxygen mask. I lean in close and can make out the hushed conversation. "I'm glad the two of you could find a way to work things out," he says.

"I am too. I have to tell you, Dad, I think she is the one. Despite all the weirdness and history, the two of us together just makes sense when we are together. I'm going to try and stay with her."

His sleepy smile says a lot about the medicated state he's in. "I'm glad to hear that. I'm a big believer in true love."

I try to keep his mind active, hold him in the here and now, and take in the moment, in case it is our last. "You're a big believer in true love?" I tease him. "Dad, you're on your third marriage and Lord knows how many girlfriends between."

He grins. "There's no one better to make the case."

"Dad, I love you, but I have a hard time following that you are the poster child for true love."

He tries to maintain eye contact as best he can, softly saying, "I've never given up on love. When I first saw your mother, I knew. I knew in an instant that she was perfect for me."

"Really?"

"She was perfect for me. Straightened me out, got me serious, made me a father and a family man." He stops to cough. "I wasn't perfect for her. I had to convince her. I had to talk her into loving me, and when I finally had her, I started to ease up. I thought I had won her, and this was my reward. There is no finish line. You can't give up working at love."

"I guess I can see that," I concede. "What about your second wife, P4... Tess?"

"You're so funny with these labels. My second wife was love at first sight. Young, and beautiful, and she wanted me. She approached me. We had that common friend, Siouxsie something."

"Siouxsie Little," I say.

His voice drifted again, as if he were trying to recapture the magic of a moment from years gone by. "Siouxsie Little introduced us at that after-work bar in Warren. Siouxsie and her brother David, good people. Fun people. We were at that bar, and she introduced me to Tess, in that tight little outfit. I knew."

"You knew what?"

"I knew I loved her."

I could feel the ambulance make its turn into the emergency drop-off and start to slow to park. The medic begins to prep for disembarking by grabbing a bag connected to the tube sticking in Dad's arm. The back door clicks and opens to half-a-dozen new faces.

I try to keep his attention on us, prevent him from worry as the cart moves through the entrance to down the hall. I lean in close, my feet working to keep up until we get to a waiting area.

"How did you know you loved Midge?" I ask.

"When I met Midge?"

"Yes, you love Midge, right?"

"I can't live without her. She was over at the house for something."

"She was over to swim in the pool at your condo," I say as blue-scrubbed staff talk among themselves in a jargon I don't comprehend.

"That's right. Your brother had graduated and brought his friends over to the condo pool that summer. She was there."

"We were all there."

"I knew when I saw her in that two-piece that she was something special." He wheezes.

"I bet you did, a hot little eighteen-year-old."

"We didn't start seeing each other until she was single. Your brother had gone off to college, and she was alone. She came to me so alone and wanting to be with me."

"It was true love?" I ask frankly.

"You don't get it, Hank." I could hear the struggle to get these last, important parting thoughts out while he could. "Love provides freedom. When you are young, it comes from your parents and family, it provides security. Later, love comes from friends; it gives you courage to explore the world. When you find someone to be with, love is a home. No matter where you go, you know you've got one place, one person to go to."

Grabbing at the plastic oxygen mask, parked for the moment in the emergency hallway, with a ring of clarity, he says, "I believe in true love. I tried to give you, your brother and sister that kind of safety and strength to be independent. You've done well. I'm proud of what you've done. I'm proud of your brother and sister too."

Fixed on each other's eyes, I say, "I'm glad you believe in true love, Dad. I'm glad you've been able to find it so many times in your life."

He squeezes my hand tightly. "Hank, people who don't find this, who don't know love, the security it brings, the freedom it provides, they find loneliness instead of the joy when alone. Instead of bringing new experiences to their life, they are endlessly searching for a place to call home. You are not like that, Hank. You are not. Are you?"

207

"I don't think so, Dad." I comfort him with my other hand lightly pressed on his forehead, smoothing down the stray gray hairs that have struggled free from his long ponytail. "I think I've found that in Erin."

"Don't give up on her," he says, giving in to the new concoction piped into his arm. Residing in the twilight of chemicals, he says, "Don't make the mistakes I made with your mother, and don't give up on love."

"I won't, Dad." I watch as his eyes close and the fight in him subsides, and I place the mask back over his mouth.

A woman in scrubs smiles and asks for my help in turning him on his side. We roll him to the side without a tube sticking in his arm, and he begins to cough instinctively. She removes the mask and places a blue plastic bowl next to him. He coughs, and a long string of dark mucus buildup pours out. It pours out and pools in the bowl, dripping from his mouth. With another series of deep pulmonary pushes, it fills the tray, and she replaces it. After ten minutes and filling three trays, he stops. She applies a moist towelette to his nose and mouth, wiping away the remains of the viscous fluids.

29

I am pointed down a hallway toward automated doors and told to wait in the room on the other side. The doors are a transition from the stark bright lights and easy-to-clean surfaces of an emergency area to the brown carpets, lounge seating, warmly lit waiting area for friends and family. Its brown drabness hides any dirt from heavy traffic. Uncertain of the time that's transpired, I look out the window to the dark, winter-evening parking lot with an orange glow of artificial lighting hanging over white marshmallow car shapes as a fast flurry of flakes fall. The room, lined with chairs, has pathways down the center to maximize the number of people able to watch a television fixed loudly on a cable news channel.

I recognize Erin the instant she rises to greet me. Next to her are Grandma and Grandpa. Next to Grandpa is Midge, mumbling to herself with a lost look on her face and the smudges of dried eyeliner and tracks of mascara. They all look to me, eager for an update.

As I start to make my way closer through the maze of chairs, Midge rises, leaves the others behind in a frazzled whimper, falls on me in an unbreakable embrace, and kisses me deeply on the lips. As she pulls away and slams her tear-filled face on my shoulder, I am taken aback by her dramatic emotions. It reminds me of when she and my brother separated. Erin has a clear audible gasp, watching this unfold. Unable to free my arms, pinned at their side, I can only say, "There, there, Midge."

Erin looks puzzled. Grandma shares the sentiment, it would seem. I can only lift my hands slightly and shrug my shoulders as if to say, "I don't understand it either." Midge begins a soft wail in my right ear reminiscent of a toddler getting a fat lip on the playground. I support her in the swaying movement. Her tears start to subside, and she gulps to catch a normal pattern in breathing.

Behind me I hear a voice from my past. "Hank?"

I try to turn and look beyond the bush of Midge's tangled hair to see Sandy in her winter jacket, a cardboard tray in hand with four coffee cups.

Overwhelmed, outnumbered, and raw with emotion, I scrape Midge off me and set her down in the nearest seat. Her wailing starts again. So I help her up and take her in my arms, rocking her like a child. Her blubbering starts to subside again as I stroke her hair. Midge adjusts her head and hands to become uncomfortably familiar with me. She has become unhinged.

"What happened, Hank?" Sandy asks. "What did I miss?"

"Yes," Erin says distinctly. "What happened, Hank?" Her question is not the same one Sandy is asking.

"Hank?" Grandma says.

"I don't know where to start," I say, looking to Erin over the head of Midge.

"How is your father?" Sandy asks. "Is he all right?"

I turn back. "Sandy, what are you doing here?"

"Your grandmother called me," she said innocently. "I drove them here."

"Grandma, you called Sandy?" I ask, pivoting Midge's body so I can look in Grandma's direction.

"I thought she would want to know," Grandma defends. "How is your father?"

"Hank," Erin repeats, looking at Midge in my arms. I can feel the smudge of oily lipstick slick on my lips. "What happened?"

"Dad," I start slowly, "is being provided fluids. He is in isolation and under observation while they get the results from some tests. There may have been a clot in his lungs."

"Hank—what happened?" Erin is insistent.

I can feel the burden of mistakes weigh on me like a giant boulder. Like Atlas? No, Sisyphus. I take a quick assessment of my circumstances. I am trapped in a maze of chairs, with people waiting for my answer, surrounded by people who are waiting for the truth. My instincts for flight or fight trigger as my synopses fire. Instant vales open in my sweat glands, pouring out the scent of fear. I cannot run and decide to stand my ground rather than lie.

"Erin, can you and I go somewhere and talk for a bit?" I ask as plainly as I can.

Midge looks to me with a twinkle in her eye I can only describe as "batshit crazy," and before I can stop her, she blurts out, "Hank and I had sex." Before anyone can respond, she adds, "Great sex."

I hear the coffee tray hit the floor and the liquid splatter over the brown carpet. Droplets of the hot substance pelt the back of my legs.

Erin, still composed, asks, "When?"

"Christmas Eve, after our breakup, before we got back together," I say factually.

"Sandy, would you be good enough to drive us home?" Grandma asks politely. "I think I'll be sick if I stay in this hospital any longer."

"Sure, sure, let me get some towels first." Sandy attempts to be responsible.

"Leave it, we're going. This kind of hospital drama should only be on my soaps." Grandma grabs her purse, and Grandpa dutifully follows.

Erin is slow to react, but clearly upset. She walks past me briskly. I call to her, "Erin, wait." It's no use. She drops the keys to the station wagon on the floor and walks away.

I'm alone with the burden of Midge, who now decides she is well enough to sit down. I wipe the smear from my face with the back of my sleeve in a first effort to cleanse myself of what has transpired.

"You had to add *great*?" I ask.

"It was," she says, looking up to me with puppy dog eyes of approval circled in the dark rings of her hot-mess makeup.

"You want to go home or stay here?" I start to make plans about kids, transportation, a toothbrush for Dad, pajamas, and deodorant.

"My folks have the kids. I called, they're fine."

"So you're staying here?" I shake my head in disbelief at what this woman will do.

"Yeah, I think it's for the best. Can I see him?"

"The nurse will come get us once he's out of x-ray and they assign him a room."

I sit across from her, watching her apply the point of a folded tissue around the lines of her eyes to clean up any streaks or runs. Her compact clicks open, and she looks in its mirror to reapply makeup. I wonder as I watch: if Midge is this capable of manipulating people to get what she wants, how talented must other women be? How much control has Erin used and when has she applied similar tactics? This is the same discussion I had with Erin only a few days ago. Am I only a pawn for women to control? How can I do so well in work relationships but be so bad at personal relationships?

The look on Erin's face will not leave me soon. It was a brave face, but I could see the devastation in her eyes as the reality of my actions began to sink in. Gone was the smile that made my heart glow over the last two days, now quashed by the downturn at the sides of her lips, the wrinkle in her brow, and the wounded look.

"We shouldn't say anything to your father about our love until he is better," she says in the act of reapplying.

"I don't think we should ever tell him about the one-time thing that took place," I say. "He should never know."

"This group now knows, and once it's out, someone is sure to tell him. Better coming from you or me than hearing it secondhand."

"Yeah." I shrug in utter disgust of her act. "I guess," I say, uncertain about most things in my life at the moment.

Happy with her quick fixes, she puts things away in her bag and settles into the chair. We are relatively alone in this room. Other small rooms down the corridor sound off from conversations from other families and friends. The volume of the news from this television is loud, disruptive to intimate conversation; it's perfect to mask this oedipal declaration from others in the ward.

I walk over to pick up my keys from the floor so no one steps on them by accident. Where is my car, and how will I find it? My suspicion is that Erin is highly unlikely to answer any texts for clues. If it's in the lot, it's under several inches of snow; in the structure, it may be parked at any level.

"You don't happen to remember where Erin parked the wagon, do you?"

"I took the Chevy Traverse."

"OK. Well, I have my cell phone. Text me if you hear anything. I'm going to look for the car."

The Henry Ford Medical Center outdoor parking area is vast. There is also an abundance of covered parking in an eight-story structure. My jacket is still in the wagon. My strategy is to start with the structure first, thinking it may be warmer. I take the elevator to the top, and a rush of winter wind blasts over me as the doors open. My pace is quick, walking down the incline of the ramp filled with vehicles. Turning the corner from the top deck, I find the environment more acceptable on the next level, protected from much of the elements. In this moment I wish I had bought a new car. GM has a new app that allows one to locate a vehicle, or at a minimum, most cars have those key fobs that sound an alarm or automatic lock. At the bottom of the ramp, I am now running for the hospital door to get inside again to warm up.

Hospitals have changed. In childhood they seemed bleak, sparse, and filled with the smells of chemical cleaners. Today they are more like a shopping mall, with food stands, shops, coffee, and comfortable seating. Now there are sculptures, indoor gardens, and play areas. I pass them all walking over to the alternative entrance.

Under the orange lighting of the parking lot, my station wagon and winter jacket sit under three inches of heavy wet snow. The footprints of others are well marked in the fresh snow, and I follow them up the first row. Erin would have been lucky to get a spot this close. Down the next aisle, I work the side of the lot, my eyes scanning for those sharp angles of the long body among newer cars shaped for fuel efficiency and low drag.

On the fifth aisle, I can feel the weight of the flakes begin to pile on my head and melt from the heat I'm producing at this slow jog. In the sixth aisle, nearly ready to break and make my way back inside, I see her—Paris the station wagon—her brown side panels sticking out from the white drifts on top.

With three pumps of the gas pedal, her engine turns over. With my jacket on, my shiver starts to slow. When the temperature gauge starts to move, I turn the heat on high to let warm air fill the cabin.

The silence is enjoyable. Alone, without the input of others, the demands of daily life aside. I click the lid of the metal ashtray open and closed. It is a noise unique to this car. I don't even know if they put metal ashtrays in cars anymore. This noise may be lost on new generations. It reminds me of a book I once read about two people who survive an off-road car accident nearly buried in a snowbank. Trapped in the car, the two live for weeks off the melted snow they can pack into the ashtray and melt with the car lighter, until a search party can find them or the battery dies out. After reading this, I specifically bought a pack of beef jerky to keep in my glove box, just in case.

I suspect phobias like these are something I've picked up from my parents. After watching something on television, Mom was quick to go out and purchase a device that would break her car windows in case of an emergency. Her biggest fear at that time was to drive into water and be unable to escape because she had power windows. Dad's fear was a bit more realistic—bladder control—but much easier to solve. Worried about something he read called "trucker's bladder" in old age, he always had that big coffee can in the backseat in the event he couldn't find a bathroom, rather than put undue pressure on his bladder. As my brother was so kind to remind me recently, I was the one who had held the can for him more than once. He did not want to stop. He did not want to hold it in, and so I held the can and turned my head. The can could be too small on occasion, so he had to pinch it off while I poured it out the window at highway speeds and brought it back within shooting range to finish off.

I hit the button on my cell phone for Erin. It dials and goes straight to voice mail. "Please call me when you can. I...would like to talk, apologize, and beg your forgiveness. Let me know you are safe."

The water rolling down the side of my face turns from the freshwater of melted snow to salty tears, given time and distance from others. For the longest time, I tried to be strong for others when my mother passed. It's unsettling to have others see me and think of her, and again I try to be strong.

It's these moments, alone, in private, that are the most emotional for me. To hear the click of the ashtray and remember mom asking me to stop, still in reach of her arm and compelled to continue. She was kind and wonderful and loved by so many, and I miss her. She would be the perfect person to talk with right now about my dad. She might understand what he is like and why we need to find redeemable qualities in our loved ones. She would be able to understand why I am compelled to satisfy the overwhelming requests from people to see me during the holidays. She would listen to me talk about snowflakes' perfection and symmetry, and my attempts to find balance and symmetry in my own life.

She would be very disappointed to find out that my dad's perfidy with women passed directly to me. Knowing this would put her in tears. I try to rationalize the moment. There is no mother. The feelings of guilt were impressed upon me in my youth by church. It is a similar sense of guilt one might feel about the natural biological act of masturbation. There are no spirits of my relatives looking down on me. It is outside the parameters of science and reason. Still, I feel as if the generations of those who lived before me are now disappointed and disgusted after watching me act on these taboos.

I can only imagine two possible outcomes when my father finds out this news. In a best-case scenario, he would feel disappointment, but over the long term, acceptance that his loving wife needed something while he was unavailable. Eventually he would come to terms and start talking to me again. In the worst-case scenario, I am the last of my direct siblings to have severed ties with the man. He would be unable to forgive me.

The buzz in my front right pocket is a text. I hope it's from Erin, wanting to meet, to talk through things, or to provide some sliver of hope that she and I have a future. Instead, it is from Midge. "Come back quick."

30

When my mother died, it seemed like there were flowers everywhere. The funeral director said the only other person who had this many flowers was Mrs. Bordine, owner of a local nursery. They had to add pages to the guest registration, then a second book, for Mom. Donation envelopes to cancer research filled the drop box over two days. Over 1,700 people came through to comfort the family. I remember the range of emotions as each new handshake started with a smile, turned quickly into tears, then raced into laughter with a cherished memory of her. They squeezed four rows of folding chairs in the hallway outside the church main congregational room. It was standing room only once the service started.

Mom's family plot was an hour north, and the parade of cars caused such a traffic jam in the middle of the afternoon, they had to relaunch the local morning news helicopter to give radio updates. My mother was loved, respected by the community, and is missed to this day. I know why her friends feel so many emotions when they see me or my siblings. It is an unwelcome reminder in their everyday life that a little piece of happiness is missing. It is why the holidays are so hard. We give thanks to be alive, for what we have, but we remember what we've lost.

Today's service for my father could not have been more different. His body, on display, displayed a crooked smirk, expressing that he may have gotten away with something, unlike Mom's peaceful smile. The pews were nearly empty in the tiny agnostic chapel. Aside from each of my six friends signing the registry individually, Pike, Michelle, Knobby, Kate, Dord, and Jean, and a few people I didn't recognize, there were Midge and the twins, my grandparents, and Sandy, who drove them.

"The kids couldn't make a second trip out after seeing him at Christmas," Grandpa says, referring to my aunts and uncles, his kids. "Maybe it's best that way; they'll remember him as part of that nice day we spent together in that restaurant."

"It's not right that a parent lose her child. It's just not right," Grandma says as she shakes her head.

"I know," I say. "Pneumonia is what the doctor said. He had gone too long without diagnosis or treatment. There was nothing they could do but try to make him comfortable in the end."

"I don't mean to be crass, Hank, but funerals are not for the family," Knobby says in a moment the seven of us share together, standing in wait at the funeral home.

"What do you mean?" I ask.

"These services, shaking hands, the ritual, only wear out the family. It makes them tired and sick."

"Yeah, it does," I agree.

"That's not for the family. That is for everyone else. Here are some flowers, *I* did something, *I* spent time, and *I* helped them. It's bragging rights on being a better person."

"Knobby, stop your shit," Jean says. "That's such male-driven thinking. *I* care. I want our good friend Hanson to stop hurting. Remember when his mom died? That sucked for all of us. She was awesome. She was the cool mom."

"She was," I say. The feeling starts instantly and uncontrollably works its way up through my body, up the back of my head, and expresses itself in the tightening of my lips. While I try to hold it back, the hot, briny tears begin to well up in the corners of my eyes and roll down my cheeks.

"Nice work, Knobby, you made him cry," says Kate.

"Holy shit, Lumpy, I don't think I've seen this before," Dord whispers.

Michelle and Jean instinctively move in and wrap me in a warm embrace. The others circle in tight around them.

"I just didn't know your dad very well, Hanson," Jean says. "I can't say those kinds of things about him."

"Even if you knew him, you couldn't say that about him," I say.

"Why the tears, Hank?" Pike asks, rubbing my back gently.

"I just realized two things," I say after a deep breath. "First, Jean was right. I am a middle child."

"Yes!" Jean takes the small victory with my admission, and I catch her making a small fist pump at her side.

"Why the hell would I need to please all these people? What good outcome did it have? I have tried for years to visit a growing list of people, include them in my life, and appease them. I should have focused on the right people, spent more time with Dad earlier. I could have helped if I had been involved earlier."

"What was the second thing?" Pike asks.

"That dad was a middle child too. He took some risky moves in life and did some bizarre shit."

As I talk, it comes to me.

"I'm him. As much as I don't like the way he treated us, or just focused on what he wanted, or jumped between women, I'm just like him. I'm hoping for true love, but have no idea what it is."

I sniffle and take the tissues handed to me to clean up.

"The family I had, that safety of being home, I need that. And now I'm an orphan."

"A thirty-year-old orphan," Pike whispers. "Lumpy, you're thirty."

"We're your family, Hank," Michelle says. "You're not alone. We've been your family for years."

Easing back a few steps from this outpouring of affection, I spoil a few more tissues in silence as my friends watch.

"I can't believe you slept with her," Knobby adds. Something intrinsic inside him or learned in the locker room allows him to find that one item and exploit it. If I did not love the man, I would hate that part of him. It is not malicious. It would be different if it were. It's the way his mind works, like a Labrador retriever picks up on a scent, tracks it down, and with gentle jaws picks at its prey and plays with it a bit before returning it as a prize for all to see.

Kate looks to her husband as if he were a child. "Don't be an asshole. Not today."

I shrug and attempt to chuckle at the reality in hindsight. "You're right, Knobby. It is a moment I want to take back. A stupid moment that slipped into a normal life, and I'll pay for it. I have been paying for it. I hope I can find someone who can see past my mistakes."

"Well, at least she's not pregnant," Dord says. "Now that would be really fucked up."

A chill runs through me. I shudder at the thought of a pregnant Midge with my child. I think back through events, the entanglement of the moment, the fumbling with the foil packet, the half-wrapped attempt; her specific complaint about the miraculous nature of the twins' birth from Father's fictitious procedure leads me to think she must be on the pill now, but it plants a seed of doubt in my mind to fester.

"Have you heard from Erin Contee?" Michelle asks.

"No. I am still paying for the mistakes I've made. I don't know that she would ever be interested in talking with me again."

"I called her," Michelle says. "I told her about you, how you are, what you were going through. She's really a great lady, I hope the two of you can work things out."

"I hope so too," I say. "I hope so too."

As if it were her cue for a staged performance, I see her at the door, signing the guest book. Her dark hair is straightened and free, and she is wearing a tasteful black outfit for the occasion. She turns from the book, enters the room, sees only us alone with the casket, and walks to the group.

Hugging Michelle, she says, "Thanks for calling me, it's good to see you." Then she expresses the same sentiment to Kate and Jean. With a slight nod to their husbands, she says, "Boys." Her final glance is to me. Uncomfortable, but determined, she steps to me and gives a hug.

"Hank, I'm sorry for your loss."

"Thank you for coming," I say, holding back the blubbering tears that preceded her arrival. "It means a lot to have you here." Telling myself that I am an adult and can handle this situation, every word she says to Michelle is lost. Her perfume penetrates my senses and still lingers in the last moment she held me. She tucks that one wild strand of hair behind her ear, a motion that I have come to discover is like a poker tell of her discomfort and not a disposition of her grooming habits. I can see the exposed collarbone that I've kissed and long for.

"Hank, stop gawking at the poor girl," Michelle says, breaking my stare. "You're creeping us all out."

"Sorry, was I gawking? Sorry, don't know where my head went," I say in all honesty. "Will you excuse me for a moment?" I force a polite grin and dismiss myself to the men's room.

The calming background music of the men's room and the unique odors try to distract me. There is a list of things left for the day's viewing. If anyone was to arrive between now and nine, I would need to be there to shake his hand. Paperwork and signatures are all in the hands of Midge. Let her deal with them. I will pay bills and give opinions, but let her make all the decisions.

I finish my business, wash my hands, and note the high pressure this particular hand blower provides, all providing distractions to think about before going back out.

Entering the room, I can see that Erin is occupied with my friends, and a new person has arrived. Standing at the casket, taking a moment to herself with the deceased, she turns back to me. It is P4, Tess, Dad's second wife. She walks right over at recognition, and we hug.

"Hank, oh Hank, I am sorry for your loss," P4 says.

"Thank you for coming. I really appreciate it."

"I must have missed the crowd."

"Yeah." I force a chuckle.

"Your father never liked crowds. I was surprised to learn that later. We met in one of the most crowded bars during its busiest times. We had a mutual friend."

"You know, he was just telling me that story the other day, how you two met through the Littles. How good you were to him. How bad he felt for the way things ended."

"Sounds like him. A little late, but still."

"Yeah."

"Well, he was a good man," she said convincingly.

"Do you really believe that?"

"Sure. He wasn't good to me, but he was a good man." She thought for a moment before continuing. "He had a real sweet spot when he wanted to be nice. I was younger than your dad, you know."

I nodded, knowing she was eleven years younger.

"And he was more experienced in life. When he wanted to show you a good time, he went all in. He was committed. I say I like Bob Seger, he gets great seats."

I smile and nod, remembering. "So good I can hear you on the album."

"So good you can hear me scream on the record. Man, I love that song. I really was a small-town girl, living in a lonely world when we met." She began to tear up a little. "We did have good times. He was a good man, but he just wasn't the right man for me."

P4 continued to tell me more details about their romance. She talked about the times when her hair was big and he dressed like Gordon Gekko, the Michael Douglas character from *Wall Street*.

"That was before his ponytail," she added. The two would be in the city of Detroit, take the riverboat cruise, dinners at the Pontchartrain Hotel, and "when you kids weren't there, mornings at the Eastern Market." It was a nice life I never knew.

"Like I say, he was a good man, Hank. You've got his good parts." She smiles one more time, hugs me, and says her good-byes.

"Who was that?" Pike asks.

"That was Tess," I answer, getting back to the circle of friends.

"Who's Tess?" Michelle asks.

"That was P4," I say.

"Holy shit, Hank!" Knobby says. "You weren't making her up. There really is a P4?"

Surprised by the question, I say, "You thought I was making her up?"

"Well," Jean says, "it's just that you have a lot of stories about a lot of parents. We've known you for years and weren't always sure, but proof, final real evidence."

Hurt by the thought, I say, "Not sure?"

"I've met P5." Erin speaks up in my defense. "On a few occasions now. He is real. I always thought if he is real, the others must be as well."

"There's a lot to take in, you have to admit," Dord says.

"Come on," Erin is quick to reply. "Hank is a lot of things, but not a liar. He has a fantastical family structure you couldn't imagine," she says with a delightful retort. "But Hank Hanson is not a liar."

They all stay until the end, standing there with me in a viewing room full of empty chairs. During the one-hour scheduled break in the evening for dinner, the staff of the funeral home decides to bring extra flowers from a viewing earlier in the week into the room. It livens things up for a little bit as I walk to examine each vase. After noticing by the third one that there is no name or card attached, I find the director and thank him for the effort. He explains that it was rare to see a wake like this one, but it happens from time to time. It is less of a reflection of the person's life, and more a reflection of the way others in that one's life view death. For many, death is something to keep distant and avoid. It is not the for the sake of the individual. Race car drivers, adrenaline junkies, and adventurists will never be found at a wake or funeral for fear of bad luck or an inability to face the realities of a shortened life. They are kind words, and it is a generous gesture.

Parting ways in the parking lot, my lifelong friends reassure me that they will see me here again in the morning and follow me to the burial.

Erin, waiting for the others to leave for some time alone, says, "I hope it didn't make things weird, showing up here."

"No," I reply. "I'm really glad to see you again. I didn't want things to end the way they did."

"Did things end?"

"Didn't they? Do not give me false hope, Erin. I don't think I could take it."

She takes my hand in hers and looks me in the eyes. "I'm not happy with you right now, Hank. You did some things that really hurt me...unintentionally, I am certain, but they still hurt."

I can hear the difficulty of being open at the back of Erin's throat. "We are even, you and me, we are square. There is nothing in each other's past that could be more surprising or split us up. I hope things did not end between us. I hope they're not over."

"No, no. I don't want them to be. I'm just ashamed," I say.

"Don't think the worst, think the best, of us," she says.

As I start to move closer, lean down for a kiss, she turns her head. "I don't know that I'm ready to stop being mad at you. I'm still mad."

"OK," I say, drawing back. "I understand that."

"How are you doing? I mean, really, how are you? Don't just be polite."

I release a cleansing deep sigh at the request from this trusted companion. My shoulders feel as if they've dropped inches below their tightened position for the first time in weeks. There is a sense of release from the drama and tension of lovers lost, family departed, and sins committed. Her question and sense of true concern for my well-being is an absolution from the burdens created and built from the inner self on display for the world.

"First—I am tired."

"I bet you are."

"Second, I am happy you are here."

"I bet you are."

"Third, I am confused by life."

Slowly, specifically, she says, "There is but one truly serious philosophical problem, and that is suicide. Judging whether life is or is not worth living amounts to answering the fundamental question of philosophy. All the rest—come afterward."

"Who said that?"

"It's the first sentence from Albert Camus in *The Myth of Sisyphus*."

"I forgot how cool you are. What's it mean?"

"Our search for meaning, for unity, for clarity, it's just empty without truth or values." She waits for it to sink in, watching me process, seeing if anything sticks in this thick head of mine, full of doubt and confusion. "All of your talk about snowflakes reminded me of it the other day, so I memorized it. Do you want to know the last sentence?"

"Yes, please."

"The struggle itself is enough to fill a man's heart. One must imagine Sisyphus happy."

My hand gently brushes her cheek, and I slowly move that strand of wild hair to the proper place behind her ear. "I can imagine myself being happy, with you."

"I can imagine that," she says.

Again, my instinct is to kiss her, and I can feel myself move in, but I resist. She looks at me, knowing. I say, "Being with you, talking to you, it keeps me from thinking about this whole other mess I call my life. I haven't thought at all about these other feelings. I don't want to think about those other things."

"I understand."

"Will you have sex with me?" I ask.

A look of surprise flashes on her face and she says, "What?"

"Will you have sex with me? I want to feel something else, something other than, well, all of it. Getting drunk, doing drugs, some other substance, it's just going to go down a dark path."

"You want to have sex as a distraction to your other feelings?"

"I want to have sex with *you* and get lost."

She thinks for a moment and says, "OK. But I'm still mad at you."

"I understand."

"I may use that against you."

"I am OK with that."

31

E rin removes the covers and sits up at the edge of her bed. Her lush, dark hair dances between her shoulder blades. Slender, elegant, with youthful skin, she could easily be mistaken for Audrey Hepburn from this viewpoint. I reach my hand out to her and touch the small of her back.

"You should go now," she says softly.

"I should?"

"Yes." Her panties are on in a flash and she reaches for her comfortable T-shirt to sleep in that is on equally as fast.

"I don't understand."

"Hank, I'm still mad at you. This was sex, not intimacy. I enjoyed myself, you enjoyed yourself, but you should go."

"Oh." It feels harsh and cold to hear these things, but she is right. I understand that she is mad.

"I—I love you, Hank," she says with hesitation. "I am in love with you. I am only going to be with you unless you do something to change that."

Partially dressed, I turn to hear her say this. I can feel the inner workings of my biology start to react. My heart seems faster, my adrenaline lifts my spirits, and feelings, already worn from the ebb and flow of emotions of the week, start to rise.

"You love me?"

"I do," she says with a tilt of her head and a look that makes me feel a fool for ever having doubting it. "I love you, but I am not happy with you, and I'll need some time to get over that."

"That is the best and the worst thing to hear all at the same time."

"It is, isn't it?"

I bound across the bed and take her into my arms. "One more kiss for the road, and for loving me."

She smiles and agrees. This kiss is long, starting out tender, stretching into sensual. It is something to be remembered and thought back on during times apart in the darkness of a lonely room. Pulling back, I hear her gasp, then say, "Oh my."

I let her down gently, safely, still holding her firm in my arms. "Don't forget."

"I won't."

I put my shirt on, my jacket, and keep her in my sight, always watching, trying to drink in any last moments of her before we part, until she is no longer mad at me.

32

It is still winter dark outside when the pounding at the door startles me awake. I shout through the blackness, "Lisa!"

My sister simply replies, "Cows won't milk themselves."

Fumbling in my unfamiliar surroundings, I find the light, which burns my eyes when I turn it on. Yesterday's pants and shirt still have the rancid airplane smell from the flight, but I put them on anyway, knowing the work about to be performed will be worse.

Lisa leads me by the glow of her tablet across the icy mud to the entrance of the enormous milking facility. Our entrance is marked "Humans" and looks like a normal door, with a slit, plastic, weather barrier just inside. There is a giant automated door for tractors to transport livestock with a big sign on it saying, "Divine Bovine." Inside she hands me rubber overalls that have boots built into the bottoms. I'm in safety yellow; she's in bright pink.

We are not the only ones awake at this awful hour. Her small crew of eight, including her husband, is busy in the wide concrete corridors of the barn, walking cows into their individual stalls for feeding. Other cows are being moved from feeding stalls to a large rotating platter holding about eighty milking positions, their udders being connected to milking machines. The giant turntable rotates slowly, milking cows, and after a complete rotation, each cow is removed and another added. Up and down the ramp, each Bos Taurus is talked to, called by name, and treated with kindness.

"Leonard Bernstein," Lisa says over the music. "They love Mahler's Titan this time of day."

"Is it day? Can you call this day?" I ask facetiously.

When she smiles, it takes me back to a time of innocence, free of the entanglements of maturity. "This is the day that the Lord has made, I will rejoice and be glad in it," she says with glee.

We go to the calving area where her husband, a fair-haired, husky, bearded farmer, is wrangling with a hoof. She is on her tablet checking the intake of the milking machines. He explains how important a healthy calf is for their business, the investment they make to ensure they feel safe among this team, and the years of production this one calf will provide. My comment that "they really make you sweat for that production" is answered by a phrase from another generation— "Horses sweat, men perspire, and ladies glow."

Lisa informs me that my hands are far too soft for any real work, so I should instead help her in the kitchen with breakfast. Owning and running a dairy farm is no easy task, and I would never assume that my talents or temperament were well suited for this line of work, but hers are. She is nurturing when needed, firm when called for, and patient the rest of the time. It consumes her life, never allowing for vacation or holiday—"those heifers would explode if we left them alone for more than two days," she has said in the past. It is focused work. It is about the health and well-being of the herd, collecting and selling milk, and maintenance of the mechanisms that allow the business to make a profit.

Snow on the farm is deceptive. It looks pure, white, and clean. Below its fluffy mantel is some of the worst mud. It is a mixture of rich fertile soil and nearly frozen water, both sticky and slick, providing uneven steps over a minefield of no traction and completely being stuck. It makes for a slow walk back to the house. Lisa, who has small plastic cleats on her boots, finds it delightful to watch her older brother in a newly designated Olympic event she now calls "heavy-duty outdoor ice tomfooleries" (which could use a better name, as the summer games will need a non-ice version).

"There are two secrets to good eggs," Lisa explains, standing over the stainless steel range. "Ratios—the right amount of egg to milk to pinch of salt. The other is a low temperature. You don't want to overcook them."

"This coffee is excellent too," I compliment. "You are very good at this."

"So, what's got you so interested in dairy cattle? You thinking about starting a farm in Michigan?"

"No, no," I reply. "I'm not all that interested in the cows. I wanted to see you. It's been too long."

She no longer looks like my little sister. Now she's a mature woman, married, with kids; the summer sun has been hard on her skin, and the Wisconsin winter winds equally tough. I can see why others would mistake her for Mom from a distance: same frame, same hips, and similar dandelion hair.

"Well, that's sweet—sorry we couldn't make it out for Christmas."

"I don't suspect you would want to go back. Recently I've been questioning why I keep up the same routine."

"How was Dad's funeral?" she asks, filling the toaster with four more slices.

"It was rather empty. Hardly anyone was at the viewings, only a handful at the burial; it was the opposite of Mom's."

"I don't think anyone will have a funeral like that again," she says. "Cleopatra had fewer people at the asp biting."

"Midge and the twins are on their own now. Things there were left in a mess, so I paid off Dad's debts and started a trust for them."

"Aren't you generous?" she says, separating the eggs with a spatula. "What exactly is a trust?"

"There are all kinds really, I set up three. There is one for Midge and the kids for living expenses, and one for each of the kids to go to college. There is this initial state of money, and a trust represents the legal rules built around it regarding how the money is used. Midge can draw money each month until the kids are eighteen. Each of the twins have a set dollar figure designed for school after they turn eighteen."

"So it's really about the kids."

"Pretty much all about the twins."

She shrugs with acceptance and says, "Well, that's good, I suppose. They need to have some type of stability in their lives. I couldn't believe the conditions you were telling me about that house—no walls, unfinished. That sounds like Dad." After a pop, she pulls the hot bread out and butters it quickly before returning to the eggs. "How are you doing on those potatoes?"

I set down my coffee and return to the task I've been assigned and neglecting. Carefully, I move each one in a fluid motion over the tin teepee-shaped slicer, with thick cuts coming out the other end. As a pile mounts, I move them to the bowl. She takes the full bowl and puts them into a hot skillet, where they start to sizzle in the warm bacon grease.

"You have a lady friend?" she asks.

"I do."

"Didn't bring her, why?"

"Complicated."

"How complicated could it really be, Hank? You like someone, you spend time with her, get married, have kids, repeat each generation."

"You know. Feelings and stuff."

"Oh yeah, feelings. Forgot my big brother had those." She chuckles. "Did you pull a Dad and cheat on her?"

I know she is joking, I know she means well to rib her brother, and as I contemplate this, she turns to realize how much I'm thinking it over. "You did. You cheated on her?"

"It's a little more complicated than just that."

During breakfast Lisa is quiet. The slurps and chewing of eating are loudest. I hear the occasional, "Please pass me the...," but that is it. Uncertain if this is normal, or if Lisa is not saying anything after telling her nearly every detail of the time between Thanksgiving and the funeral, I quietly sit on my part of the bench, enjoying delicious eggs and bacon with toast.

Shortly after finishing, the men go back to the barn while Lisa and I start to clean. We scrape plates into the compost bucket for the pigs, then rinse and place the plates into the dishwasher.

"Hank," Lisa finally breaks the silence. "I'm kind of creeped out by your story, and I am not sure what to say to you."

"I can understand that. I've made some bad choices recently."

Taking my coffee cup, she fills it from the fresh brewing, and hands it back. "Looking out for those kids, well, I can see that. Midge? I do not see what strange hold she has over you men. What need could you possibly have that she fills?"

"I don't know."

"Dear brother, you should do everything you can to make certain that Erin can forgive you, and separate yourself from Midge. I suggest a restraining order."

My chuckle slowly turns to the realization that she is not joking. "Really? You think I need to go to that measure?"

"I do. Why do you think Mark moved away and never wants to talk to them again?"

"Um, because Dad married his old girlfriend."

"That's only part of it."

"Dear God, it's worse than that?"

She sits down at the table across from me, her own cup of coffee in hand. "It is."

Lisa begins to tell her tale.

It happened over a weekend excursion downriver for a "dad's weekend" when I was away at camp for two weeks. Mark and Midge were dating in high school, and Lisa was in middle school. Dad and P4 lived downriver. There is this awkward instance where they are at Belle Isles on a Saturday afternoon to picnic, and they split up into an odd grouping. Mark, Tess, and Lisa are at the picnic table when Dad and Midge go off to the concession building or looking for the bathroom. A while later Lisa runs up to the building to use the facilities, but never runs into them. After she is done, she looks around for a bit and discovers Dad and Midge stolen away in a less-traveled area. At first Lisa is not sure what she walked in on, but slowly she put the parts together, saying, "Nabokov would have called Dad a lone traveler or changed his name to Humbert."

The words coming from my little sister's mouth describe how all the faith and confidence she had in her father liquefied in one instant. It rang true from her tone.

For the rest of that summer, which I never really understood, Lisa locked herself away in her room every weekday, only showing up to the table for meals. When it came time to go down to Dad's on weekends, she was always spending it with a girlfriend. She kept it inside and wasn't able to articulate her shock, her confusion, or disappointment to anyone. It was only later when she eventually told Mark. After he stopped dating Midge, after Dad and Tess ended things, she opened up to him.

"I had no idea," I said. "I thought you were older when you first found out, that it was after P4 and Dad split up."

"They split up because Tess found out about Midge," she explained. "Think about it. Seventeen-year-old Midge having sex with forty-something Dad, who is married to twenty-eight-, twenty-nine-year-old Tess, huge problem there. You were fourteen, which makes me eleven. Dad and Tess are divorced four years later, and two years after that, Dad marries Midge." She stops to perform the math in her head. "That means Tess was how old?"

"Tess was twenty-one when she married Dad," I say.

"Holy shit? Really?" She stands and walks over to a jar on the counter, adding a quarter from her pocket.

"She was. This would have made Dad, oh, thirty-eight during the summer you describe." I look down to my coffee cup, trying to take in everything. "I'm glad I wasn't so lecherous."

"No, you just fucked your thirty-four-year-old stepmother." She reaches for her pocketbook, pulls out a five-dollar bill, and stuffs it into the jar.

"Yeah, short and sweet description." I sigh at the notion. "Still hurts when I hear the truth."

"The worst of it was when Midge wanted to get back with Mark," she adds.

"What? When did that happen?"

"Oh—you don't, it's why Mark moved away. You must have been away at school at that point."

"Why, what?"

"Midge came back to Mark. She came back to him in tears, asking that he take her back. It got very dramatic. Mark, completing work on his advanced degree, still driving into Detroit every day for school, with his high school sweetheart, still living with her parents, and she wants him to give up on all of that. She wants to get back together and tells him she is pregnant. She won't stop calling or coming to the house. That is when Tess and Dad split up.

"Midge starts to threaten to kill me, frequently, in a very real and scary way. It's when Mom has to call a lawyer and gets a restraining order."

I stop her to say, "That's when I found out Dad and Midge were dating."

"Dating." Lisa smiles and tilts her head.

Her look is one of empathy, that after years I am finally figuring out things she has already known.

"You were a pretty naïve kid, Hank. There was a lot going on in those days." Lisa pours a little more coffee and joins me at the table again. "Thank God I'm away from all that drama. I do not think I could keep up. I prefer cows and kids with a loyal husband."

"I remember things differently. The timing is all messed up in my head, like a photo album that's been dropped, and you have to put all the pictures back in the right order." The light of the morning starts to break the edge of the horizon and spills into the kitchen.

"Time to get the kids up for school," she says. "Are you going to be all right?"

"What? The kids are just getting up. How many hours have we been awake now? It's like half the day has gone by."

As she starts to walk away, she gets in one last dig. "We let the newbies take a nap on the first day."

33

Still exhausted from my visit on the farm, I spend my drive in the rental car from Dulles to McLean hoping to get some actual sleep when visiting Mark. My check-in at the Holiday Inn Express is quick. I unpack in minutes, keeping most of my clothing in the roller bag in hopes of doing some laundry.

My nap lasts longer than planned, and I make it to Mark's about fifteen minutes late. His wife is as lovely as I remembered. Now blond, she holds on to sun-touched skin from the Florida winter break vacation, showing freckles on her toned arms. A former field hockey player at university, she holds a slight limp in her gait. Their two kids are adorable and well behaved—a couple of towheads getting the latest Disney movie songs stuck in my head from the repetition over dinner. The perfection of how his life appears makes me question if I was adopted. How can I feel so different from either of my two great siblings? Both have wonderful marriages, are successful at what they do, and in addition have phenomenal families. I am missing some type of balance that they have been able to latch onto.

After a lovely meal, Mark takes me into the basement, where he's assembled his man cave filled with a bar, darts, pool table, and large-screen television.

Pouring me a drink, Mark says, "I got a call from Lisa this morning."

"You did?"

"She told me all about your visit." He smiles. "She tells me you are soft and weak. Not built for the farm."

"It's true. I'm never going to be a dairy farmer."

He reaches into the freezer and pulls out two cold rocks, then places one in each of our brown liquors. "I told her you weren't smart enough for bioengineering."

I laugh, knowing this is about as funny as he gets. "That's true. I don't have the brains you have."

"So that leaves you as the Tin Man, all heart." He holds his glass up to mine, and they clink. "I appreciate you keeping me updated on Dad's arrangements and all, but I have to be honest, I'm not all that interested in those affairs."

"I know. It's just that, well, I thought you should know. That's all. There may be a point when it matters, or you have questions, and well, now you know." I can tell I am rambling. There is no logical answer for why I have done this. He is accurate that it's about heart. "How are things at the Hughes Center?"

"We're making great strides in our work. I enjoy the new facilities, and the team I lead is efficient." He sips at this glass. "What kind of rental car did you get?" Mark slips into his standard line of questions each guy from Detroit must ask at some point during a conversation.

"It's a Chevy Impala," I say, supporting the corporate line.

"Nice?"

"I think so. You know it's a rental, but Paris is so old that everything in it seems high tech. The engine-to-weight ratio is well balanced, the steering is precise, and it even has noise cancelation in the cabin for a quiet ride. That's a pretty great ride in my book."

"Yeah." He thinks for a bit. "You know that since the reorganization, the product out of Buick has been exceptional. I imagine it's helped Chevy as well."

Mark can be hard to read in person. Talking about cars is a fallback when faced with talking about feelings. So I try to ease into the next level of intimate topics with him by saying, "You've got a great family, Mark. They are very nice. You must be proud."

"Thanks, Hank. I'm very fortunate." He looks back at his drink. "You know, when we were kids you wouldn't stop following me around. Everything I did, you wanted to do too."

"Yeah, brothers," I say.

"I did all the work. I found all the good music to listen to, and you got to listen to my records, tapes, and CDs," he says.

"Still have them," I say.

"I find a cool shirt, start to figure out how to dress, you get the hand-downs."

"Yeah," I say, a little bitter. "I get hand-downs, no shopping at the mall for lazy afternoons with mom."

"Hell, you should be grateful I showed you the way. You didn't have to put up with all that heart," Mark stops in midsentence.

"Everything OK, Mark?"

"I've been getting these phone calls in the last few weeks," he says.

"What kind of phone calls?" I ask.

"They're from Mary," he explains in a dour tone that sounds like dad. This is the name Midge used in high school.

"Oh, those kind of phone calls."

"She isn't supposed to call me, you know."

"I know," I say.

"She says she's sad that Dad died. She says she's lonely." He finishes off the rest of his drink in one quick gulp. "She says she's pregnant with your child." He reaches for the bottle and pours another.

I cough on the hard liquor and bold statement. "What?"

Having a sip of his second, "She tells me the two of you hooked up, and now you're going to be a daddy."

The night, that awful night, shoots back into my head again. My mind replays the moment, unwrapping the packet, fumbling with the foil, and going forward in the moment. I shake my head in disbelief. In my heart I know that it was difficult to get on in the dark, but it did go on. It was on.

"I thought she was just being crazy Mary, you know, like the old days, now that Dad is gone, back to her old habits of threatening people, manipulating people, to get what she wants," Mark says. "It's a joke, right? It's messed up. But then Lisa calls." His voice starts to become unbalanced. "She tells me about your visit. She confirms that story, about you and Mary."

"You see, Mark, that's one of the reasons I wanted to come see you, face-to-face, to set things straight. I wanted to make sure you got the whole story about Midge."

His face, now nearly purple in color, holding things back. "Set the story straight? There's little room for finesse or augmentation—it happened or it didn't."

Still ashamed, I breach the thorny subject head-on. "It happened."

Mark turns his head and mutters beneath his breath. He is so disgusted; he can't even look me in the eyes. "Just like Dad. You are just like Dad." Infuriated, he starts to walk away, bottle in one hand, glass in the other. His voice is hushed, filled with spit and rage, in an attempt to keep this from his perfect family upstairs. "You think about yourself, you think an apology will fix things you've broken." He starts to point and jab in the air, nearly spilling the bottle on each strike. "I loved her. I loved Mary. But she fell in love with some other guy, broke my heart, and I find out that other guy is my dad. What the fuck, Hank? Then a decade later you feel like twisting that knife? *Et tu, Brute? Et tu?*"

Instinctively I put my hands up in defense, try to use a soothing voice, calm him down. "You have nothing to worry about, brother—you have a beautiful wife, much hotter than Midge ever was, great kids—"

"If you like her so much, why don't you fuck her too?"

"Hey—hey now." I try to ease back. "It's not like that, Mark. You weren't there those last few weeks with Dad. It was a weird pressure cooker of emotions."

"Yeah, and you just popped Mary," he says in a cutting tone. "Nice."

We stand face-to-face, inches apart, my older brother, heaving boozy breath, ready to give me a good licking. Not very different from being a kid in the backyard, but this time won't end in noogies and pulled punches.

"I came here because I love you and you're my brother," I say firmly. "I wanted you to know the truth and ask for your forgiveness."

"Just like Dad—said nearly the same thing. If you love me so much, why did you do it in the first place? Where was your head while this was happening?" He pauses and backs down from his ready position. "You don't love me. You barely know me."

"We're brothers, Mark."

"Which means what, exactly?"

"Which means," I say, stepping back, "that your forgiveness is important to me. Explain to me what I'm missing here?"

"Mary was my first, Hank. My first. You don't get over your first that easily. I thought it was true love, real love. You don't get over that easily either. You remember what I was like in high school, all study, no friends. When she and I started dating, it was different. No one ever paid attention to me like that, cared about me like that. I was, I don't know, mapping a course of my heart that any other person would later have to pass through."

"First love, it's different," I say.

He huffs. "It is, especially at that age. I was just looking at pictures from back then, and everything we did, we did together. There was lots of hand-holding and kissing, and you would think we couldn't be apart for more than a few minutes. It's like I had to learn a whole new lexicon, one with her as part of it."

"I've never heard it described that way."

"It's true, it was real. We were discovering everything together. We discovered sex together. And yeah, at first it was fumbling around, and trying to get things right, but then it got to something real, real sex. Knowing how each other's energies merged, how to make her feel a certain way, building trust. Everything else after that is just a reference, pointing back to that time."

"Wow, that is, I didn't know, Mark. You were going over old photos recently. I didn't know."

"So when I found out that she was seeing someone else, when I found out that it was Dad, of all people, my life started to dissolve, unravel. Things fell apart. I couldn't do anything the rest of that summer."

"Later, it was Mom's restraining order. She forced you to move on, change schools." Things started to connect in my mind. "Mom put the restraint on to protect Lisa from the threats. She had you move away and change schools to keep you away from Midge. You would have taken Midge back if it weren't for that, thrown all those years in college away, for Midge?"

The sound of the bottle hitting the carpeted basement floor makes a thud so loud, it should have broken. A female voice from the top of the steps calls out, "Everything all right down there, boys?"

Mark calls back to his wife, sweetly covering his drunkenness. "Fine, honey."

"Mark, *are* you all right?" I ask.

He picks up the bottle and steps behind the bar for clean water and a wad of paper towels for the liquid that dribbled out in the drop. "I am. This is a tough trip down memory lane. It is a journey I avoid taking at all costs. I think you should go, Hank. I don't want"—he stops himself short and rephrases—"I can't live in the past, Hank. I'm not built for that. I'm the Scarecrow, my specialty is in the brain," Mark says with polite restraint from the floor, cleaning up the spill.

"Thank you," I say.

"For what?"

"For listening. For not throwing a punch. For being my brother. I hope that you can forgive me. I am very sorry to have done this. I'm sorry to have hurt you."

He looks up, eyes red, emotional. "I'll call you in a few weeks."

"OK." I nod. "OK."

"Hank?"

"Yeah Mark."

"Mary isn't pregnant. I was making that up to fuck with you."

"You son of a – I deserved it."

34

"Affectionate contempt is the best a parent can ever hope to receive from their children," Grandpa explains. "You're not a father, so it may be a stretch of the imagination for you."

"Isn't that a contradiction in terms?" I ask.

He turns his aging body in the deep recliner to find a better position and makes a chafing noise of skin on waxy leather. "It is," he says. "It's a total contradiction, but then so are children. You love them, shape them, scold them, try to point them in the right direction and give them the tools they need to survive in life. In return"—he sighs—"in return all you get is unrestrained emotion mixed with selfishness. If one of our kids were to do something without a motive or without an expected emotional payout, it would be a surprise."

I shake my head in disbelief. "What? I've never heard anyone talk like this before about their kids, especially you."

"I'm old, Hank. I don't really care what others think about me anymore, and they've formed their opinions about me long ago."

I turn to the couch, where Grandma sits looking exhausted from life. Her warm smile and maternal glow have left since Dad's passing. Her will to live lingers on the finest thread. Her days are now dangling on Grandpa's routine.

"What do you say, Grandma?"

Disengaged from what we have said, she looks to me and feigns a smile. "What's that, dear?"

"Affectionate contempt. It's what Grandpa says is the best you can hope for from children."

"Well, I agree with your grandfather. It doesn't make them bad people, but the relationship parents and children share is different from any other one may have. There were often times when I didn't like or agree with my mother over the years, but she loved your grandfather. And he"—referring to Grandpa—"couldn't stand his father, left home when? When you were fifteen? He wanted nothing to do with him, but the few times I met him, he was a lovely man to me." Looking out the window to the dozen yellowish-green spring finches dangling from the bird feeder. "I don't care if they hate me for the way I raised them, the disagreements we had over what time to be home, which boy to date, money. I just want them all to outlive me. But that's not going to happen now, is it?"

SPRING

35

Opening day for the Detroit Tigers is the true mark for the start of spring in Detroit. Often weeks after any groundhog's declaration or official date on the calendar, the snow on the ground finally starts to melt down to smaller, more manageable piles of black, icy dirt and grime, on that first day when the umpire shouts out, "Play ball" in the official season.

We have tickets for standing room only among the 40,000-plus fans crammed into every corridor and corner of the park. Verlander is pitching well, and Prince Fielder looks promising. By the fourth inning, Pike and I step aside to grab another beer while Dord and Knobby stay with the ladies.

Making our way to the concession stand, Pike says, "You know most of the shit you've gone through could have been prevented."

"Tell me about it, brother," I say, bumping shoulders with a passerby.

"Really, I've been thinking about it. Go back to that night, when you and I were at the bar, and we shook on a promise." He weaves in and out of the crowd, keeping up. "If you had just kept that promise, not told Erin, Sandy wouldn't have known, and I could have told Michelle rather than the euchre night e-mail incident." His thoughtful tone stops me. "If only you had kept your promise."

I reach out to him, placing my hand on his shoulder, and look him in the eyes, congesting traffic in the middle of the thoroughfare. With the crowd pressing to squeeze around us, I say, "You're right. This is all the result of me breaking my word to you, Pike. I am sorry I did that to you."

He gives me that goofy grin I have gotten a hundred times. "I forgive you. I was never angry. It just came to me the other night, and I wanted to let you know. In case, in case you hadn't figured it out for yourself."

"Are you and Michelle back together?"

"We are. Things are better now than before. We're better at talking through things, I think."

"That's good to hear. I'm glad something good could come of my mistakes. I never thought my actions would have such an impact on other's lives."

Somewhere along the railing overlooking the Fox Theater and the Fillmore's marquee, I see P5 ahead of us, beer in hand, leaning against a high-top table for support. It's a rare sighting to see him in this state. We go to him.

"Hey, hey, how are you doing there?" I ask him. Pike, holding my beer, watches as I try to help stabilize him.

"Hank!" he says in a drunken delight. "Hank, good to see you."

"How many of these have you had?" I ask, taking the cup from his hand.

"We have a luxury box, and I came out to walk around for a bit. I may have started a little early today." He slurs and mumbles.

"Pike, this is P5, P5, this is Pike," I say without thinking.

"P5." He laughs. "I get a number. That's as close as you can get to Hank; but 5 isn't bad. I was married to P1. I bet Pike isn't your real name, is it? He gave you this name."

"No sir," Pike says. "It's a name that connects to my identity, not something given to me before I even had a personality."

P5 thinks for a moment. "You're right. I should be happy to have a nickname. It's actually more personal."

"Are you enjoying the game?" I ask him.

"Ah, it's work, so I thought I would walk around a bit, eat something," P5 repeats, tilting his head down and away.

"I'm going to set these down and grab us a few dogs, Hank," Pike says, setting down our beers and walking back to the line.

"I'm just not one for drinking this early in the day," P5 tells me.

"Yeah, you have to pace yourself," I say. "One water for every two beers."

"Now you tell me." He takes a long and cleansing breath. "Hank, when was the last time you spoke to Erin? Six weeks now?"

A bit surprised at the quick change in conversation, I say, "I text her every day. I dial her number and leave a voice mail three times a week, hoping she'll pick up or return a call."

"If I asked if you love her, I bet you'd say yes, but I don't think you know what love is." His face is grim and slightly green. "You're just a kid." He starts to sway and then leans into the table. "You've never looked at a woman and felt completely exposed. Sure, you've been laid, but you wouldn't know about sleeping in hospital rooms for months, doctors and nurses giving you looks after visiting hours."

His words come out sloppy, but understandable. "You wouldn't know about the feeling that there was this perfection placed on this earth just for you, and you had to be her guardian angel, holding her hand, stroking her hair, and looking into her eyes, watching her fade away. You do not know about love and loss because you've never loved anyone more than yourself, taken that chance, dared to be open completely to another human being. You can't even call people by their own names; they remain distant to you, a number and a designation." He has reached a level of intoxication my friends refer to as the honesty stage.

"You're right—I haven't had that in my life. Still—I haven't given up." I put my hand on his shoulder and help steady his stance, provide a comforting pat. "I thought I found that in Erin Contee. I thought I had found a reward for working hard, for living a good life." I lean in closer, so he can hear me over the crowd's cheer. "But there is no reward. There is no finish line. Working hard is just my nature. The life I live is not good or bad, just the choices I make and have to live with. You had my mom. You are so happy to have been with her. Life was enjoyable, but she was no angel, and you were no saint. You are no saint. You were both just doing what you thought was right, what was best for each other. You'll find that happiness again if you allow it to happen."

He looks up to me from his half-hunched position on the table, his eyes red from rubbing them, then leans in and hugs me. "I miss her, Hank. I miss her."

I pat his back. "I know you do; I miss her too."

Pike arrives with a cardboard tray stacked with three hot dogs between two bottles of water. He sets the first one in front of P5 and says, "Eat these two slowly," then removes a bottle of water. "Drink this with them. You're going to be fine."

P5 starts to remove the red and white paper wrapped around the franks.

Pike looks to me and asks, "Honesty stage?"

"Yeah."

"Public honesty stage. You don't often see that in a grown man," he says, shaking his head.

His mouth still full of hot dog and bun, P5 says to me, "When did you get all wise, Hank?"

"After both your parents die," I say, "you get a new perspective on life. There's a clarity about which things are important, what you need to accomplish in the time remaining, and there are new questions."

"New questions?" P5 mumbles while masticating.

"Sure," I say. "What's the direction of my life? Who am I going to be today that might make them proud and avoid the mistakes they made?"

His expression changes from a balanced content of eating to one of surprise. He scans the area and sees that trash tub steps away. Reaching the tub just in time, he pushes one person out of the way and begins a retching noise that sounds like Chewbacca from Star Wars.

Pike looks to me and smiles, saying, "Dads are underrated."

"How do you mean?" I reply, watching P5 purge his system.

"You hear all these studies on moms being a vital part of development, and there is so much research invested in women's health, which is great, don't get me wrong," he says, picking up his beer from the high-top. "I'm all in favor of it, but something is lacking when it comes to dads. My dad's the best. He was there for me to talk to and socialize with, and he never thought I had a bad idea, but he helped me to form concepts and ideas by talking through them." He turns to me to say, "I don't think your dad did that for you."

"Maybe he didn't know he was supposed to," I say.

"Did five try?" Pike asks.

I think for a moment and say, "I was too old at that point. Three and five were nice guys, but they weren't that."

"Too bad. But your mom was there."

P5 starts to come back up from the tub, and I hand him some extra napkins that are unsoiled. "Yeah, she was there."

"Maybe that's why they spend all the money and time on moms," Pike says. "They are there."

"Maybe," I say, offering P5 the water bottle. "Maybe."

36

I did not recognize her at first, with shorter hair, new glasses, and dressed in fewer layers for warmer weather. It should have been the first clue that I had not seen Erin in what seemed like forever.

"Hank!" She hugs me with slender summer arms ready for tanning. "How are you?"

I can barely hear her with the loud crowd and music on the first floor. Her arms around me fill my heart with joy. "Fine," I say loudly. "Good, how are you?" I ask, letting go.

"Good, good," she shouts.

Looking her up and down, I say, "I like your new look. It's brighter, ready for spring."

"I am ready for warmer days." Her smile is luminous.

"There is something, something I can't place my finger on, that's different. What is it?" she asks.

I lean in to her ear so she can hear me. "I don't know."

"It's something. You seem so happy. It's been too long." She speaks loudly to talk over the crowd. "I should have known you would be down here for the game. Are you here with the gang?"

"I am. They are all here somewhere." I nod my head.

"Oh good. I'd like to say hello to Michelle and the girls."

When she says it, I know things are over. I can tell she has not returned my calls not because of needing time to think or get over things, but because it is over. Her new look, her new brightness, it is because she's moved on. She has returned to a state of happiness present when we first met, a level of self-confidence regained after going through the traumatic messed-up shit I call a life.

"Yeah," I say, trying not to change my tone or happiness to see her, keeping that mask of joy in check. "They would love to see you again, I bet. It's been far too long." I am curious. There are questions to ask, gaps in time to explain, but I do not ask. I refrain from appearing clingy; I refuse to pressure her into a place that may scare her away. There will be no emotional outburst in public, no scene I regret later.

"It's been a while."

I read her touch on my shoulder as an expression that she cares at some level, even if it is only sympathy for my downfall, which was caused by my own bad decisions.

"Almost two months, I would guess," I say.

"I get your messages; I hear your voice mail," she says. I cannot read her in this crowd. Is it sympathy? Is it pity?

"Good, good, I'm glad to hear that." It is too loud in here to have a real conversation. I cannot tell with any sense of certainty how she feels, what she is thinking. I can only try to talk over the crowd of happy fans and music.

"I like to hear what's going on in your life," she says.

I am reading too much into the statement—my life, her life, so separate, and not our life. It's difficult to know what to say in a moment like this. My feelings are in check. I suppress the desire to grab her, take her in my arms, and ravish her with kisses. I resist the urge to take her aside and have "a talk" in an area more private. I want to know every detail since we last spoke, that moment in her room when she was wearing that nearly transparent tee fresh from the height of climax.

"I'm happy to do it. Would you like to come say hi to the gang? Have a drink?" I offer with gracious restraint.

She pauses to think and looks off in the distance to something or someone. I can't tell. "Ah, I would really like to, but...maybe later?"

"Cool," I say. "No need to explain. We are on the second floor. We have a table. If you get a chance, join us. There is plenty of room. You can swing by and say hi. You know, if you have other things going on, we can always catch up later. We have each other's numbers." I smile.

"We have each other's numbers," she says before a quick embrace and peck on the cheek. She squeezes her way through the bodies of the packed bar until she is gone.

"Erin is here," I say, leaning in to Michelle so she can hear me.

"She is?" Michelle is excited at the news. "Where? Did you tell her to come by the table?"

"I did. I don't think she is coming over."

"Oh." Michelle sounds disappointed. "Was she with someone else?"

"I don't know. I didn't see anyone, but it was odd."

"Odd. The worst way to find things," she says in a tone of condolence.

"So there I was," Dord starts. "Standing at the urinal of Comerica Park after the Tigers win. The men's room is packed. The line is huge. All these people are trying to hold it while waiting in line. I am doing my business when I hear this guy to my right say loudly, 'Hey, buddy, nice dick.'

"I turn and see it's Knobby, and play along. I say, 'Hey, yours is pretty nice too.'

"Suddenly, the place goes silent. All you can hear is the sound of men clenching up and zippers closing."

Dord and Knobby play this scenario out frequently in public; however, this time, Dord is telling the story with a fresh black eye. This is a new addition to the tale. It is a twist that keeps things interesting. Dord keeps things interesting.

The individual parts each adding up to more than the sum just makes sense. After Erin and I last saw each other, I was optimistic. I never doubted we would get back together. Yet I can see now that she was being kind. It may not have been her intent at the time that we were done, but things had gotten too weird. I had gone too far over the line for forgiveness, and now all I could do was try to forget my first true love.

I think of Mark. When Erin left me, I was a homeless orphan who needed to do some growing up. Being successful or having money did nothing to make me a better person; it only allowed me the ability to live like a college student far longer than I should have. It sheltered me from the need to be more of an adult, to be a better man than my father. Eventually I will learn to live without Erin Contee. I may even love again. For now I should treat those I am fortunate to have in my life better, make certain they know I care for them.

"Hi, Lumpy, is this seat taken?" she asks with one hand on my shoulder.

"Erin!" I say, getting up quickly from the table. "I wasn't sure if…"

She smiles. "How could I pass up time with my Lumpy and his friends? I had to tell the people I was with to move on without me. You can give me a ride home later, right?"

I grab the empty chair and move it next to mine while she hugs the girls and says hello to the boys.

"We have some catching up to do," she says, sitting up cozy to me.

"We do," I say with a newfound joy. "I have milked cows, shoveled pig manure, gotten drunk with my brother, moved into a house, and bought a new car."

"What happened to Paris?"

"Oh, we'll always have Paris. The new car will let her rest in the garage while I restore her."

After, she tells me her tales from the last two months, including details on her job as a graphic designer, adventures she had training her cat to use the toilet instead of a litter box, the time she got a flat tire but the state of Michigan paid her fifty dollars for pothole damage, and her discovery of a new favorite cocktail.

Then she says none of it was the same without me.

"There is something absent in my life, like it doesn't happen unless I can tell you about it."

She looks to me tenderly, openly, a twinkle in her eye and her same ribbon of hair standing out rebelliously from the rest. "What have *you* learned since last time?"

I pause.

I look at her.

Then, taking the rectangular paper place mat with advertisements out from under my plate, I fold it in half and rip it carefully into two separate squares. I take the one square to fold it.

"Snowflakes are wonderful things."

I fold the paper again.

"There are at least thirty varieties of snowflakes. Each has six sides. Some have arms."

I tear at the edges.

"Some have points. Others are cylinders. No two are ever exactly the same." Near the center, I tear more away.

"Particles float around the heavens and attach to raindrops. The environment has a lot to do with the type of snowflake you get. When it is cold, you get simple snowflakes that are flat, like plates. When it is colder, you get needles and prisms. When it is supercold, you get columns, and when a particle and a water droplet join together, in low temperatures, they grow edges and arms, get heavy, and fall to earth as a snowflake."

I unfold the paper…it is not elegant.

"The perfect snowflake is rare. It is hard to find. Most just turn out the best they can."

"That's nice work. Can you make a swan?" Erin asks playfully.

"I can make two things, ugly snowflakes and snowballs."

I crumple up the other paper square into a ball and toss it in her direction.

"I've learned that you are my rare and beautiful snowflake, and I know that together, we have symmetry."

Erin Contee smiles and kisses me with a passion and friendship I have never known in my life.

I have found the greatest woman.

I know this now.

I will work every day to keep her in my life, to keep our love alive.

AUTHOR BIOGRAPHY

Paul Michael Peters is an American fiction writer who lived in both Philadelphia and Toronto after studying at Second City in Chicago. He has since returned to his beloved mitten-shaped state, Michigan, settling in Ann Arbor.

Peters made his literary debut with *Peter in Flight*. *The Symmetry of Snowflakes* is his second book. You can follow him at http://paulmichaelpeters.com/.

—

Made in the USA
Middletown, DE
20 March 2015